Dark God

DESTINIES CONVERGE

THE CHILDREN OF THE GODS
BOOK SIXTY-ONE

I. T. LUCAS

Dark God Destinies Converge is a work of fiction! Names, characters, places and incidents are products of the author's imagination or are used fictitiously and are not to be construed as real. Any similarity to actual persons, organizations and/or events is purely coincidental.

Copyright © 2022 by I. T. Lucas

Published by Evening Star Press

EveningStarPress.com

ISBN: 978-1-957139-19-7

Kian

A cup of coffee in hand, Kian stood next to the floor-to-ceiling window of his office and surveyed the village square below.

This early, only a few of the café tables were occupied, and further ahead the playground was still deserted, but the sight of the lonely swings swaying in the gentle breeze no longer saddened him.

His village was growing.

They now had two teenagers, two toddlers, two babies, and one more on the way. Some evenings, Parker and Lisa stopped by the playground while walking Scarlett, sitting on the swings and talking while the dog chased critters in the bushes. In the afternoons, Phoenix and Ethan often played in the sandbox or on the jungle gym, with Eva and Nathalie sitting on the bench and chatting while watching their children.

It warmed Kian's heart to see mother and daughter and their little ones enjoying the place.

Fates willing, soon the playground would be teeming with children and their parents. Kian could see Allegra and Eve on those swings when they got a little older, with him gently pushing his daughter, Dalhu pushing his, and Syssi and Amanda sitting on the bench and enjoying each other's company while watching their mates with their daughters.

Jacki and Kalugal's son would arrive next, and hopefully, more couples would conceive soon. He knew of several who were actively working on it and not bashful about sharing their journey to become parents with others, and he suspected that there were still others who chose not to make their conception efforts public.

Now that Ronja had transitioned, Merlin might be tempted to use his potions to have a child with her, but not yet.

The transition wouldn't be complete for another six months, and Ronja shouldn't and probably couldn't get pregnant while her body was still changing. Besides, she was enjoying her immortality and restored youthful appearance and was in no rush to become a mother again.

Sari and David hadn't decided yet if they were going to start actively working on having a baby either, but Merlin had given Sari the recipe for his fertility potions to take with her to Scotland. When they were ready to start, their doctor would prepare it for them, and perhaps some of the single ladies would like to use it to try to increase their chances of conception as well. Dormants and unrelated immortals were slowly trickling into the clan, but until the flow increased, the old ways of ensuring the clan's survival were still just as valid as they had been before they had discovered their first Dormant.

As a knock sounded on the door, Kian turned around. "Come in, Shai."

"Good morning." His assistant strode into the office with a stack of files tucked under his arm and a tray with two paper cups in the other. "I see that you've already gotten coffee." He put the files and the cardboard tray on Kian's desk.

"I can always use another." Kian plucked one of the cups from the tray and sat behind the desk.

"Let's start with this month's budget," Shai said.

"Are there any changes from last month?" Kian removed the lid from the paper cup and took a sip.

Shai pulled out a single printed page and put it on the desk. "William hired Darlene as his administrative assistant, and he's asking for you to approve her salary."

That was a surprise.

"I thought that the plan was for you to hire her as your assistant." Kian glanced at the amount William was requesting to cover her salary. "That seems reasonable." He lifted his eyes to Shai. "Did she refuse your offer?"

"I didn't make it. Geraldine brought it up with her as an idea, but Darlene said that she preferred not to work with family."

Kian arched a brow. "Most everyone in the village is family."

Other than Kalugal's men and the three Kra-ell, everyone else was related either by blood or by matehood.

"She said that she didn't want to work for her mother's mate, which is understandable. I wasn't too keen on it either. If I wasn't happy with Darlene's performance, I couldn't dismiss her without upsetting Geraldine. So I'm glad she came up with the idea to help William organize the lab's paperwork. He needs help more than I do."

Kian wondered whether working together would result in a romantic relationship. Clearly William and Darlene weren't fated mates, or they would have already been together, but that didn't mean that they couldn't form a loving relationship without that special bond.

Then again, even though Darlene was the granddaughter of a god, she still had a better chance of successful transition if her inducer was her fated one. Bridget's latest theory was that the bond was an enhancer, an additional catalyst, but not absolutely necessary if the other catalysts or the Dormant's genetics were strong enough to initiate transition without it.

In Darlene's case, her genetics were superior, but her age was a big impediment.

"Any other new items on the budget?" Kian pulled the page toward him.

"William also needs some remodeling done, but he left the pricing to you. At the moment, our two Perfect Match machines are right next to each other, separated only by fabric partitions. He wants to put up actual walls to create two dedicated rooms with proper soundproofing, so the participants will have more privacy."

"Understandable. I'll have Gavin take a look and design a dedicated space for them." Kian smiled. "It started as an experiment, but the virtual adventures have become so popular that it is time to rethink the operation." Leaning back, he crossed his arms over his chest. "Perhaps we should start charging a fee to cover the remodeling cost and the technicians' salaries. William has two people doing it full-time now."

"Good idea, but we should delay charging for the service until it's no longer in the middle of William's lab."

"Good point."

As Kian's phone rang, he glanced at the display. "Speaking of Perfect Match. It's Gabriel."

Shai arched a brow. "Does he call you often?"

"Not at all." Kian accepted the call. "Hello, Gabriel."

"Good morning. I actually need to speak with Syssi, but I only have your number."

Kian didn't remember giving it to the guy. Syssi was the stock owner and sat on the board of the Perfect Match

Virtual Fantasy Studios, but all communications with the other directors were done through email.

"Are you calling a board meeting out of schedule?"

"This is unofficial business, at least for now."

"Syssi is unavailable at the moment, but I can forward your message to her. What is it about?"

"It could be nothing, but we might have a buyer for the company, and I wanted to know if she's at all interested in selling."

Kian's hackles rose. "We are not interested. If you and Hunter want out, Syssi and I can buy your shares."

"We are not interested in selling either, but Hunter and I are curious to see how much this guy is willing to pay. We are going to throw a crazy number at him and see if he bites. Syssi is the majority stockholder and a board member, so Hunter and I thought that we should at least let her know that we are having the meeting, and if the two of you want to attend, you are more than welcome."

"Since we have no intention of selling, you can entertain yourselves without us. Just out of curiosity, though, how much are you going to ask for?"

"Twenty-five billion dollars."

Kian barked out a laugh. "The company is not worth even a fraction of that."

"It might be one day," Gabriel said. "We are still in the initial stages of creating awareness for the technology. If we find ways to reduce costs and make it more affordable, the demand for the service will skyrocket."

"That's true. Who's the guy?"

"Someone named Tom Hartford. I couldn't find any information on him, so it's either a fake name, or he's a recluse who doesn't have social media profiles."

"The name is probably fake, and the guy is most likely a competitor who wants to get his hands on the technology, or he's a nutcase."

"A nutcase with a lot of money. Hartford was a client, and he fell in love with his Perfect Match lady. He bought roughly a quarter of a million worth of sessions to share with her, but since she has a medical condition that makes it unsafe for her to enjoy the service, we can't allow her to continue. He wants to buy the company so they can keep sharing adventures in the virtual world."

The technology was meant to provide solutions for people with disabilities, so Kian couldn't imagine what kind of medical problem could preclude someone from participating.

"What's wrong with her? And why can't he just meet her in real life?"

"He did. The lady has a severe heart problem, and she's a double amputee. She had an episode during their last session and was rushed to the hospital, which is why we can't allow her back. Naturally, we refunded all of their tokens, which was painful. That was a lot of money."

That was most unfortunate, and Kian could understand the guy's motives. Hartford was in love, and he wanted to make his lady happy any way he could.

Swiveling his office chair, Kian looked out the window. "Now I get why you're meeting with him. It's not curiosity about how much he's willing to pay but about you feeling guilty for refusing them access to the machines. But wouldn't it be easier for everyone involved to just allow them to continue and make sure that the lady has medical supervision?"

"I wish we could, but if we allow her back after our insurance company has officially disallowed it, they will cancel our coverage, and we can't operate without insurance."

Kian wondered if there was anything he could do about that. This wasn't a normal case of a couple seeking thrills. It was a solution to a very real problem, and he could empathize with the guy. If he were in his shoes, and Syssi was the one who needed the virtual world to do all the things she couldn't do in the real one, he would have sought to buy the company for her as well.

"Try to talk to the insurance people and convince them to change their policy. We could also apply for additional insurance as a medical facility. If we want to offer service to hospitals, that's a necessity."

"I'll talk it over with Hunter, and we will see what can be done. So your and Syssi's answer is a no for sure? Even if he's willing to pay twenty-five billion for the company?"

Across the desk, Shai cleared his throat. "There is a lot the clan could do with our share of twenty-five billion dollars. Especially since you've just bought a cruise ship for a quarter billion."

Kian covered the mic with his thumb. "The shares belong to Syssi, not to the clan. So the money from the sale will be hers to do with as she pleases."

"I didn't know that."

Kian uncovered the mic. "First, let's see what the guy says. Personally, I'm not interested in selling, but ultimately, it's not my decision. It's Syssi's. If there is anything concrete on the table, and Mr. Hartford provides proof of funds, I'll discuss it with her and let you know how we wish to proceed."

Mia

"Good morning, family." Toven walked over to the breakfast table and leaned to kiss Mia's cheek before taking his seat.

He seemed more cheerful than usual, and his eyes shone with that inner light Mia had noticed on several occasions when he'd been either excited or aroused.

The first couple of times she'd thought that he was wearing contact lenses that reflected the light at certain angles, but in all the time they'd been together, she hadn't seen any of the paraphernalia that came with using contacts.

She'd been noticing more and more oddities about him, but none of those peculiar quirks took away from the incredible person he was or from how much she loved him.

So what if the guy never slept more than four hours a night and still looked fresh as a daisy in the morning?

Some people didn't need a lot of sleep. And then there was his bat-like hearing and eagle-eyed sight.

Face it, Mia. Your boyfriend is an alien.

Mia smiled. She had absolutely no problem with having a hot alien for a boyfriend. It would explain why he had no family and no friends, as well as the glowing eyes, the negligible need for sleep, and the superhuman senses.

How had he gotten so rich, though? Maybe he could conjure gold out of thin air?

Stifling a snort, Mia reached for the toasted bagels to hide her amusement. She was a creative person with an active imagination, and she had read too many science fiction novels, including some that had romance and even erotica mixed in.

Toven unfurled a napkin and put it over his slacks. "The email from Perfect Match finally arrived last night, inviting me for a meeting with Gabriel and Hunter at the Beverly Hills branch."

"Hallelujah," her grandfather said. "It only took them a week to get back to you. When is the meeting?"

"Tomorrow morning at ten." He turned to Mia. "Do you want to come with me?"

The idea horrified her.

Parading the poor disabled girl in front of the founders would be an effective tactic to put pressure on them to make concessions, but she hated being pitied, and she would hate even more being put on display.

Mia shook her head. "I'm sorry, but I can't. You will have to use other methods of persuasion than showing them the poor girl with no legs who they are denying access to their virtual adventures." She grabbed another toasted bagel and stuffed a piece of it in her mouth.

"That's not why I want you to come with me." Leaning over, Toven took her hand. "I need you for moral support. You are my partner, and I want us to enter this adventure together."

Way to make her feel guilty for wrongly accusing him. She should have known better, but despite his heartfelt words, she still dreaded going to that meeting.

"If you really need me, I'll come, but I'd rather not. I know nothing about business, and I'll feel awkward and stupid just sitting there with nothing to say."

"Mia Berkovich." Her grandmother used her stern voice. "You are not stupid, and you are not allowed to call your-self that."

Mia stifled an eye roll. "I didn't say that I was stupid. I said that I would feel like I was because I don't know enough about virtual reality technology or about running a business to contribute anything useful." She looked at Toven. "Besides, I don't have time. I need to finish the illustrations for my publisher by Friday. He was kind enough to extend the deadline because of our trip to Switzerland, but I can't keep giving him excuses."

The truth was that she was almost done, and if she really wanted to, she could have taken a break for a couple of hours to accompany Toven to the meeting. But despite his best intentions she would still be the subject of pity, and whether he wanted to use her for emotional blackmail or not, her being there would have that effect.

Toven seemed to have gotten the message and nodded. "I don't want you to do anything you are not comfortable with." He lifted her hand to his lips and kissed the back of it. "On another subject, the demolition part of the bathroom should be done today, and since the rest of the remodeling work is not as noisy, we can go back to working over at our house during the days. I prefer for us to be there so I can supervise the job."

The demolition had started yesterday, and Toven had made several trips to the house to see how the construction crew was doing. "The house is fifty feet away. You don't need to be there to supervise the work. You can walk over a few times per day."

"If we are there while they work, they won't take two-hour-long breaks or spend half of the time chatting. I want that bathroom done as soon as possible." He gave her a meaningful look.

As her grandmother chuckled and her grandfather grimaced and hid his face behind his coffee mug, Mia's cheeks got warm.

It wasn't difficult to guess why Toven was in such a hurry to finish the project. He didn't want to continue spending his nights in her room at her grandparents' house, and until the wheelchair-accessible bathroom was ready, they couldn't move into his place.

They hadn't announced plans for their living arrangements yet, but her grandparents had no doubt figured it out by now. Nevertheless, she needed to make it official, and she dreaded that conversation.

The other thing Mia was dreading was Toven's expectations. She still hadn't let him see her fully naked, and once they moved in together, she would have to get over that hurdle, but she wasn't ready.

Heck, she didn't know if she ever would be. They'd found a good way to make love with her prostheses on, and she'd even let him see more of them, but not all.

Perhaps he would be happy with her getting fully naked but wearing her legs, so to speak?

Mia had seen photos of models and ballerinas flaunting their prostheses, and it didn't look gross at all. She could do that. Would fishnet stockings and a sexy garter belt be too much? Would it boost her confidence or make her feel silly?

A decision like that required a consultation with her besties, but first some browsing was needed, so she would have a selection to show them.

Toven

"Are you sure you don't want to come with me?" Toven pulled Mia into his arms. "You don't have to say anything. I'll do all the talking."

He'd tried to convince her to come last night, but it had been no use.

"I'm sure. You don't need me there." She kissed him lightly on the lips. "Good luck."

With a sigh, he let go of her. "I need to get going if I want to get there by ten."

Curtis looked at his watch. "It probably won't take you two hours to get to Beverly Hills, but you never know with L.A. traffic, so it's better not to take chances."

Mia followed him to the foyer. "I just want you to know that if they don't want to sell you the company, I'm not going to be disappointed. I already have all I need to be happy." She smiled. "We will make our own adventures in the real world."

He kissed the top of her head. "We will, but it's no longer just about you and me. The more I think about it, the more I want to own that technology and make it available to those who would benefit from it the most."

Toven was aware that he was falling into a trap similar to what he had allowed himself to fall into before. He'd wanted to help humans live better lives, but they hadn't been receptive to his message, twisting it around and committing atrocities in his name. He'd failed time and again, and it had nearly destroyed him.

This time, however, his goals were less ambitious.

He wasn't looking to change human nature at its core, and he wasn't trying to eradicate all of humanity's evils. All he was attempting to do was help those who couldn't enjoy their lives to the fullest due to disabilities by providing them access to fully immersive and realistic virtual experiences. It wasn't as lofty a goal as those he'd had in his younger years, but it was more achievable.

Waiting patiently behind his granddaughter, Curtis gave him a reassuring smile. "If you need help crunching the numbers, I'm your man. Call or email me, and I'll make sure no one is cheating you. There is no substitute for having a numbers person in your corner to look out for your interests."

"I appreciate it." Toven let go of Mia and awkwardly embraced the man for a brief moment.

He'd never been overly affectionate with his real family, but Mia and her grandparents were huggers, and he was starting to warm to their ways.

"Come here." Rosalyn pulled him into her arms. "I'm keeping my fingers crossed for you."

"Thank you." Toven lifted his satchel off the entry table and slung the strap over his shoulder. "I'll call Mia as soon as the meeting is over. I don't want you having to keep your fingers crossed for too long." He winked at her before walking out the door.

Rosalyn had arthritis, which he hoped to remedy with his blood transfusions, but he hadn't figured out a way to do that yet. For some reason, sneaking into the couple's bedroom at night and thralling them into deep sleep seemed disrespectful, but that was the only idea he'd come up with so far.

It would be even more difficult to do when the bathroom remodeling was done, and he and Mia moved out of her grandparents' house.

If he told Mia the truth about who he was and what was the real reason she was feeling so much better, she could help him devise a plan, but he hadn't figured out a way to do that either.

He no longer had the excuse that her heart was too fragile to handle a revelation of that magnitude, and his idea of preparing her in the virtual world was not practical. Even if the owners of Perfect Match agreed to sell him the company today, it would take months for the deal to be finalized, and until he owned it, he and Mia couldn't avail themselves of the service.

Could he wait months to tell her that he was a god?

He could, but he shouldn't. They were a couple, and there should be no secrets between them.

Then again, he wasn't the only one who was holding back. Mia still refused to let him see her fully naked, but that wasn't on the same level as keeping his real identity from her.

Letting out a breath, Toven typed the address of the Beverly Hills studio into the navigation system, and when the software calculated that it would take him an hour and a half to get there, he cursed under his breath.

If he made it on time, it would be a miracle.

Toven shook his head. He was an immortal, and time used to move differently for him. But now that he was living in Mia's human reality, time had become a precious commodity, and he'd become impatient.

Vrog

"Do you know why Kian wants to see you in his office?" Wendy refilled her coffee mug and sat down next to Vrog.

He'd been wondering the same thing ever since he'd gotten the text summons last night, but he hadn't asked. When the boss wanted to see him, he was just going to show up. It could either have something to do with the journals he'd brought back with him from the compound or questions regarding the clan children's education.

"His text only said that there was a matter he needed to discuss with me. I assume it has something to do with schooling. Maybe he's already making an educational plan for his daughter and his niece."

Vrog loaded two more pieces of carpaccio onto his plate. It was the only form of raw meat that didn't gross Wendy out, and it had become his daily breakfast with her. Four days a week, Vlad had an early shift at the bakery, and

Vrog made a point of waking up at three in the morning to share a cup of coffee with him before he left for work. As much as he liked Wendy, he loved the mornings he got to spend alone with Vlad.

Wendy laughed. "Allegra is just a baby. It's too early to plan her future education."

"It's never too early to start. Some parents have a plan in place even before their children are born. Getting into the right preschool can determine the child's entire future."

"That's crazy." Wendy cradled her mug between her palms. "Those parents are obsessive."

Vrog shrugged. "They want the best for their children. In China, getting into the right school has a huge impact on a person's future." He sighed. "I really need to go back. As capable as Dr. Wang is, he's not the head of school, and if standards slip even a little, we will lose students."

Wendy pouted. "I don't want you to go, and neither does Vlad. Is it because you are disappointed with Aliya?"

"In part," he admitted. "But I need to go back regardless."

Wendy put her mug down and crossed her arms over her chest. "Phinas doesn't come by anymore. I asked Aliya about it, and she shrugged it off, saying that he's working late, but Yvonne hinted that he's no longer a contender."

"Yvonne, Aliya's roommate?"

"That's the one. Aliya might not tell me everything because she knows I'll probably tell you, but her room-mates know what's going on."

"It doesn't make any difference. If it's not Phinas, then it's someone else. Aliya made it clear that she's not in a rush to commit to any one male, and it's her right to flirt with whomever she finds pleasing."

"She doesn't really flirt with anyone. Don't forget that she came here with almost no social skills, so what we might have thought of as flirting was her way of being friendly. She's learning, though. Now that she understands about the intricacies of male-female interactions, she is a little more reserved with the males. Before rooming with Yvonne and Bernice, her only role models were Wonder and me, and we are both mated, so we can get away with more joking around with the men because they know we are taken. Having two single roommates is good for her."

"I'm glad, but that doesn't change the fact that she shows no interest in me."

Smirking, Wendy pulled out her phone. "You stopped coming by the café, so maybe she thinks that it is you who are no longer interested." She scrolled until she found what she was looking for. "But I think Aliya is worth the extra effort." She handed him her phone.

Vrog's eyes widened. "Why does she wear so much makeup? She's beautiful without all that warpaint."

Wendy barked out a laugh. "Spoken like a guy. I think she looks stunning, and when you see her, make sure to tell her that."

"I don't plan on going to see her, and if she wants to see me, she knows where to find me. Kra-ell females are not shy."

Wendy shook her head at him. "Aliya might look more Kra-ell than human, but I have a feeling that her character and her emotional makeup are more heavily slanted toward her human side. She's quite sweet and mellow, and she's not at all bitchy like the pureblooded Kra-ell females."

"They are not bitchy. They are assertive and uncompromising, which in human society is acceptable for males but less so for females. You wouldn't think of their behavior as negatively if they were male."

"Not true. I would just call them jerks or assholes instead of bitches. I wouldn't accept such demeaning behavior from anyone."

"The Kra-ell males don't think of it as demeaning."

Wendy snorted. "That doesn't mean anything. They live in that society, and that's what they've been taught was right from the moment they were born. Human females also used to believe that they were the rightful property of their husbands. It took a few brave freethinkers to challenge those beliefs. But that's a discussion for another day. You need to go to the café, talk to Aliya, and make her see that you don't hate her."

Vrog was taken aback. "I don't hate her. Why would she think that?"

Arching a brow, Wendy leaned closer. "First, you stopped coming to the café, and then you asked Alena to get Aliya a new place to live. What else is she supposed to think?"

That was supposed to be a secret, and he was sure that Alena hadn't said a thing about it. But maybe Ingrid had spilled the beans?

"How do you know that?"

"I'm not stupid, and neither is Aliya. Just go talk to her, Vrog, and let her know that you are still interested. What's the worst that could happen?"

"She'll hurt me again," he admitted.

"She won't. Besides, not knowing for sure where you stand with her is hurting you already and makes it difficult for you to decide what to do next. Forget that Aliya is half Kra-ell and treat her like a normal human female. Ask her how she's acclimating to the clan, compliment her looks, and if she responds with smiles, ask her out on a date."

Toven

As soon as Toven walked through the door of the Beverly Hills Perfect Match Studios, the receptionist greeted him. "Good morning, Mr. Hartford."

He wasn't surprised that she remembered him from his previous visit. When he wasn't shrouding himself to look like an ordinary human, Toven was difficult to forget.

"Good morning." He returned her smile.

She picked up the phone, announced his arrival, and pushed to her feet. "They are waiting for you in the conference room. Please, follow me."

He fell into step with her. "Is it the same room Dr. Brenna used the last time I was here?"

"No, that was her office." The receptionist stopped in front of a set of double doors. "This is the conference room." She knocked before pushing one of the doors open.

"Thank you." He walked past her.

Three people sat around the oblong table—the doctor whom he'd met before and the two men he assumed were the founders.

The dark-haired man rose to his feet and offered him his hand. "I'm Gabriel Barnes."

"A pleasure to make your acquaintance, Mr. Barnes." Toven shook the guy's hand. "I'm Tom Hartford."

"Hunter Anderson." The other guy extended his hand without getting up.

Nodding, Toven shook it as well and then smiled at Brenna. "I'm glad that you are joining us today. Your medical expertise will no doubt be needed."

She smiled brightly. "Perhaps. But I'm here more out of curiosity and to support Gabriel and Hunter."

Toven swallowed the taste of disappointment her comment elicited. He would have liked to have Mia by his side at the negotiation table, but she'd been adamant in her refusal, and he hadn't wanted to push.

"We have good news," Hunter said. "The reason we took so long to get back to you was that we were scrambling to find a solution to Mia's problem. The impetus to create Perfect Match was to provide people with disabilities with an option to experience things they couldn't otherwise enjoy. If we couldn't accommodate Mia, then we were failing our original mission statement, and that didn't sit well with either of us."

Toven wanted to point out that most people with disabilities couldn't afford three-thousand-dollar sessions, but he wanted to hear what they had managed to accomplish.

"Go on."

"We talked with our insurance provider," Gabriel took over for his partner. "We told them that we wanted to reclassify part of what the studios were doing as therapeutic procedures, and we asked them what needed to be done to enable us to provide services for people with disabilities. After all, if medical facilities can obtain insurance, we should be able to get it too. I'll spare you the details of the back and forth, but basically they need three things." He smiled at his wife. "A doctor on staff, which we have, a psychological evaluation of the benefits that virtual adventures can provide disabled people, and an iron-clad contract between the participants and the studios that protects us from lawsuits in case something goes wrong."

Toven arched a brow. "I remember signing a very detailed contract that said you are not responsible for any resulting health consequences, mental or physical, including death and suicide."

"Which you signed as Tobias Navon," Hunter said. "In our efforts to protect our customers' privacy, we were shooting ourselves in the foot." He waved his hand around the room. "There are no cameras anywhere, and we don't ask for identification. We have no proof of who actually signed the contract. That will change right after our lawyers prepare the new contract. We will video the entire signing session, starting with a verbal explanation of all potential risks and the clients repeating and confirming that they understand, and ending with their signature. The recording will be stored on a secure server and will not be accessible to anyone without a court order. It will only be used if legal action is taken against the studios, claiming physical or mental injury or complication resulting from participation in our virtual adventures."

"You will lose some clients," Toven said.

Brenna nodded. "We factored that in but decided that the benefits outweighed the potential losses. In summary, you and Mia will be able to continue your virtual adventures. Not right away, of course. Everything takes time, and it will probably be months before we have everything in place, but it's better than never, right?"

"Indeed. But my desire to buy your company is no longer just about Mia and me. I want the service to be available to people who can't afford to pay thousands for a few hours of living a fantasy."

Vrog

Vrog kept his head down as he made the trek to Kian's office. After the disaster that his virtual adventure had turned out to be, he dreaded bumping into the dominatrix he'd been partnered with, and since he didn't know who she was, every unmated female was a suspect.

For the past three weeks he'd been holed up at the house, and if not for the meeting with Kian he wouldn't have left this morning either.

Wendy thought that his reluctance to socialize was because of his disappointing relationship with Aliya, and she wasn't wrong, but it was just one more reason he'd been avoiding the village square.

"Good morning." A female smiled as she jogged by him.

Thankfully, she didn't stop.

Would he ever get over the awkwardness with every clan female he didn't know?

Probably not.

It was time to go back to his school, but the problem was that he no longer thought of it as his primary home, and he dreaded returning to his lonely existence. Vrog had a family in the village, and it included not only Vlad and Wendy, but also Stella, Richard, Margaret, and Bowen.

Who would have thought that he would befriend the mate of his son's mother, the guy who had beaten him to a pulp and who'd hated his guts for the first few weeks of his stay in the village? Now they were all one big family, meeting for dinners at either Vlad and Wendy's home or the homes of the two other couples.

Vrog also enjoyed not having to hide his otherness. The clan people had accepted him even though he wasn't one of them, and they'd accepted Aliya as well, for which he was grateful. With her alien looks, life on the outside was difficult.

His options were to choose the school as his base and treat the village as a destination, or the other way around, or divide his time equally between the two.

Aliya was another variable in the equation though, and if he gave it another shot and things warmed up between them, he would have to factor that into his decision.

Wendy was right about one thing. He'd given up too soon and hadn't fought hard enough for Aliya.

Given that his prior approach had failed, he was inclined to take Wendy's advice and treat Aliya like he would a human or an immortal female. He would take the initiative, and if she didn't respond well to that, he would do the mature thing and have an open and honest discussion with her so he would know once and for all where he stood with her.

With the decision made, Vrog felt lighter and more optimistic than he'd felt in weeks.

Vrog had never been good at just accepting his fate and not fighting for what he wanted, and he'd hated the feeling of defeat Aliya's rejection had brought about. Then the catastrophic virtual adventure had done a number on his self-esteem, but it had also been a wakeup call.

It seemed that the Mother didn't want him paired with a clan female, which brought him back to Aliya.

Feeling a renewed bounce to his step, Vrog took the stairs up to Kian's office two at a time, and when he found the door slightly ajar, he knocked anyway.

"Come in, Vrog," Kian said in his usual gruff voice.

"Good morning." Vrog walked in and closed the door behind him.

"Please, take a seat." Kian rose to his feet, motioned to one of the chairs in front of his desk, and then sat in the other.

"Thank you." Vrog sat down.

"I'll get straight to the point." Kian crossed his legs at the ankles. "We need a school for the village children, and we don't have anyone who is qualified to start one. Callie decided that she wanted to be a chef more than she wanted to be a teacher, and I don't have any other candidates. I know that you have your hands full with your school in China, but any help you can give us would be appreciated."

"I'm not sure what it is that you want me to do. I run a high school. What you need is a preschool."

Kian sighed. "That's the problem. Before approaching you, I talked to Zelda, who established the high school our older kids went to, but she's never been a kindergarten teacher, and she's retired. I need to brainstorm ideas with someone who at least has some experience in establishing a school from the ground up."

"You don't have enough children for a preschool. I would suggest finding one clan member who loves children and is willing to run a daycare. It would be best if that person goes through some training first, even online, so they will know how to keep the children engaged in stimulating activities."

Nodding, Kian steepled his fingers on his knee. "Can you help me interview people and provide a list of activities?"

"Again, I'm not an expert on early age education. I can look into it, but a daycare is a short-term solution. If I were you, I would build a private school outside the village that will serve human children as well as clan children. Then you can hire human teachers, and your primary problem will be solved."

"Not really. The girls turn immortal as toddlers, and anyone who spends time with them would start noticing that their scraped knees heal too fast, that they are too strong, can hear and see too well, and there is always the risk of them telling their friends and their teacher things that they are not supposed to. Nathalie has to keep coming up with creative excuses for Phoenix's stories, and she dresses her in long-sleeved shirts and pants in case she falls and gets a scrape."

"I understand." Vrog nodded. "Then the daycare option is what you need to go for, and the parents will have to homeschool the girls until they are old enough to know to be careful and to know how to keep their identity a secret. Perhaps you should concentrate on building a middle school somewhere near the village. At twelve, clan children will be old enough to interact with human children, and the occasional slip-up can be covered up."

"I agree. Is that something that you will be willing to do? Other than Zelda, we don't have any clan members who are qualified to create a curriculum, and she's not interested." Kian raked his fingers through his hair. "Phoenix is almost three years old, and I don't think Nathalie and Andrew will survive homeschooling her for the next nine years. She's a rambunctious little girl, and she needs structure. We need a better solution."

"I'll give it some more thought." Vrog mimicked Kian's pose and crossed his legs at the ankles. "I need to go back to my school soon, but I'll try to come up with some ideas for you before I leave."

"How soon do you plan to leave?"

Vrog smiled apologetically. "I should have left weeks ago."

"That doesn't answer my question."

"I know, but I can't give you a date yet. It might be in a few days, or it might be in a couple of weeks."

"Let me guess." Kian smirked. "It depends on a certain brunette who works at the café."

"You are not wrong."

Toven

After the receptionist brought in coffee for the four of them, Gabriel smoothed his hand over his almost black hair. "You are preaching to the choir, Tom. A disabled friend was what prompted Hunter and me to start working on the Perfect Match technology, but dreams met reality, and we needed to make the studios commercially viable. I love what you want to do, but I doubt that you will be able to actually pull it off. Besides, Hunter and I put our lives into this, and we can't just walk away from it."

Toven nodded. "I understand, and I have no wish to kick you out. I have no technical background, and I would need your expertise to keep running the studios. You can stay on as directors, and we can negotiate your pay, the amount of stock you will retain, and all the other details, but I want to be in control of the company. How much of the stock do the two of you own?"

"Forty-eight percent," Gabriel said. "Our silent partner owns fifty-two percent."

That wasn't good. It meant that the decision to sell or hold was mainly the silent partner's. Hunter and Gabriel probably had a veto clause, and the partner couldn't sell without their approval, but if Toven managed to convince them, the partner might still refuse to sell.

"Have you discussed my offer with your partner?"

Gabriel nodded.

"Did you calculate how much you would be willing to sell the company for?"

Gabriel and Hunter exchanged glances, and then Gabriel smiled. "Twenty-five billion dollars, which is much more than the studios are currently worth, but we included in our calculations the value of the technology, which is revolutionary and has enormous potential."

Given the three humans' smug expressions, they expected him to walk away from the deal, but the thing was that he'd been prepared for them to come up with an exorbitant amount precisely for the reasons Gabriel had mentioned.

The possibilities of what could be done with their virtual technology were fantastical.

"Sold." He smiled at them. "Where do I sign?"

The three were visibly taken aback.

"Do you even have that kind of money?" Brenna asked.

"I anticipated you would want to see proof of funds, and I brought it with me." He opened his satchel and pulled out a printout. "This is one of my gold depositories in Switzerland." He pushed the page toward Brenna.

She lifted the printout and examined it. "The name on the account is blacked out. How do I know it's even yours?"

"How else would I have access to it? The Swiss don't release information about the accounts of their clients, or their gold depositories."

"How do you have so much money?" Brenna handed her husband the printout. "I've never heard your name before you came to talk to me, and when I googled it, you didn't come up on any of the lists of the richest people in the world."

"That's because it's not a fortune that has been amassed in the modern era. It's very old money. This gold has been in my family for hundreds of years."

"That's incredible." Gabriel handed the printout to Hunter. "Can we keep this? We need to show it to our silent partners."

Toven frowned. "Is there more than one?"

"They're a couple. The shares belong to the wife, but they are both involved with the company."

"I see."

That was actually good news. Toven had always had better rapport with females. They were softer, more compassionate, and the wife would probably be more sympathetic to Mia's plight.

"I would like to meet your partners. Can you set up a meeting?"

The two exchanged glances again.

"We can try," Gabriel said. "They like their anonymity, and they are not inclined to sell. But given the amount, they might be more agreeable to negotiate, especially if we can come up with an agreement that will leave us access to the technology."

"Of course." Toven closed his satchel and rose to his feet. "Please try to arrange a meeting as soon as possible. With twenty-five billion dollars, I can probably develop a technology like yours from scratch, and if you and your partners refuse to sell, I will do just that. I prefer to save myself the time it will take, but I want you to be aware that whether you decide to sell or not, your technology will not remain the only show in town for long. You will soon have competition on your hands."

Aliya

⚜

Aliya's heart had skipped a beat when she'd seen Vrog walking toward the café, but then he'd ducked into the office building, and the hope that had bloomed in her chest had been smothered.

He was not coming back.

She'd lost him, and for what? For a pipe dream about having both him and Phinas?

What a joke that had turned out to be. It had been fine to fantasize about having a harem like a proper Kra-ell female, but when push came to shove, Aliya had found out that she wasn't a true Kra-ell.

She had thought that she'd been attracted to Phinas, but when he'd made a move on her during the get-together that her roommates had organized, her attraction to him had fizzled out as if it had never been there. At the time she'd blamed fear and inexperience for freezing up, and she thought that spending more time with Phinas would help her relax around him, but when he'd taken her hunting in the nearby canyon, things between them had gotten even worse.

Phinas hadn't said anything, but it had been quite evident that he'd been repulsed by her drinking blood straight from the animal source. Apparently, knowing that she needed to hunt for blood was not the same as witnessing it, and since that night she hadn't seen much of him.

"Don't look," Wendy whispered. "But Vrog is heading this way. Be nice to him."

Aliya pretended to shrug it off. "I am always nice to him. I wasn't the one who severed contact between us. He chose to ignore me."

"Hello, Vrog," Wendy said with exaggerated cheerfulness. "Aliya will take your order." She grabbed a rag. "I need to wipe the tables."

"Hello." Vrog sat down on one of the barstools. "How have you been, Aliya?"

"Fine." She forced a smile. "And you?"

"Fine."

That was not what Aliya had heard. Wendy had told her that Vrog's virtual hookup hadn't turned out well, and the adventure had been terminated only minutes after it had started. But he refused to talk about it, so Wendy didn't know what happened, only that it hadn't gone as well as he'd expected.

"What can I get you?"

"The usual."

"A soy cappuccino with a roast beef sandwich?"

Vrog smiled. "I'm surprised that you remembered."

"How could I forget? You ordered the same thing each day for weeks." She pushed a strand of hair behind her ear. "I assumed that you got tired of eating the same sandwich every day, and that was why you stopped coming."

She knew perfectly well that hadn't been the reason, but it was an opening for him to explain the cold shoulder he'd been giving her for weeks.

"It wasn't the sandwich I got tired of."

"Was it the cappuccino?" She batted her eyelashes with mock innocence.

Leaning forward, he looked into her eyes. "It wasn't the cappuccino either. I got tired of watching Kalugal's right-hand man flirting with you."

"Why? Were you jealous?"

His eyes kept her hostage. "What do you think?"

"I think that's very un-Kra-ell of you. Kra-ell males don't get jealous."

"Oh, I think they do. They are just not allowed to show it. Do you think women who are forced to share a husband because their religion says that's their duty are not jealous? I'm sure that when the husband takes a second wife, the first one cries herself to sleep for months, but she puts on a dutiful and accepting face because she can't do anything about it. No one asks her if she's okay with him taking another woman to his bed."

Aliya swallowed. "I never thought of it like that. I thought that the males didn't mind sharing and being shared."

Letting go of her eyes, Vrog leaned back. "In the Kra-ell males' case, they don't have it as bad as those human females. They are free to accept invitations from the other females in the tribe as well. The Mother was wise to encourage at least two females to share a harem of males. It makes it a little less painful and a little less humiliating." He leveled his eyes on her again. "Unless love is involved. I can't see a male who's in love with a female being okay with sharing her, and the same goes for the females. In my opinion, the tribe system was created out of necessity, and not out of an innate preference for multiple partners."

Aliya let out a breath. "That's a relief. I was starting to think that I wasn't being true to my heritage and that my human half is messing me up."

Vrog smiled. "Care to elaborate?"

"I don't think I can handle sharing either."

41

Vrog

❧

Aliya's admission boosted Vrog's confidence. It seemed that Wendy had been right, and Aliya thought more like a human female than a Kra-ell.

"That's good to know. I don't like the idea of sharing one bit."

Suddenly looking uncomfortable with their conversation, Aliya turned toward the cappuccino machine. "I should start on your coffee." She chuckled softly. "It's good that the café is not busy right now. I'm neglecting my duties."

Maybe he should let up a little. He'd been overly insistent and blunt in his initial pursuit of Aliya, and that had either scared her or turned her off.

"Speaking of duties, I should go back to my school," he said.

Aliya looked at him over her shoulder. "Are you planning to leave soon?"

"I was, but then Kian asked for my help with starting a school for the village children, and I'm debating what to do. I might be able to help him plan the logistics and maybe even the curriculum, but I can't stay to run it, which was what he probably hoped I would agree to."

It was an opening he hoped Aliya would use to tell him not to go.

For a long moment she didn't comment, focusing on the cappuccino she was making for him. When it was ready, she put it on the counter in front of him. "I know that the international school is your life achievement, but at some point you will need to let it go. You're not aging at the same rate as humans, and you can't get away with pretending to be human for much longer. You could sell the school now and use the experience you gained to establish a new international school here. I don't mean in the village; I mean in Los Angeles. That way, you'd still be doing what you love, but you would be close to Vlad and Wendy."

She'd forgotten about his sandwich, but since he wasn't there to eat, he didn't remind her.

"It sounds like you don't want me to leave."

"I don't."

"Why? Would you be sorry to see me go?"

"Of course." She smiled tightly. "I don't want to be the only hybrid Kra-ell in the village."

"You are not. Emmett is coming back at some point."

"No, he's not. From what I heard, after he and Eleanor complete their mission, they are going straight to Safe Haven. The clan bought it from him, and they are going to convert it into a place for humans with paranormal talents. Or something like that. I just overheard people talking about that, so I'm not sure I got it right. But in any case, Emmett is taken."

Vrog grinned. "But I'm not."

She wrinkled her nose. "You're not taken by a woman, but you are taken nonetheless. Your school is your mistress."

Was that the problem?

Aliya had found a home here, and since he hadn't committed to the village, she couldn't commit to him.

Instead of reacting to her comment though, he asked, "Would you like to go out with me on a date?"

"A date? What's that?"

"It means doing something enjoyable together. We can go to a restaurant in the city, see a show, a movie, a concert. Whatever you like."

She wrinkled her nose again. "I don't think I'm allowed to leave the village. Phinas had to ask Kian for permission to take me hunting in the nearby canyons."

Vrog felt as if she'd just punched him in the gut. "Why did you ask him to go hunting with you? He's not Kra-ell. You should have asked me."

"You seem fine without blood."

"I can do without, but I'm still Kra-ell, and I can still hunt like one. You should have asked me."

For some reason, the idea of taking Aliya hunting, of assisting her to catch her prey had awoken some primitive instinct that resonated with him, resulting in an intense arousal.

"Yeah, I guess I should have." She smiled nervously. "Maybe next time. Now that it's not my only source of sustenance, the blood I took will last me for a while."

"If Kian allowed you to go hunting with a former Doomer, I'm sure he would allow me to take you out."

"I'm not sure of that at all. Kian is a suspicious guy. He might think that the two Kra-ell hybrids are conspiring against him."

Vrog huffed out a laugh. "To do what?"

"I don't know. Sell him out to Jade or something."

"Jade is gone, and we don't even know if she's alive." He leaned over the counter and took her hand. "If Kian agrees, will you go out with me this Saturday?"

She hesitated for a split second. "Where do you want to go?"

"Let's start with dinner at a nice restaurant, and if we are in the mood, we can find a nightclub and go dancing."

When Phinas had suggested it, she'd seemed excited.

"I don't know how to dance. Do you?"

"Not really, but we can observe the humans on the dance floor and imitate them. It shouldn't be too difficult."

"One of my roommates is a dancer. I can ask her to teach us."

That sounded like a great opportunity to spend more time with her. "I would love to take dance lessons with you."

"I'll ask her and let you know."

"Good deal." Vrog finished his cappuccino and rose to his feet. "But first, I should talk to Kian."

Mia

"The UPS truck is here." Mia's grandmother pushed the curtain aside. "Did you order something?"

Mia shook her head. "Not recently. Maybe the delivery is for Tom."

"The driver put it in our mailbox. I'm going to see what it is." She walked out the front door and left it open as she retrieved the package. "It's for you." She brought in a medium-sized envelope and handed it to Mia. "You must have forgotten that you ordered something. It happens to me all the time." Her grandmother chuckled. "I have fun twice. First, when I place the order, and the second time when I get a surprise delivery." She shook her head. "And people say that getting old is no fun."

"I didn't forget." Mia tore the envelope open and pulled out the contents. "Leg warmers? I certainly did not order them. What am I going to do with leg warmers?"

Her grandmother took the empty envelope and looked inside. "There is a note." She pulled it out and handed it to Mia.

"It says that it's a gift from your friend Frankie." Mia turned the note over to see if there was anything written on the other side. "She's losing it. I need to call her and ask what's the idea."

If it was a present from anyone else, Mia would have taken it as a cruel joke, but Frankie would never do that.

Taking the phone and the package with her, she walked to her room, sat on the bed, and texted her friend. *Leg warmers?*

Her phone rang a moment later. "Do you like my brilliant idea?" Frankie asked.

"I think that you're losing it. What am I supposed to do with leg warmers?"

"Isn't it obvious? Use your imagination."

Mia shook her head. "I don't need to keep my prostheses warm, so am I supposed to put them on my arms instead of a sweater?"

"No, silly. Those are thigh-high, so you can use them to cover the prostheses while getting naked with Tom. Problem solved."

"You are brilliant."

They'd talked about getting sexy fishnets with garters, but the idea had been scrapped for practical and esthetic reasons.

"I know. You're welcome."

"It's a coward's way out, but I'll take it." Mia tucked the phone between her ear and her shoulder and pulled the leg warmers off the cardboard insert they were scrunched on. "They are thick enough to cover what needs covering. I just hope that they are long enough too."

They were black with a silver thread woven through to give them some glam, and she could pair them with a sexy black babydoll, provided that she still had it and hadn't donated it to charity like she'd done with most of her clothes from before the event.

"Give them a test run," Frankie suggested. "Put them on and strip naked. If you look good, which I'm sure you will, snap a picture and send it to Tom."

Mia chuckled. "I'm not taking naked pictures of myself and sending them. They could get stolen and spread all over the internet." She shuddered. "With how freaky people are, they could turn viral. But if I can find my black babydoll, I might do that. Just not while he's in a meeting with the Perfect Match people. I don't want to distract him."

"Right. That wouldn't be good. I hope that he buys the chain so Margo and I can get limitless free runs."

"You bet."

"I have to go," Frankie whispered. "My boss is giving me the stink eye. If you end up snapping a sexy picture, send it to me. I want to see how my idea worked."

"I will. Talk to you later." Mia ended the call.

Where could that babydoll be? She didn't remember giving it away, so maybe it was still in her lingerie drawer?

Leaving the leg warmers on the bed, she walked over to the dresser and pulled the drawer open. Her bras and panties were organized in two neat lines, and there was nothing else in there. Maybe it had fallen to the drawer below?

Her T-shirt drawer was a little less organized, or rather a lot, and Mia pulled out all of the contents and dumped them on top of the dresser to sort and to refold. She found what she was looking for pressed between two T-shirts she hadn't worn in years.

Excited butterflies flapping their wings in her stomach, she walked over to the door and locked it.

Stripping down to her panties, she pulled on the babydoll even though it had a musty smell and needed laundering, and then sat down on the bed and pulled on the leg warmers.

Pushing up, she turned to regard herself in the mirror.

She looked okay, but not great. The flimsy babydoll just didn't go with the thick warmers. Perhaps a long T-shirt would do better? Snatching one from the top of the dresser, she pulled the lingerie off and put the black T-shirt on.

"Much better." Mia took her phone, snapped a picture of her reflection, and texted it to Frankie.

Her friend's reply arrived a moment later. *Sweet and sexy. An irresistible combination. You look awesome.*

Smiling, Mia turned around and used the phone to see the reflection of her backside. It wasn't bad either.

The question was whether she should wear the leg warmers for Toven tonight or wait until they moved into his house and had more privacy. Her grandparents' bedroom was at the back of the house, but still, for her first time naked with Toven, Mia didn't want to worry about making too much noise.

Vrog

Vrog left the café intending to call Kian and ask for another meeting, but on second thought, he realized that rushing in without a plan was a bad idea.

Instead, he decided to go on a walk and gather his thoughts.

He needed an excuse to see Kian again, and asking permission for Aliya to leave the village should come after he'd offered Kian something of value.

The boss wanted a school for the village children, but they were too few and too young to create a vibrant environment, which Vrog considered essential not so much for the quality of their education as for the socializing and character growth that was no less important.

For the first few years, or maybe even decades, the school would have to incorporate human children to provide the needed numbers as well as diversity, but it would also need to safeguard the immortal children's identity and hide their enhanced senses and abilities, which would be difficult to control for the younger ones.

A boarding school like the one Vrog had founded in China would be a good solution, but he doubted that clan families would want to part with their precious children, and it also wasn't a practical solution for little ones like Phoenix. But what if the school was part boarding and part day school?

He'd visited a lucrative private high school in Los Angeles that had a small boarding program for students from China. The administration had purchased two homes adjacent to the school and put a teacher with his or her spouse in charge of each. The foreign students attending the high school resided in those two homes.

How could he apply the same formula to younger children, though?

Perhaps the homes could be run by the clan families, and the human children would come from the foster system?

That would solve the problem of kids seeing strange things and reporting them to their parents, and it could also be a great service to the community, but Vrog doubted that clan families would be willing to live outside the village.

Besides, even if some were willing, Kian wouldn't want them out of its protective sphere.

But what if the school and the homes serving as dormitories could be built close to the village? The village's security system could encompass the school compound, and the families wouldn't have to travel far to spend time with their friends.

In addition, some of the single clan members might want to become foster parents. Many craved children but couldn't have them, and fostering could fulfill their need to nurture.

Perhaps they could even search for children with paranormal talents? Could the clan pick and choose which children it wanted to foster?

The more Vrog toyed with the idea, the more excited he got about it. Instead of attracting rich parents who wanted the best education for their children, he could dedicate his time and expertise to helping children who didn't have parents to ensure a good future for them.

Maybe he could even search for throwaway Kra-ell offspring like Mey and Jin. Those two had been lucky to get adopted by caring people, but those exhibiting more pronounced Kra-ell features like Aliya had probably not been as fortunate and had either been fostered or had languished in orphanages.

Would Aliya consider joining him on a search for more abandoned second-generation hybrids?

Probably not.

She was happy in the village, and she wouldn't be inclined to leave, but he was sure that she would find his newfound mission admirable and would support his efforts.

Vrog shook his head.

He'd allowed himself to get carried away. From trying to find a solution for the clan children's education, he'd somehow gotten to searching for abandoned Kra-ell descendants. Building a hybrid boarding school with foster children would be difficult enough to pull off. Adding the Kra-ell element could wait.

Spotting a bench a little further down the path, he pulled out his phone, walked over, and sat down to text Kian. *I have an idea for a school that I want to run by you. Do you have time to see me again today?*

Kian's response came a few seconds later. *Come to my office now.*

Vrog replied, *I'm on my way.*

Kian

When Vrog was done explaining his idea for a hybrid school, Kian leaned back in his chair. "What you suggest is complicated. I need to give it some thought."

A couple of hours ago, Vrog had seemed uninterested and dismissive, and now he was full of grandiose plans that exceeded what Kian had in mind, turning the project into a monster.

Kian wasn't at all sure that he wanted to get involved with the human fostering system. He didn't know much about it, but foster parents were probably frequently visited by officials to evaluate the care they provided to their charges. The last thing the clan needed was that level of scrutiny.

"I understand." Vrog nodded. "It's a much more expensive undertaking than what you originally had in mind."

"Finances are a secondary concern." Kian crossed his arms over his chest. "I don't know much about the foster system, but Jacki grew up in it, so she might be able to shed some light on it for me. I like the philanthropic aspect of your idea, but my primary concern is providing the clan children with the best environment to learn and socialize. I need it to be a safe place for them to be themselves, a place that is protected from humans and from our enemies. Sending my daughter to a school that is outside the village borders goes against my fatherly instincts, and I'm pretty sure that Syssi is not going to like it either." He uncrossed his arms and leaned forward. "On the other hand, Nathalie enrolled Phoenix in a human preschool, so maybe not everyone would be opposed to your idea."

"While you contemplate my proposal, do you want me to start working on a plan?"

Why was the guy suddenly so eager to build a school for the clan?

Kian narrowed his eyes at Vrog. "This morning you seemed uninterested, and now you can't wait to start. What has changed?"

Vrog's lips lifted in a small smile. "Can I be frank with you?"

"I won't tolerate anything else."

Vrog cleared his throat. "My interest in Aliya shouldn't come as a surprise to you. I was very open about my intentions towards her from the very start, but she hasn't been receptive. The Kra-ell do not form strong instinctual bonds like immortal couples do, and our tradition puts the burden of initiating a relationship on the females, so when Aliya didn't indicate an interest in me, I backed away and waited for her to come to the realization that I was her best choice. I think she's starting to accept that, but I also realized that she needs me to act more like a human or an immortal male than a Kra-ell. And that means I need to be the one to make the first move."

Kian stifled a chuckle. "Kra-ell, human, or immortal, male or female, it doesn't make a difference. You should always go after what you want and not wait passively for it to come to you."

"I agree. After our meeting this morning, I went to the café and invited Aliya on a date."

"Good for you. I assume she said yes?"

"She did, but she was concerned that you might not allow her to leave the village. I want to take her to a nice restaurant in the city, and maybe a show or a movie. We both live with roommates, so entertaining at home is not the best option."

"No, it's not." Kian sighed. "Which reminds me that I need to take my wife out of the village too. We haven't done anything as a couple since Allegra was born."

"So, do I have your permission to take Aliya out?"

A mating between Vrog and Aliya would definitely be a good thing. Kian couldn't keep Vrog in the village against his will, but he preferred him where he could keep an eye on him. Not because he didn't trust the guy, but because Vrog was exposed in China. If the hostile Kra-ell ever came back and found him in his school, his knowledge of the clan could be a problem. Kalugal could compel him to keep silent, but the Kra-ell might have an even stronger compeller who could override Kalugal's orders.

Obviously, Vrog's renewed interest in the female was what had prompted the change in attitude toward building a school for the clan. If the two mated, Vrog would stay in the village, and he would need a project to sink his fangs into.

"I have no problem with you taking Aliya out, and I trust both of you not to intentionally betray the clan, but I always prefer to err on the side of caution. I will need Kalugal to reinforce his compulsion on both of you to keep the existence of the clan and the village a secret and to return here after your date."

"Of course." Vrog dipped his head. "Thank you. Also, would it be okay for me to borrow Vlad's car? I don't have a mode of transportation."

For a brief moment Kian considered offering Okidu's chauffeuring services, but then another idea popped into his head, prompted by Vrog's comment about his and Aliya's living situation. If things went well, they would need a private place to get intimate.

"Did Vlad tell you about the cabin where he and Wendy fell in love?"

Vrog nodded. "Wendy told me about her stay in the remote mountain location with Vlad, Bowen, Leon, and Richard. She was a very negative young lady before spending time in that cabin, and her companions helped change her worldview and turn her life around. She is grateful to all four of them, but especially to Vlad."

"Naturally. Love is transformative." Kian opened his laptop and pulled up pictures of the place. "Several clan couples have found love in that cabin, and my wife says that its walls are imbued with it. You could take Aliya on a romantic weekend in the woods and stay within those love-imbued walls." He turned the laptop around to show Vrog.

"It's lovely, but I'm afraid it's premature. This is going to be our first official date, and I doubt Aliya will be willing to be alone with me for the entire weekend."

"You never know." Kian turned the laptop around and closed it. "One thing could lead to another, and given that neither of you has a place of your own, you might miss a great opportunity to take your relationship to the next level. I'll give you the address, the directions, and the code to the door, and if the timing is right and the lady is agreeable, you can take her there. Just text me before you head out there so I can notify security. If you go there unannounced, you'll encounter a shitload of trouble, so don't forget."

"I won't. Thank you." Vrog pushed to his feet and offered Kian his hand.

"You're welcome." Kian shook it. "I wish you the best of luck."

Vrog

Excitement bubbling in his chest, Vrog strolled back to the café.

He found Aliya delivering a tray to one of the tables and waited until she was done to approach her.

"I spoke with Kian, and he's fine with us leaving the village, but he conditioned our outing on Kalugal reinforcing the compulsion on us. Also, in addition to keeping the community a secret, he wants Kalugal to compel us to return to the village at the end of our date."

It occurred to Vrog that if Aliya agreed to go with him to the cabin and they stayed for the weekend, the compulsion might be a problem. Technically though, it could be considered part of their date and worked into the compulsion, but if he wanted to keep the option a secret from her, he needed to contact Kalugal beforehand and explain.

"That's great." She gave him a shy smile. "When are we going?"

"Is Saturday evening a good time?"

She nodded. "I'm looking forward to it."

"Wonderful." He leaned and kissed her cheek.

Her big eyes widened in surprise, but she smiled, so it was all good. "Do you have a car?"

"I'll borrow one from Vlad or Wendy."

Hopefully, they would be okay without a car until Monday morning. Wendy worked in the village, so she wouldn't be too inconvenienced if he took hers, but Vlad needed to be at the bakery at four in the morning, so if they took his they would need to return Sunday night.

"What time should I be ready?"

He hadn't thought it through yet, but if he made reservations in a restaurant for five in the afternoon, they should leave the village at four.

"Is four o'clock okay?'

She nodded. "Will you stop at the café tomorrow as well?"

He wasn't sure that was a good idea. If he started hanging around the café again, he might do or say something to ruin their date. He preferred to play it safe.

"I have a big new project to work on, and the café offers too many distractions, but I might stop by to get a coffee and a sandwich."

Aliya winced. "I forgot your sandwich. Let me make it for you now."

"That's okay. I need to go home and start working on plans for the clan's new school. I'll grab some leftovers." He smiled. "Goodbye, Aliya."

"Goodbye." She shifted from foot to foot. "It was nice seeing you again."

"Hopefully, we will be seeing much more of each other now." Vrog turned around without waiting to see her expression.

Heading back to Vlad's home, he made a detour to stop by Aliya's new place. He didn't have her roommates' phone numbers, but he knew where the house was, and he needed their help.

During the five-minute walk he formulated what he was going to do, and as he climbed the steps to the front porch, he took a deep breath and straightened his shoulders before knocking on the door.

A slim woman wearing exercise clothing opened up. "Vrog, what a nice surprise. Aliya is not home."

He offered a prayer to the Mother that the woman wasn't the dominatrix from his virtual adventure.

"I know. I just spoke to her at the café. I want to talk to you. Bernice, right?" He had a fifty-fifty chance of being correct.

"In the flesh." A puzzled expression on her face, she opened the door all the way. "Please, come in."

"Thank you."

She motioned for him to take a seat on the couch. "So, what did you want to talk to me about?" She sat on one of the armchairs.

There was no roundabout way to ask for what he needed. "I invited Aliya on a date this Saturday, and when I asked Kian to approve the outing, he offered me the use of the clan's cabin. I told him that was premature since it was our first date, but he suggested that I keep it as an option in case Aliya was agreeable."

Bernice smirked. "I had no idea that you were such a naughty boy, Vrog. Go on."

"Since I'm not going to suggest it unless I feel that Aliya is open to the idea, I can't tell her about the optional plans, but she will need a change of clothes, and that's what I need your help with. I need you to pack a bag for her without her knowledge. I'll put it in the trunk and pull it out only if Aliya agrees to spend the rest of the weekend with me at the cabin."

Bernice tapped her finger on her full lips. "That might be a problem. Aliya's wardrobe is modest, and she will notice if something is missing. I will have to pack something of mine for her. You will also need food and wine and other goodies for a romantic weekend in the cabin. But leave all that to Yvonne and me, we can take care of everything."

He hadn't expected that. "Thank you. I truly appreciate your help."

She waved a dismissive hand. "Yvonne and I were team Phinas until he blew it. Now we are team Vrog."

He lifted a brow. "I didn't know there were teams dedicated to Aliya's suitors. Do you mean like cheerleading teams?"

She barked out a laugh. "You've got it. Anyway, Phinas messed up, although I'm not sure how and why. All I know is that Aliya is no longer interested in seeing him." She leaned her elbow on her knee and her chin on her fist. "You got a good chance with her. Don't blow it."

"Care to elaborate? I could use some advice from Aliya's friends."

Bernice grinned as if he'd given her a great compliment. "With pleasure. Aliya might be thirty years old, but she's a teenager at heart. She has big expectations, and she pretends to be confident, but she needs to be treated with care and approached gently. Don't rush her into things she's not ready for, but don't wait for her to initiate things either."

"I'm confused," he admitted. "How will I know what she's ready for?"

"Take a tiny step and observe her reaction. If she's agreeable, you can take another tiny step, and if she's not, retreat and wait for a cue."

"That sounds complicated. I was under the impression that contemporary women no longer played those games."

"Well, some of us do, and some of us don't. It depends on many factors but mainly on the level of experience." She winked. "Besides, it's not just about sex, right? You like her, and she likes you, and you have many things in common. You need to focus on that."

Syssi

❦

"She's getting so big." Amanda lifted Allegra from her stroller and kissed the top of her head. "Evie looks tiny in comparison."

Oridu came out of the kitchen and bowed to Annani. "Shall I serve lunch, Clan Mother?"

"Not yet." Annani handed him her teacup. "But I would appreciate fresh tea for my guests and for me."

"As you wish, Clan Mother." Oridu bowed and retreated to the kitchen.

"How is Eve's sleep cycle?" Alena asked.

"Good." Amanda sat down with Allegra in her arms and glanced at her daughter, who was sleeping in her baby carriage. "She sleeps six hours straight at night and naps throughout the day. She's the most serene baby I've ever seen."

Syssi took the colorful padded blanket out of the baby bag and spread it on the floor. "Allegra is constantly rolling over. I put her on her belly so she can play with her toys, and a moment later, she flops on her back."

"That's what she's supposed to do," Alena said.

"Yeah, but she can't flop back and starts crying." Syssi took her daughter from Amanda and put her down on her tummy with several plush toys within reach.

Allegra cooed at the stuffed butterfly and then promptly flopped onto her back.

Syssi sighed. "I'd better put her in the baby gym." She reached into the storage compartment under the stroller and pulled out the toy.

Annani smiled. "Babies these days have such wonderful toys."

"What toys did the babies of the gods have?" Syssi asked.

The gods had been such advanced people, and they cherished their children. They must have had wonderful toys for their babies.

"I do not remember." Annani leaned to touch the soft arch of the baby gym. "I do not think any babies were born to the gods during my time. But the babies of immortals had rattles and stuffed toys that were made by hand. Even the gods did not have sewing machines."

"Making clothing was so time-consuming," Alena said. "It took a skilled seamstress three days to sew a simple dress."

Amanda sat on the floor next to Allegra. "I'm so glad that I was born in the modern era after the invention of the sewing machine." She pushed one of the toys hanging from the arch, so it swung back and forth to Allegra's delight. "I need to go back to work in two weeks. I'm still trying to figure out the logistics of being a mother and having a job." She looked up at Syssi. "When are you planning on coming back to the lab?"

Syssi cast her an apologetic look. "I enjoy being a mother too much to go back full time, but I'm willing to work a few hours a day, provided that I find a solution for Allegra." She turned to Alena. "Can you be her babysitter? I don't trust anyone else with my baby."

"Orion and I still plan to visit my children in Scotland and then continue to Paris and meet Yamanu and Mey there."

Syssi waved a hand. "I was just joking. I need to find a clan female who's a mother and who loves babies." She looked at Allegra's sweet face. "How am I going to part with her even for a few hours, though? I'll miss her too much. But on the other hand, I need to get out of the house and interact with adults, or I'll go nuts."

"I might have a solution," Amanda said. "We can bring our daughters to work with us and hire a human nanny to watch them. I can convert my office to a nursery." She folded her legs under her. "I can move my desk to the main lab and work from there."

"That's a great idea." Syssi joined Amanda on the floor. "That way, we will never be far from our babies, and we can go into the nursery any time we want to cuddle them."

"Then it's settled." Amanda pushed up to her feet and walked over to her purse. "I'll start work on my office right away, so it's ready in two weeks." She pulled out her phone and started typing on the screen.

"Who are you texting?" Alena asked.

"Ingrid, of course. I need her to go to the university, take some measurements of my office, and design the nursery."

Amanda's decisiveness was one of the things Syssi appreciated most about her sister-in-law. She was a doer.

"Speaking of Ingrid," Alena said. "How are things between her and Kalugal's chef going? Did they move in together?"

"They did not." Annani accepted a new teacup from Oridu. "They are seeing a lot of each other, but they are not in a rush to live together."

As Oridu handed each of them a teacup, Syssi thought about how strange it was that other than Edna, none of the clan females found true love with Kalugal's men. There were plenty of hookups, and some couples had even moved in together, but none had bonded.

She took a small sip from the tea and then put the teacup on the coffee table. "Don't you find it strange that none of the former Doomers have bonded with clan ladies except for Rufsur?"

Annani sighed. "I hoped that more truelove matches would be found, but I am not really surprised that it did not happen. Back in the time of the gods, most couples were not truelove mates, but they still formed loving relationships without the bond. In fact, I am surprised that all the transitioned Dormants and their partners are bonded mates. It must be because the Fates brought them to us."

Amanda chuckled. "Then who brought Kalugal and his men to the clan, the devil?"

"Of course not." Annani uttered an indignant huff. "We do not believe in a devil, Amanda. It was also the Fates, but they only intended for Kalugal and Rufsur to find truelove mates. Maybe they were the only ones who earned the boon."

"That's an interesting hypothesis." Amanda tapped a finger on her lower lip. "Most of the clan females hook up with more than one of Kalugal's men, so they avoid getting addicted, but I wonder what will happen to the couples who are exclusive once the addiction sets in. It's almost as good as the bond at keeping people together."

Kian

Kian glanced at his watch. It was almost noon, and the meeting with the prospective buyer for Perfect Match should have ended already. He'd hoped Gabriel would call to tell him how it went before he had to leave for lunch at his mother's, but it seemed that the meeting was taking longer than it should, especially given that they were not interested in selling.

The call came when he got to the staircase.

"What's up, Gabriel? Did Hartford agree to shell out twenty-five billion dollars?"

"He did."

Kian stopped in his tracks. "You're joking."

"I'm not. He even brought proof of funds. He has mountains of gold in a depository in Switzerland."

"Who is this guy, and how come I've never heard of him before?"

"He said that it's old money that's been in his family for hundreds of years."

"Do you have a recording of the meeting? I want to see what he looks like."

"We don't, but that's going to change soon. To ensure our clients' anonymity, we didn't want any surveillance cameras in the Perfect Match studios, but once the new contracts are ready, we will install a camera in one of the offices."

"That's for public consumption. I'm sure you have some hidden around."

"I assure you that we don't. If you want, I can send you a picture of the avatar he created for himself. It looks a lot like him."

"That won't do. What do you and Hunter want to do? Do you want to sell?"

"We discussed it, and half of twenty-five billion dollars is a lot of money. We can use some of it to keep developing our virtual technology and at the same time never worry about money again. In addition, he offered to keep us in the company as directors and let us retain some of the shares. His offer is just too good to pass up, and I think we can negotiate a deal that will be satisfactory to all parties."

Despite his gut instinct telling him to decline the offer, Kian couldn't argue with Gabriel's assessment. At the very least, he had to pretend to consider it.

"I'll discuss it with Syssi and let you know."

"Don't take long. Hartford said that he wants to move forward with the deal as soon as possible, and that if we decline his offer, he's going to use that money to develop the technology from scratch and become a very well-funded competitor. I don't think he was bluffing. I don't want to pressure you, but if you don't want to sell, you'll have to buy Hunter and me out and pay us forty-eight percent of what he offered. That's what the contract between us states."

"I'm well aware of what's in the contract. I will let you know in a couple of hours." Kian ended the call.

Gabriel was bluffing. He and Hunter would never use that clause. It offered them the option of getting bought out at whatever the market value of the company was at the time, but it also stipulated that they would be prohibited from developing any similar or new virtual technology. The two were too young to retire and too passionate about what they were doing to enforce it. However, if they did, he didn't have the money to buy their share.

When Oridu opened the door for him, Syssi and his sisters were already seated around the dining room table. "Good afternoon, everyone." He walked over to Syssi and kissed her cheek before turning around and crouching next to Allegra. "Hello, beautiful."

"*Bwooo.*" She started kicking her legs and lifted her arms to him.

Smiling, he picked her up and kissed her cheeks one at a time. *"Bwooo* to you too." He took her with him to the dining table.

"She was happy playing on the floor," Syssi said.

"She's happier in her daddy's arms." He kissed the top of Allegra's head. "Gabriel called."

"And?"

"Hartford is willing to pay twenty-five billion dollars for Perfect Match and leave Hunter and Gabriel in charge."

Amanda whistled. "That's a lot of money." She grinned at Syssi. "My brother has been investing in stocks for decades, and you outperformed him with one stock. Not bad, Syssi. Not bad at all."

Syssi blushed. "I just believed in the company. I never expected to profit from it like this."

"Do you want to sell?" Annani asked.

"There is a lot we could do with that money."

"Like what?" Amanda asked.

"We could run more rescue missions. The Guardian force is stretched to capacity, but with that much money, we can hire human teams and expand the fight. Besides, Gabriel said that Hartford wants to make it accessible to people with disabilities, and apparently, he has the funds to do it. The question is whether he's sincere. If he wants the company for the technology and what he can do with it to make even more money, then I'm not sure I want to sell." She turned to Kian. "I would like to meet him and bring Andrew along. I need to know what Hartford is really planning to do with Perfect Match."

Kian nodded. "Text Andrew and find out when is a convenient time for him."

"I'll do it right now." Syssi pulled out her phone and texted Andrew.

His stubborn brother-in-law still refused to quit his government job at the anti-terrorism department. His excuse was that he didn't want to relinquish access to all the classified data he was privy to, but Kian had a feeling Andrew just wasn't ready to sever ties with his human past yet. Regrettably, Turner suffered from the same affliction, keeping his hostage-rescue operations going.

When Syssi's phone pinged with an incoming text, she lifted it and read Andrew's answer out loud. "I can do it Monday morning. The earlier, the better."

"Ask him if ten o'clock is good. I don't want to be stuck in rush hour traffic."

Syssi texted the question, and a moment later, Andrew replied with a thumbs up.

"May I serve lunch now, Clan Mother?" Oridu asked.

"Yes, you may."

As the Odus came out of the kitchen with platters laden with food and put them on the table, Kian got up, walked over to the baby blanket, and put Allegra down. "Are you going to play nicely and let Daddy eat?"

"*Bwooo.*"

"I will take that as a yes."

Toven

"You shouldn't have waited for me." Toven kissed Mia's cheek, pulled out a chair, and hung his satchel on the back of it.

"Nonsense." Rosalyn handed him a platter heaped with rosemary chicken and tiny potatoes. "We had a snack earlier to tide us over. A family should eat together."

"Thank you." Toven scooped up two pieces of chicken and a handful of potatoes onto his plate and dug in.

It had never been the case in his family, but he liked Rosalyn's mama-goose attitude much more than the rigid formality he remembered from his mother's house. His father had always been a rebel, informal and warm, but since his parents hadn't been mated, Ekin hadn't resided with them, and most of Toven's childhood meals had been either taken alone or with his mother.

Regrettably, things hadn't been much different in his own household. His wife had been a goddess, and she followed the same rigid rules of conduct. Perhaps that was why he'd traveled so much. Whenever he'd stayed in one place for too long, Toven had felt stifled. He craved the freedom of going places where no one knew who he was and where he didn't need to follow anyone's rules.

That hadn't worked out so well either.

He was still a god, enamored with the ideals of his people, and he'd deluded himself into thinking that he could copy Ahn's civilizing methods in another part of the world. Upon reflection, Toven realized that what he'd lacked was Ahn's ruthlessness. The head god had pursued the gods' objectives regardless of the cost to his subjects and even his own daughter. If Ahn hadn't promised Annani to Mortdh, history would have taken a different route.

Curtis put down his fork and wiped his mouth with a napkin. "Given how quiet you are, I assume that the meeting didn't go well."

"On the contrary." Toven took a sip of water. "The founders came up with an amount they were willing to accept, and I agreed to it. I also offered to keep them on as managing directors, which I think was the tipping point in the negotiations. Hunter and Gabriel didn't want to give up their life project, but the money appealed to them. They want to make a deal, and I'm waiting for them to schedule a meeting with the silent partners."

"Is there more than one?" Mia asked.

"The shares are owned by the wife, but naturally, both she and her husband are involved in the decision making." He turned to Mia. "I think it would be advantageous for you to accompany me when we meet with them, and it has nothing to do with your disability. It's about the principle of mirroring. They make business decisions together and therefore would be more positively inclined to negotiate with another couple."

Mia put a hand over her heart. "I don't want to pull the sick girl card, but just thinking about participating in a power meeting like that makes my heart race. I'll feel like a fish out of water."

Toven took her hand and kissed it. "I don't want you to do anything that you're not comfortable with, but just give it some thought. It took the founders days to get back to me and schedule the first meeting. I don't expect the second one with the silent partners to happen any time soon. You have plenty of time to decide."

Mia nodded. "I will try to get used to the idea." She smiled. "Maybe I should get a new business outfit that would make me feel more confident."

"Anything you need or want is yours." He turned sideways and covered their joined hands with his other one. "If you're done with the illustrations, we can go shopping for new outfits tomorrow."

"That's so sweet of you." She leaned and kissed his cheek. "I can't tomorrow, but maybe on Friday. I'm meeting with my publisher and the writer tomorrow afternoon."

"Do you need me to come with you?"

She shook her head. "It's just an informal meeting to finalize the story. I can handle it by myself."

As Toven's phone rang, Mia sucked in a breath and her grandparents tensed, probably expecting it to be news about the meeting with the silent partners.

Pulling it out of his pocket, he gave them a smile. "It's just the contractor."

"Oh." Mia let out a breath.

"Hello, Bobby."

"Hi. We finished the hot mop in the shower, and we need to let it dry, so we are leaving early today. Did you speak with the tile store? We need it delivered by midday tomorrow."

"I did, and they promised to be here early in the morning."

"Excellent. My men will be there to help unload it."

"Thank you. Enjoy the rest of your day."

"You too." Bobby ended the call.

"It seems like we can go home early today and put in some work." Toven picked up his knife and fork.

Mia smiled. "That's great. I need to put a few finishing touches to my illustrations for tomorrow."

Rosalyn smiled under her breath. "Ah, to be young and in love."

Curtis huffed. "There is nothing wrong with being old and in love."

"You're absolutely right, my dear. There isn't." She leaned over and kissed his cheek.

Mia

It was the perfect opportunity to try out the leg warmers, but Mia had to be discreet about it. She couldn't just put them on and walk out of the house. It wasn't cold outside, and even if it was, her prostheses didn't need warming.

"I need to collect my things and change into something more comfortable." She patted her tummy. "The chicken was delicious, and I overindulged. Now my waistband feels too tight." She smiled at her grandmother and got up.

"Are you going to wait for me?" she asked Toven. "Or are you going to the house?"

She still couldn't call it home, not in front of her grandparents. She really needed to sit them down and tell them that once the bathroom remodeling was done, she was moving in with Toven. It wasn't a big deal. They were still going to share two or three meals daily, but emotionally, it was a big step.

"I'll wait for you." Toven pushed to his feet, kissed her cheek, and then sat back down to finish his tea and chat with her grandparents.

She was so grateful that he got along so well with them. He seemed to genuinely like them, and they regarded him as a son. Technically, he could be their grandson, but somehow that didn't seem to fit. He was such an old soul.

Back in her room, Mia locked the door as quietly as she could and then walked over to her closet. She needed something that could be worn over the leg warmers without them being noticeable. The black wide-leg trousers would do the job, but they were too fancy for an afternoon at home. Besides, her excuse had been a full tummy, and the pants were high-waisted and had buckles on the front.

The other choice was a long blue skirt. She could bunch the legwarmers, so they were hidden, and the skirt had an elastic waist, so it worked well with her excuse.

Sexy lingerie was in order as well, but the best she could do was a matching set of black bra and panties that was pretty, but more practical than seductive.

Standing in front of the mirror in the black lingerie set and the black leg warmers, she liked what she saw. She looked sexy. Not perfect, but Toven would think that she was, and that was all that mattered.

The long skirt was next, and she matched it with a short T-shirt that exposed her midriff when she stretched her arms up. A brush of mascara, some lip gloss, and a squirt of perfume, and she was ready to go.

As she walked out of her room with the strap of her large bag slung across her body, Toven stopped talking mid-sentence and stared at her.

"You look beautiful, Mia. Is this your new power outfit?"

She laughed. "It's not but thank you for the compliment. Ready to go?"

"Indeed, I am." He rose to his feet and took his satchel before turning to her grandfather. "We will continue our discussion over dinner."

Her grandfather nodded. "Remind me. At my age, I'll forget what we were talking about the moment the door closes behind you."

Toven chuckled. "You're not fooling anyone with that old man nonsense, Curtis. You are as sharp as a fox."

Her grandad smiled. "Once I remember what I was talking about."

"Dinner is at six-thirty," her grandmother called from the kitchen. "Don't be late."

"We will be here." Toven wrapped his arm around Mia's middle and led her out the door. "We have four hours until dinner. What do you want to do with them?"

"Go over my illustrations," she said innocently. "I need to make sure that everything is perfect for the meeting tomorrow."

"And once that's done?"

"Then we will see."

As Toven opened the door to their house, she walked in expecting everything to be covered with dust, but the remodeling crew had left the house as clean as they could, and all the windows were open. Only a faint smell of tar remained from the hot mopping.

Toven put his satchel on the dining room table. "I hope the smell doesn't bother you."

"It's not so bad." She walked over to her favorite armchair and sat down. "It's good that we don't have to sleep in here tonight." But she had every intention of making good use of the bed for other activities.

The question was how to surprise Toven. Should she go into the bedroom, take her clothes off, and walk into the living room wearing only the lingerie and leg warmers? Or should she lie on the bed and call Toven?

The second option seemed more appealing, but he might wonder what she was doing in there and follow her. Maybe she should use the secondary bathroom to get undressed?

And then what?

Toven

Mia looked so delectable that all Toven could think about was taking her to bed, but she had work to do.

That could wait for after he'd had his fill of her, but he couldn't just throw her over his shoulder and carry her to the bedroom caveman style. She was too delicate for such rough play, and she wouldn't appreciate it. Though if he wasn't mistaken, he'd detected a slight whiff of arousal hiding under the stronger smell of her perfume, so maybe Mia had some naughty plans of her own.

"I'm going to check what they've done in the bathroom today."

"Okay." She smiled at him. "Call me if there is anything interesting to see."

He nodded, but his phone going off in his pocket stopped him in his tracks.

It wasn't the contractor because he'd already spoken to him, and Mia was right there next to him. The only other people who had this number were from Perfect Match.

"Hello," he answered.

"It's Gabriel. Does Monday at ten in the morning work for you?"

"It's perfect. Same place?"

"No. Our silent partner is very concerned with security and keeping his and his wife's identity a secret. They are going to provide me with the details on the morning of the meeting. I'll text you the address Monday morning when I get it from them. All I know is that it's going to be somewhere in downtown Los Angeles."

"Can I at least know their first names?"

"It's up to them if they want to share them with you during the meeting. When they first showed interest in our company, we only knew the husband as Mr. X."

Those people were even more paranoid than he, which was no small achievement.

"Don't forget to account for traffic. You need to give me the address at least an hour and a half ahead of time."

Gabriel chuckled. "Where are you staying, the boonies?"

"I'm staying in a very nice suburban neighborhood. But if your silent partners are that secretive, perhaps I should be too, so I'm not going to tell you where it is."

"I have a good idea where that might be. We know where Mia Berkovich lives, and you are probably not too far from her."

Damn. He was so obsessed with Mia that he was neglecting his own security.

Once the negotiations were done, he would have to compel everyone involved to keep his identity and his involvement with the company a secret. Hunter and Gabriel would continue to be the public faces, and he would be the new silent majority partner.

As Toven switched the phone to his other ear, he noticed Mia's pinched expression and gave her the thumbs up. "It's a big city, Gabriel, and that could be anywhere, so I don't think you can find me that easily. Thanks for arranging the meeting."

"You're welcome. See you Monday." Ending the call, Toven returned the phone to his pocket.

Mia looked at him expectantly. "So, you're meeting with the silent partners Monday morning."

He nodded. "That gives you a lot of time to get used to the idea of coming with me. Today is only Wednesday."

"Four days is not that long." She got up and walked up to him. "But I will use them to talk myself into going."

"You are so brave." Pulling her into his arms, he kissed her softly on the lips. "And I'm so proud of you."

She chuckled. "I'm not brave. I'm a big coward who just doesn't give up easily."

"That's bravery." He moved to her side, leaving one arm around her. "Are you accompanying me on my inspection of the bathroom?"

"Yes, I am." She lifted her smiling eyes to him. "If I chicken out of going with you to the meeting, I can at least say that I supported you in something."

He stopped and turned to her. "What you have done for me is nothing short of a miracle, so never belittle the value of your support."

She looked at him with puzzlement in her eyes. "You keep saying that, but it's not true. You've done much more for me than I've done for you."

He shook his head. "Before you entered my life, I existed, but I wasn't living. You restarted my heart. I felt love again for the first time in forever. Then you shared your grandparents and your best friends with me, making me part of a family again. You can't put a price on that. You can't buy it, and you can't negotiate for it, and you can't even conquer it in battle. It can only be given out of love."

"Oh, Toven." She wound her arms around his neck. "I love you so much."

Mia

"I love you too, sweetheart." Toven dipped his head to look into her eyes. "Why are you crying?"

"I'm not crying." Mia chuckled. "I'm tearing up because I'm emotional." She wiped the tears away with her thumbs and took in a long breath. "Let's see that bathroom."

"Okay." He kissed the top of her head before releasing her.

"The new enclave for the bathtub looks awesome." Mia leaned against the doorjamb.

"It's going to be a luxurious retreat once it's done." Toven inspected the work. "It was a good call to install a bay window and put the tub there. It opens up the space."

That had been her idea and the reason the remodeling project had been extended by a week. Mia was excited about the beautiful new enclave and the jacuzzi tub that would be installed there, even though she wouldn't be able to use it. Well, technically she could, but it would necessitate Toven carrying her into the tub, which was a big no-no. At least for now. She couldn't wear leg warmers in the water, and her waterproof prostheses were basic and much uglier than her regular ones.

"We can put some potted plants on both sides of the niche." She walked over to the bay window and pointed to where the plants should go.

"I can't wait for us to enjoy the tub together." Toven embraced her from behind and kissed her neck.

Swallowing the lump that had formed in her throat, Mia turned around with a smile on her face. "It's going to take a long time for this bathroom to be completed, but the bedroom is just fine for what I have in mind."

"And what's that?" Toven pretended innocence.

As usual, when he got aroused, his eyes started glowing, but by now she was used to it, and it was a very convenient tell. She didn't have to guess whether Toven was in the mood for love.

Not that he ever wasn't.

Her guy was always randy, and it was just one more thing she loved about him.

Taking his hand, she led him to the bedroom. "Close the curtains." She smiled up at him. "This show is just for you."

He practically leaped to do as she asked, moving way too fast, which meant that she was forced to do the striptease in front of him.

Oh, well. Maybe it was better like that.

Now that the curtains were closed, the room was nearly dark, making it a little less scary. He could still see her, and she could see him, but it was dark enough to provide the right ambience.

"Sit on the bed," she pointed.

He did as she asked and crossed his legs. "Am I getting a show?"

"Yes, you are." Mia grabbed the bottom of her T-shirt and tugged it over her head. "But you have to stay on the bed and not move until I'm done."

Smiling, he tucked his hands under his thighs.

As Mia pushed her thumbs into the elastic of her skirt, she closed her eyes and imagined that she was a cyborg— a beautiful, powerful, enhanced female that was sexy and knew how to please a man.

Perhaps once she could participate in a virtual fantasy again, she could request a cyborg as her avatar and a futuristic city as the environment for the adventure.

Taking a deep breath, she pulled the elastic on both sides as far as it would go and pushed the skirt down without touching the leg warmers.

When the skirt hit the floor, Toven's breath hitched. "You are absolutely stunning and so brave. Can I touch you now?"

"Not yet. I'm not done."

His enthusiasm wasn't faked. He really believed that she was gorgeous, and with him looking at her with such hunger, Mia felt that she was.

Reaching behind her, she unhooked her bra, and holding the cups to her breasts with one hand, slid the straps off her shoulders one at a time. When they were down around her biceps, she let the bra fall to the floor.

"Can I touch you now?" Toven's voice sounded like a cross between a growl and a hiss.

"Not yet. One more thing to go." She hooked her thumbs in the elastic of her panties, pulled it far as it would go, and removed them just as carefully as she had done with the skirt.

Toven

Toven didn't know whether he was more stunned by the sheer beauty of Mia's nude body, or by her courage and the inventive solution she'd found to make herself feel more confident about stripping in front of him.

It wasn't the full reveal he'd hoped for, but it was a tremendous step forward.

"You can move now," she whispered.

Rising slowly to his feet, he walked over to where she stood. "I'm speechless."

He kissed her, pouring all the love and admiration he felt for her into it while his hands roamed over her bare back, sliding down to her small bottom and then circling back up to cup her breasts.

"Fates, you're perfect." He dropped to his knees in front of her and kissed her right where her lips parted.

"Should I worship you with my tongue?" He nuzzled the place he'd kissed.

"Yes," she breathed.

He wanted to do that right there but standing for long periods of time was difficult for Mia, and he intended to take his time. Pushing up to his feet, he wrapped his arms around her and carried her to the bed, but he didn't lay her down. Instead, he set her on the edge of the bed and knelt again.

"Spread your thighs for me, love." He helped her by lightly pushing them apart.

Toven wanted to see all of Mia, he wanted to devour her, but up until this moment he hadn't been privy to all of her treasures. She'd always kept her pants partially on to conceal her prostheses from him, and the long, footless socks were an ingenious solution that freed her to finally offer herself fully to him.

"Beautiful." He pressed a kiss to her petals. "Thank you for giving yourself so fully to me." When he swiped his tongue on one side of her sensitive nubbin and then the other, Mia's thighs trembled, but her throaty moan assured him that it was from pleasure and not discomfort, so he pressed on, drawing slow, lazy circles around that bundle of nerves but refraining from licking at it directly.

"Toven," Mia whispered. "You're tormenting me."

"Shhh. I've got you, sweetheart." He added a finger to the play, then two, pumping them slowly in and out of her.

Flicking his tongue over the most sensitive spot at the apex of her thighs, he hooked his fingers inside of her and pressed on the spot that was guaranteed to send her shooting to the stars.

Mia threw her head back, and the sound she made as she climaxed was the sweetest music to his ears.

Toven was out of his clothes in two seconds flat, and as he climbed over Mia, he'd never been more excited about making love in the missionary position.

Gliding into her welcoming heat, he looked into her eyes. "I love you."

"I love you too." She lifted her lips to his and kissed him.

Making love to Mia face to face was indescribable, and it was testing Toven's formidable self-control to its limits. He'd had thousands of lovers, but none had ever made him feel like he was going to die if he didn't spill his essence into her.

When his fangs started elongating, and he could no longer maintain the lip lock, he reached into Mia's mind and thralled her to close her eyes and keep them closed until she came down from her trip to the clouds.

Usually, that was all that was necessary. After he bit her, she soared on the wings of euphoria, and when she drifted back to earth, more often than not she didn't remember the bite. On the rare occasion that she had, he'd thralled her to forget it, but again, very little had been necessary, and she didn't seem to suffer any ill effects from his gentle thralls.

As rational thoughts became too difficult to hold on to, and his climax neared, he licked Mia's neck and then carefully bit her.

She cried out, not in pain but in pleasure, and as he pumped her full of his venom, she came again, and this time he joined her.

When his own tremors subsided, he retracted his fangs, licked the spot to heal it, and rolled to the side with Mia in his arms. It usually took her a couple of hours to complete the trip, and he loved holding her and keeping her safe while she soared on the wings of pleasure.

Watching her blissed-out expression and stroking her back, Toven felt his heart swell with love, but his happiness was marred by the secrets he was keeping from Mia. He still needed to tell her the truth about who he was and what he'd been doing to her, but with each passing day it was becoming more difficult to come clean.

Mia would be so angry with him for not telling her the truth weeks ago, and he couldn't stand the thought of seeing the disappointment in her eyes, or worse, causing her distress.

She was already stressed enough about accompanying him to the meeting, so telling her now would be ill-advised.

He would tell her everything after Monday. Well, almost everything. The gods had kept many secrets from their immortal offspring and the humans they'd been in charge of, but none had been more fiercely guarded than the healing properties of a god's blood. As he had learned, the rumors had been grossly exaggerated, but his blood was still potent and valuable enough for humans to kill for.

For Mia's safety as well as his own, he had no choice but to keep that one secret from her.

Mia

"What do you think?" Mia closed the one button of her new cropped jacket. "Do I look formidable?"

Margo regarded her with a critical eye. "You look pretty and professional."

Mia had spent half the day shopping with Toven, and he'd been incredibly patient while she tried one outfit after another. She'd finally settled on a fashionable gray suit. The pants were wide legged with a high waist that accentuated her slim build, and the jacket was cropped with three-quarter sleeves. It was a very feminine suit, but it was also stylish and work appropriate.

As usual, Toven had insisted on paying for it, and she hadn't argued because it was definitely not in her budget. Besides, with how rich he was, she felt it was ridiculous to argue with him over what he regarded as small change.

For some reason, it was really important to him that she attend the meeting with the silent partner, and she wanted to be there for him, but she was still not a hundred percent decided.

"That's not good enough." She sighed. "I need to look intimidating, so no one will ask me questions. Any suggestions?"

Margo chuckled. "You couldn't look intimidating even if you wore a biker-chick getup with a switchblade sticking out of your pocket and tattoos all over your chest. That vulnerable china-doll face of yours isn't going to scare anyone, but it's also your greatest weapon. No one expects you to have balls."

"I don't have balls." Mia cast Margo a mock glare. "But I'm trying really hard to grow a pair." She unbuttoned the jacket, hung it on the back of the chair, and sat next to Margo on the bed. "I ran out of excuses not to go. My publisher accepted my illustration and didn't ask for any corrections, and I have time before I need to start working on the next book, so I can take a break."

"I don't know why you're so scared of going to that meeting."

Mia arched a brow. "Wouldn't you be? Hunter and Gabriel are geniuses who've invented incredible technology, and their silent partners are a power couple who are no doubt super-rich. Tom is richer than King Midas, and he's accustomed to dealing with people like them. I'll feel like a little mouse in a den of lions."

Margo wrapped her arm around Mia's shoulders. "But when the biggest and scariest lion of them all, the king of the beasts, is your boyfriend, you have nothing to fear. He won't let anyone belittle you."

Letting out a breath, Mia leaned her head on Margo's shoulder. "He promised not to involve me in the conversation unless I wish to participate. All he wants is for me to be with him, and he doesn't mind if all I do is listen."

A knock sounded on her bedroom door, but before Mia could say come in, it opened and Frankie walked in. "I detest Friday rush-hour traffic." She dropped her purse on Mia's desk and then regarded her outfit. "That looks nice."

"It comes with a jacket." Mia got up, pulled the jacket off the back of the chair, and shrugged it on. "How do I look?"

"Gorgeous." Frankie sat on the bed next to Margo and smirked. "But what I want to know is whether you made use of my present."

Margo frowned. "What present?"

"A pair of sexy leg warmers," Frankie said. "My solution to Mia's striptease problem."

Margo's eyes widened. "That's genius." She turned to Mia. "Did it work?"

"Splendidly." Mia felt herself blush. "But that's all I'm going to say on the subject." She did up the button again and examined her reflection in the mirror. "I wish the meeting wasn't in the morning, so you could do my hair and makeup." She ran a hand over her short, dark hair. "I thought that this hairdo was going to be easy to maintain, but it turned out to be a major hassle to keep it nicely styled. I'll probably let it grow out."

Her friends gaped at her as if she was speaking in a foreign language.

"What?"

"That's all you are going to say on the subject?" Frankie squawked. "Really? After all the brainstorming I did to help you out? I want details, girl."

"Me too." Margo crossed her arms over her chest. "Start talking, Mia."

Kian

As Kian regarded the long dining table with his family seated around it, he realized that Friday had become his favorite day of the week. He actually looked forward to hosting the family for dinner instead of dreading it like he used to before Syssi had entered his life.

With how large the family had become, every Friday dinner felt like an event. It was also a good time to share news and get unsolicited advice, which he sometimes listened to and was glad of.

The days of him seeking solitude were long gone, mainly thanks to Syssi's gentle and always supportive influence, and lately thanks to Allegra's arrival and the joy of having her in their lives. He was a changed man, and he liked the new Kian much more than he'd liked the old one.

Kalugal tapped a fork against his wine glass. "I want to make a toast." He pushed to his feet. "To our family and to many happy sailings aboard the new cruise ship yet to be named." He turned to Kian. "Congratulations."

Stifling a groan, Kian lifted his glass. "Thank you, but the ship is not mine. It belongs to the clan."

As usual, rumors had spread through the village like wildfire, and by now everyone knew that he'd purchased a ship.

"I know." His cousin sat back down. "I'm looking forward to the upcoming weddings."

"Who else is getting married besides Alena and Orion?" Nathalie asked.

Smiling at Dalhu, Amanda took his hand. "Since the whole clan is going to celebrate for an entire week, Dalhu and I should seize the opportunity and make use of one of the nights to finally get officially mated." She turned to Alena. "If you don't mind, that is. If you want it all to be about you and Orion, I totally understand."

Alena cast her an incredulous look. "Are you kidding me? I would love it. The more reasons to celebrate, the better. If we could have a different couple celebrate their mating every night of the cruise, that would be even better."

Orion didn't seem as keen on the idea as Alena, but he was smart enough to keep it to himself.

"You might just get your wish," Annani said. "Vlad and Wendy already postponed their wedding date by a month, so perhaps it would be a good idea for them to wait a little longer and have it on the cruise as well. It would save them the hassle of organizing the party themselves." She turned to Kian. "I assume that we will have human staff to take care of everything?"

"Of course."

Kian still had many details to figure out, but he trusted Ragnar to shoulder the project. The only thing he needed to take care of was the renovation, and he'd already hired a contractor who specialized in that.

"How much did the ship cost?" Kalugal asked.

Kian narrowed his eyes at him. "Why? Do you want to buy a bigger one?"

Kalugal laughed. "Not at all. I'm not interested in the hospitality business."

"You still haven't told me which business you are interested in."

Kalugal twirled the wine glass between his fingers. "I told you that I'm interested in innovative startups, and that was the honest truth."

"I believe that you haven't lied to me, but I also know that you are not telling me the entire truth."

"Boys," his mother said with a smile. "This is a family dinner, not an arena for you to play in. You can do that later when you go out to smoke your cigars."

Kian groaned, but Kalugal just smiled back at her. "My apologies, dear aunt. I will change to a subject that is of interest to everyone. After listening to Aliya talk about growing up in the Kra-ell compound, it occurred to me that she might have subconsciously recorded conversations between Jade and the other pureblooded females that she overheard as a child. I know that accessing such distant memories is very difficult, but you've done it successfully in the past, so it could be a good idea for you to do so with Aliya. We might get some more clues about the Kra-ell."

"I would do that gladly. I have not met Aliya yet, and I think it is about time that I did." Annani turned to Alena. "You are on friendly terms with her, so you should be the one to introduce the girl to me."

Alena chuckled. "She is going to freak out. I need to warn her not to prostrate herself at your feet."

"Well, I am a goddess. It would not be the first time someone did that."

As the two discussed the matter of introducing Aliya to his mother, Kalugal leaned closer.

"I heard that you got a very sweet offer for your little side hustle."

It was irritating the way the guy knew everything that was going on right as it happened.

Kian cast him a glare. "Did you install listening devices in my office?"

Both eyebrows hitching, Kalugal put a hand over his heart. "Why would I do a treacherous thing like that?" He smirked. "I just have the best possible spy at my side."

He leaned to kiss Jacki's cheek. "You know how it goes. Syssi told Amanda and Alena, Alena told Ingrid, and Jacki heard it from her. I don't think there is even one person in the entire village who hasn't heard about the twenty-five-billion-dollar offer for Perfect Match. Is it worth that much?"

He should have told Syssi to keep the details of the offer a secret, but since Kian had no intentions of selling, it wasn't really important if everyone knew. In fact, he didn't mind Kalugal getting a little jealous. None of the startups he was investing in had ever gotten an offer like that.

"Not in the slightest. But whoever owns the technology can use it to develop even more fantastical ways to escape the real world, and there is a lot of money in that."

"Right." Kalugal smoothed his hand over his goatee. "Maybe I should offer that guy some competition." He winked. "With two vying for the company, you might get even more for it."

Kian shook his head. "You don't have that kind of money."

Or did he?

Kalugal sighed. "Regrettably, I don't. I would if I liquidated a large chunk of my businesses, though." He frowned. "Maybe Perfect Match is worth it. If that Hartford guy is willing to pay so much for it, I would be a fool not to look into it."

Surprised by the extent of Kalugal's wealth, Kian kept his expression impassive and shrugged. "I don't want to sell the company, but Syssi wants to meet the guy and hear what he has to say. Ultimately, it's her stock and her decision whether to hold it or sell."

Aliya

"You look amazing." Bernice stood behind Aliya and combed her loose curls with her fingers. "Your hair is so thick and luxurious, but it doesn't hold a curl for long." She picked up a bottle of hair spray. "I hope this will help it last through the weekend." She lifted a section of hair and sprayed underneath it.

"I just need it to stay styled until the end of tonight." Aliya closed her eyes to keep the hairspray from irritating them.

"Yeah. Still." Bernice kept lifting sections and spraying underneath them to create volume.

Aliya tugged on the short stretchy skirt Yvonne had loaned her. "I don't feel comfortable in a skirt. Why can't I wear pants?"

The skirt was black, the midriff-exposing T-shirt was red, and on top she wore the cropped leather jacket Yvonne had loaned her when she'd first moved into the house and had refused to take back.

"You wear pants every day to work. You need something different for going out." Bernice put the spray away and fluffed up Aliya's hair. "All done."

Her roommates, who'd been firmly team Phinas, had switched sides and were now devoted supporters of Vrog, psyching her up for the date as if her entire future depended on it.

Were they already tired of her and hoping that Vrog would take her off their hands? She'd been an accommodating roommate, going along with most of what the two had come up with and doing her share of the household chores.

They had no reason to want to get rid of her.

When the doorbell rang Aliya took one last look in the mirror, tugged her skirt a little lower, grabbed her purse, and took a deep breath before walking out of her bedroom.

"Hello, Aliya." Vrog gave her a thorough once-over. "You look beautiful."

He looked dashing in a white button-down shirt and charcoal slacks, his black hair brushed back, and his face clean-shaven.

Should she compliment him back?

"Thank you." She tugged on the short skirt again. "You look very nice." That sounded so lame. "Are we stopping by Kalugal's place first?"

"He's waiting for us at the pavilion."

"Okay." She turned to her roommates. "Thanks for helping me get ready. Are you going to be here when I come back tonight?"

Smiling like she was hiding a secret, Yvonne shook her head. "Bernice and I are going to a club, and if we get lucky, we won't be back until tomorrow morning." She stretched on her toes and kissed Aliya's cheek. "I'm crossing my fingers for you to get lucky too," she whispered in her ear.

"Are you going to a gambling club?" Aliya asked.

Bernice chuckled. "Yeah. Kind of. Have fun, you two." She winked at Vrog.

"Thank you. We will." He took Aliya's hand.

When they were a few feet away from the house, Aliya shook her head. "Ever since I told them that we were going out on a date, they've been acting strange."

Vrog tilted his head. "In what way?"

"They were even more excited about it than I was."

He smiled. "I'm glad to hear that you're excited about going out with me."

"I'm excited about leaving the village for the first time since I arrived. Well, except for my hunting expedition with Phinas, but that doesn't count. We didn't go anywhere. I didn't get to see the city yet."

It was true that she was excited to finally leave the village and see Los Angeles for the first time, but she was even more excited about going out on her first date. Still, Vrog didn't need to know that she'd never gone out with a man before.

He seemed a little disappointed, but he covered it well. "Aren't you curious about the places I'm going to take you tonight?"

She turned to look at him. "Aren't we going to a restaurant?"

"We are, but it's not just a place to have a nice meal. You wanted to go dancing, so I found a restaurant that has a live band performing on the weekends and a dance floor."

"Sounds exciting." She wrinkled her nose. "Bernice and Yvonne gave me dance lessons, but I'm not very good."

When Vrog had first asked her out, and she'd suggested that they both take dance lessons with her roommates, he'd seemed excited about the idea, but somehow she hadn't had the nerve to call him and ask him to join her.

Aliya was a disgrace to all Kra-ell females. Why was she so damn timid around men? She was supposed to be confident and commanding. She should have been the lead, not the tail.

"Neither am I." Vrog squeezed her hand. "We will just watch the humans and imitate what they do."

Vrog

"Thank the Mother." Aliya let out a breath when the lead singer announced that the band was going on a break. "They are so loud that I still hear ringing in my ears."

Vrog had hoped that she would love the place, but once again he'd been wrong about what Aliya wanted, and this time he'd asked for advice, so it wasn't even his fault.

Bernice had recommended the restaurant as the best possible place for a first date, but apparently, she didn't know Aliya as well as she thought she did either.

Aliya didn't like how loud the band was, she didn't like how packed the dance floor was, and she hadn't wanted to dance. She hadn't enjoyed the food either, but she'd made an effort to pretend that she did.

"Would you care for dessert?" asked their waiter.

"I would like some coffee," Aliya said.

"And for you, sir?" he asked Vrog.

"The same. Thank you."

As the guy left, Aliya leaned back in her chair. "You are always so polite. I'm still trying to figure out when it's appropriate to say please and thank you. The customs here are different."

"You're doing wonderfully." He gave her a reassuring smile. "It's not easy to acclimate to a new place, a new language, a new society, and you are doing that very fast."

"I'm trying." She sighed. "But I make mistakes."

"We all do. Don't beat yourself up over it."

"Why would I do that? I don't practice self-flagellation, and I don't understand people who do."

He stifled a snort. "Neither do I. It was just an expression. To beat yourself up doesn't mean literally hurting yourself. It means feeling bad about something."

"Oh." She chuckled. "English is so full of idioms. How do you learn all of them? Is there a dictionary I can study?"

"You can look them up on the internet."

"Right." She pulled her phone out of the pocket of her tiny leather jacket and cradled it in her palms. "I'm amazed at how many things I can learn from watching YouTube, or from Wikipedia, and all that information is accessible with the help of this small device. Technology is amazing." Her eyes sparkled with mischief. "Who could have ever imagined that a machine can transport you into a make-believe world and allow you to experience it as someone else without remembering who you are in the real world?"

"Yeah. That's not always a good thing."

"Right. Wendy said that something went wrong with your virtual adventure. What happened?"

"I'd rather not talk about it." Vrog was grateful for the waiter's arrival with their coffees.

As soon as the guy left though, Aliya pressed on. "I figured that if a virtual adventure is like a dream, it can't be guaranteed to be good, and that's why I don't want to try it. But what I'm curious about is how you managed to get it stopped. Is there like a hidden exit door that you instinctively know will get you out of the nightmare?"

"There isn't. The only reason my session was stopped was that my body went into distress, and the technician realized that something had gone wrong. I got lucky."

Her big eyes turned enormous. "Did you get injured?"

"Yes."

"How?"

Vrog sighed. He could end it at that and refuse to tell her any more details, but that would achieve the opposite of what he was after. If he wanted them to get closer, letting her in on a secret he hadn't told anyone else could be just the thing to do.

"Promise me that you won't tell anyone."

She put her hand over her heart. "I vow to take your secret to the grave with me."

"It's so embarrassing." He shook his head and then looked around to make sure that no one was within earshot. "Naturally, I chose the Kra-ell adventure." He lowered his voice. "When I filled out the questionnaire, I modeled my desired partner on a pureblooded Kra-ell female."

Aliya smiled knowingly. "You mean Jade."

"Naturally. In our society, the most dominant female is the most desirable. What I didn't take into account, though, was that my description would be interpreted very differently when applied to a human or an immortal female. The clan female I matched with was a sadistic dominatrix who got off on inflicting pain."

Aliya tilted her head. "Is that not what Jade would have done?"

"Not like that. Jade, or any of the other pureblooded females, would have put up a formidable fight, during which they would have no doubt inflicted pain in the form of biting, scratching, kicking, and punching, but they would never have whipped me as part of the sexual experience. Whipping was done as punishment in the compound. It was never part of sex."

Aliya gasped. "You got whipped in your own adventure? That's horrible."

He nodded. "After my tech stopped the session, the female sent me a note, apologizing for the misunderstanding. She explained that she enjoys inflicting pain, but only on willing partners." He leaned forward. "Since I don't know who she is, I can't look at any of the unmated clan females without suspecting them of being my tormenter. It makes staying in the village very uncomfortable for me."

"That's terrible." Aliya reached for his hand and clasped it. "I'm so sorry that you had such an awful experience."

Vrog laughed nervously. "I guess the Mother decreed that I deserved the punishment."

"For what? You are such a good man."

"For not staying steadfast in my pursuit of you. I shouldn't have given up so easily."

Aliya

～∽～

A liya's heart did a strange thing, contracting with pain for Vrog's suffering and then guilt for being responsible for him believing that he deserved the punishment.

She hadn't done anything to deserve his devotion, and yet he gave it unconditionally.

Was it because she was the only hybrid Kra-ell female available to him?

Aliya wanted to believe that he wanted her because of who she was as a person and not her genetics, but that was stupid wishful thinking. He didn't know her well enough to even like her, let alone love her.

The thing was, she didn't know herself either. Most of her life had been about fighting for survival, and ever since the Kra-ell compound had been destroyed, her interactions with others had been limited. She hadn't fit in with the Mosuo children, and had always felt like the odd one out, but at least she'd been part of a community. After her mother died, though, she'd lived in nearly complete isolation for fourteen years, and her sense of self had shrunk to a very few basic tenets.

Survival, honor, and adherence to the Mother's commands as best as she understood and remembered them.

"You didn't deserve a punishment, let alone such a horrible one." She let go of Vrog's hand. "And I don't deserve your devotion. I've done nothing to encourage you."

He gave her a tight smile. "I should have asked you out on a date weeks ago."

"I told you that I didn't want to be pressured."

"Would you have said yes?"

She nodded. "Probably."

"Then it was a mistake not to do it. A date is not a big commitment, and it wouldn't have put pressure on you, but it would have allowed us to get to know each other better."

She huffed out a breath. "We lived in the same house. We had plenty of opportunities to talk."

"But we didn't talk because the whole situation was awkward, and it put much more pressure on you than a date would have done. Residing in the same house was another mistake."

Upon reflection, she had to agree. Moving out had been a huge relief. Yvonne and Bernice didn't expect anything from her, and if she wasn't in the mood to socialize, she could stay in her room and watch television and no one would get offended. She couldn't do that while living in Wendy and Vlad's house. She'd always felt like every move she made and every word she said had been observed and analyzed.

"You are right." She let out a breath. "It wasn't comfortable for either of us, and I agree that going out on dates is less stressful."

He tilted his head. "Did Phinas ask you out on a date? I mean, after you moved into the village."

"He knew that I wasn't allowed to leave, but he used to come to the café nearly every day."

"Why did he stop?"

It was on the tip of her tongue to blame Phinas's work schedule for his absence, but Vrog had been honest with her and told her about his horrible virtual experience, and she could do no less.

"I'm not sure what turned him off. Maybe it was my reluctance to become intimate with him when he made a move on me, or maybe it was seeing me hunt and drink blood from an animal, or maybe both."

Vrog's eyes flashed red. "What did he do?"

"Nothing. He just stopped showing up at the café the same way you did."

"I meant when he made a move."

She shrugged. "Nothing to get upset about. Bernice and Yvonne invited him and a couple of his friends to a wine and cheese party, and he must have assumed that I was just as lustful and free with my physical affections as my roommates. When it became clear to him that I wasn't, he backed off, but naturally he was disappointed." Feeling her cheeks burn with embarrassment, she pushed a strand of hair behind her ear. "I'm not like the immortal females, I'm not like the Kra-ell females, and I'm not like the human females either. I don't know who I am like, and I don't know how to act around men."

Vrog leaned forward and took her hand. "You don't need to be like anyone else. You only need to be like you."

Vrog

Aliya nodded. "You are right. I miss the hunt. I miss the sense of freedom and exhilaration, the wildness. It was all stifled because Phinas was with me, and I could sense his disgust." Her eyes momentarily flashed red. "He thought that I was an animal."

If Phinas wasn't Kalugal's second-in-command, Vrog would have challenged him to a duel. But since they needed Kalugal's help, that would be a mistake. If not for Kalugal compelling Vrog and Aliya to keep the village and the clan a secret, Kian wouldn't allow them to leave.

"Did he say that?"

"No, but I could feel it. I thought that I was imagining it, but then he stopped coming to the café, which proved that I was right."

"He might be busy at work. I heard that Kalugal is working on a big project."

Aliya smiled. "That's what I keep telling myself and everyone who asks, but I know it's not entirely true. That's okay, though. I lost interest in him as well."

Vrog wanted to know why, but he decided it would be best to stop talking about the other contender for Aliya's heart and focus on winning her for himself.

"If you want, I can take you hunting." He smiled seductively. "I find the prospect of hunting with you very exciting."

Her eyes widened. "I didn't know that you hunt."

"I do, but not frequently. It's not always possible during my travels and even while I'm at the school, and I don't need blood on a regular basis. It's more of a treat for me."

The other reason he kept hunting to the minimum was that it spurred his innate aggression, and afterward it took him weeks to regain his composure. People expected the head of an international school to be highly cultured and refined, and that was the mask he needed to don while recruiting new students.

Aliya grinned. "You've got yourself another date. When can we go hunting?"

Was it a good time to bring up the cabin?

It wasn't the romantic context he'd hoped for, but it was a great opportunity nonetheless.

"The clan owns a cabin in a remote mountain area. We can go hunting there and spend the night at the cabin." When her eyes clouded with suspicion, he quickly added,

"It has two bedrooms and a loft. Wendy and Vlad stayed in it for a while, and they fell in love while there."

Her expression softened. "So that's how you know about it."

Damn, when he pulled out her bag from the trunk along with all the food her roommates had cooked for them, she would know that he'd had it planned. He needed to fess up now.

"Actually, Kian told me about it when I asked his permission to take you out of the village."

She frowned. "Why?"

Vrog swallowed. "He said that since neither of us has a private residence, we might need a place where we could be alone. I told him that it was our first official date and that we were just getting to know each other, but you know how he and his people are." He smiled nervously. "Everyone sees the world through their own prism."

Aliya chuckled. "For once, I understood what a phrase means."

It was good that she was still in a good mood. Once he told her that he'd actually acted on Kian's suggestion, she might not be as agreeable.

"I have another confession to make." He reached for the wine glass and emptied it down his throat. "I liked Kian's suggestion, and I thought that if things went well, we might make use of the cabin. I asked your roommates to pack a bag for you just in case." When she glared at him, he lifted his hands in the air. "I didn't presume anything, and I don't expect us to do anything. We can just spend a nice time together at the cabin and sleep in separate rooms. But we don't have to do even that. It's totally up to you."

For a long moment, Aliya regarded him with a frown on her beautiful face, but then she let out a breath. "I don't like surprises, and I'm glad that you told me your plans now. I would have been very angry at you if I realized later that you tried to deceive me."

"Surprise, not deceit. It's a matter of intention."

"To me they are one and the same." She folded her arms over her chest.

He lifted his hands again. "I promise never to surprise you again."

"Good." She unfolded her arms and pushed to her feet. "You promised to dance with me."

"I did, and I will." He followed her up and took her hand. "Let's go."

Aliya

⸙

The hunt had an unexpected effect on Aliya. Arousal shouldn't have been part of it, and yet she was so consumed by it that she could barely stop herself from attacking Vrog.

Maybe it was the adrenaline rush from tackling a large bear and overpowering it with Vrog's help, or maybe it was the animal's blood that they'd both shared, or the freedom and exhilaration of running through the woods and leaping over obstacles, or perhaps it was finally seeing the powerful Kra-ell male under the civilized veneer that he wore so well, but she'd never wanted a male more than she wanted Vrog.

"Race you to the cabin!" he called before sprinting ahead. "Whoever wins gets a kiss!"

Laughing, she sprinted after him.

With her body fueled to the brim, Aliya could keep on running for miles, but the cabin wasn't that far away, and at the rate they were going they should reach it in ten to fifteen minutes.

Vrog was still faster, so Aliya knew that she was going to lose, but she didn't mind. It would have been better if she won, though, and he had to kiss her.

She'd never been kissed, but she'd seen enough movies to know what to do.

More or less.

Vrog had done a lot of confessing on their date, so perhaps she should follow his lead and confess her inexperience. She'd already given up on her fantasy of being a proper Kra-ell female with a harem of males and had accepted that her needs and urges were more human in nature than Kra-ell. Would that be a turn-off for Vrog?

He'd requested a dominant female for his virtual adventure, so obviously that was what his sexual fantasies were all about, but maybe he was wrong about that as well?

Nah, that was unlikely.

He had plenty of sexual experience, with human and immortal females, so if he still fantasized about a dominating Kra-ell female, he'd probably found the humans and immortals lacking.

Sex was so confusing, and Aliya was tired of the doubts and the insecurities. She wanted to just tell Vrog the truth and let him take it from there. It either worked out between them, or it didn't.

She just hoped he would be honest with her as well.

When she reached the cabin Vrog was already there, leaning against the front door with his arms crossed over his chest and a smirk on his handsome face.

"I won."

"Obviously." She climbed the stairs to the front porch and sauntered over to him. "Are you going to open the door?"

"Not before I get my prize. I'm owed a kiss." He beckoned her with his finger. "Pay up."

Smiling, she walked up to him, leaned over, and kissed his cheek. "Prize paid." She leaned back.

His arm shot around her middle and drew her to him. "That's not the kind of kiss I meant, and you know it."

His body was all hard planes against hers, and the simmering arousal that had abated during her run had flared again. "How about you kiss me," she suggested, her voice sounding oddly raspy.

"That wasn't the deal. I said that whoever wins gets a kiss, not gives it."

"I didn't agree to your terms. If you want it, you will have to kiss me."

Wrapping an arm around her, he lifted a hand to her nape. "Do you want to fight me?"

Of course, he would misunderstand. He still thought of her in terms of a Kra-ell female.

"I don't." She looked into his luminous eyes. "I have a confession of my own if you care to hear it."

"You can tell me anything."

"I've never been kissed before, and I'm afraid to do it wrong. I've never even been held like this before, and the last thing I want is to fight to get free of your arms." Losing her courage, she averted her eyes. "I'm sorry to disappoint you, but I realized that despite the way I look, I'm more human than Kra-ell. I want to be loved, I want to be cherished, and I don't want to fight or hurt you or anyone else unless it's in self-defense."

When she felt his hand leaving her neck, her heart squeezed painfully. He was going to push her away and tell her that he was disappointed and that he could have any human female he wanted. But his other hand stayed on her back, and his finger hooked under her chin and turned her head up, so she had to look into his eyes.

"I must be more human than Kra-ell as well because I also want to be loved and cherished, and the last thing I want is to hurt you. I want to give you only pleasure."

"But you wanted a dominant female for your virtual adventure."

"I wanted to give the Kra-ell way a try. I wanted to see if I could enjoy it, but the truth is that I've never been aroused by the prospect of forcefully subduing a female while she bit me, not to drink from me but to cause me pain." He smiled. "I tried to convince myself that once my Kra-ell instincts were triggered, that sort of aggression would come to me naturally. But even after the hunt and the blood lust it evoked, my feelings for you remain tender." He cupped her cheek. "So you see, we are perfectly matched."

Vrog

Vrog had suspected that Aliya was a virgin, but to hear that she'd never even been kissed had him harden to the point of pain. It had never mattered to him before whether the women he'd been with were experienced or not. In fact, he would have probably turned away and looked for someone experienced, but the thought of being Aliya's first brought out something primal in him that he couldn't even blame his Kra-ell upbringing for.

Her mouth was mere inches from his, and her long, lean body was surprisingly soft against his chest. As he dipped his head, she parted her lips and met him halfway, and as their lips fused in a soft kiss, she moaned so sexily that he nearly came in his pants.

He wanted her so badly, but given her virginity, his seduction plans would have to be amended. For now, kissing was all that he allowed himself to do.

Swiping the tip of his tongue over the seam of her lips, he urged her to open for him, and when she did, he slipped it into her mouth. With a guttural groan, he tightened his arms around her, and his hips moved of their own accord, grinding against her mound.

If she noticed how hard he was, she didn't seem to mind, her hands clutching his shoulders, her nails digging into his skin, not to hurt but to hold on, to take more of him.

He wanted to give her everything she'd ever wanted, but they were still standing outside the cabin's front door, and even though there was no one around for miles, there were cameras mounted on the fence, and he didn't want to give the Guardians watching the feed a show.

With a groan, he let go of her mouth and leaned his forehead against hers. "We should get inside."

Panting, she murmured a yes, but she didn't move an inch, and her fingers were still clamped over his shoulders in a death grip.

He didn't want to push her away. "I need to turn around to input the code."

"I'm sorry." She let go of his shoulders and took a step back, dropping her gaze to the floorboards.

He already missed the warmth of her body. "Don't." He cupped her cheek. "There are cameras everywhere, and I don't want to give anyone a show, but the moment this door closes behind us, your lips are mine again. I will never get enough of them." He brushed his thumb on her well-kissed lower lip.

Her fangs were slightly elongated, and the sight of them peeking from under her upper lip had his shaft twitch.

She laughed nervously. "Hurry up, then."

His fingers shook as he typed in the code, and he had to do it twice before getting it right. The moment the mechanism released the lock, he pushed the door open, grabbed Aliya by her waist, and hoisted her into his arms.

Kicking the door closed behind them, he walked to the couch and sat down with her on his lap. "Where were we?"

Her eyes glowed in the dark, the red hue indicating arousal, not aggression. "You were kissing me." She smiled, flashing him her fangs, and his arousal kicked up.

There was no way she hadn't felt it through the thin fabric of the leggings she'd put on for the hunt. Did she even know what it was?

Yeah, of course, she did. She'd grown up in a Mosuo village, and those people were not shy about sex.

Transfixed by the sharp gleaming points, he murmured, "I can't wait to feel your fangs in me."

As the glow in her eyes intensified, she swiped her tongue over her fangs. "I've never taken from a man or a woman. I only ever took from animals."

Vrog was a hair away from spilling in his pants, and if Aliya bit him he was going to orgasm for sure, but he didn't care. He wasn't going to take her tonight, or the next, or the one after that, so he might as well enjoy what he could until she was ready for more.

"Take from me."

"I don't want to hurt you."

She was so damn innocent. "Your bite is going to bring me pleasure. In fact, I'm likely to orgasm, so if that's something that might bother you, perhaps you shouldn't."

Shifting in his lap, she rubbed her soft bottom over his shaft. "It's not going to bother me." She trailed her fingers over his neck. "Have you ever been bitten before?"

He shook his head. "You're going to be the first one to take from me."

"So how do you know that you're going to like it?"

He'd bitten plenty of females before, and he'd experienced their reaction, but that wasn't something Aliya would want to hear right now.

"I've heard the pureblooded males talk about the pleasure of the bite." He tilted his head sideways. "Bite me, Aliya. Don't make me beg for it."

Wrapping her palm over the back of his neck, she closed in slowly, and as her lips touched his skin, his eyes rolled back in his head. But she didn't bite him. Instead, she kissed his neck and then licked it.

"Please," he murmured.

She kissed his neck again, and then scraped it lightly, driving him to the very edge of orgasm. When she finally struck, the pain of the twin incisions was the stuff of decades of fantasies, and when the suction started, he jerked up, and a massive orgasm exploded from the tip of his shaft.

Aliya didn't release him until the last of his tremors subsided, drawing out his pleasure until there was nothing left for him to spill, and when she withdrew her fangs and licked the puncture wounds closed, it was much too soon.

Aliya

〜

Vrog's blood had been better than anything Aliya had ever tasted before, so delicious, so rich, that she'd had to force herself to withdraw her fangs from his neck before she took too much.

It had been better than the best delicacies she'd ever tasted, and she licked every last drop that had dripped down his neck and then swiped her tongue over her fangs to get the last of it.

Had she taken too much?

His head lolling back, his eyes closed, he looked half-dead, but given the smile lifting his lips he didn't mind the brush with death.

"Are you okay?" She ran her fingers through his thick hair.

"I'm more than okay." He opened his eyes and smiled at her. "But I need a shower." His arms tightened around her. "This was the best orgasm I ever had, and I wasn't even inside of you."

Her cheeks heated. "I think I need a shower too."

"Sorry about that." He lifted her and put her down on the couch beside him.

There was a large stain on his pants, but it wasn't responsible for everything that was soaking her leggings. The bite had been incredibly arousing, and although she'd never experienced an orgasm before, she was sure that she'd come very close to having one while sucking on Vrog's vein.

"Where is the bathroom?" She pushed to her feet.

Would he suggest that they shower together? And if he did, would she agree?

"It's between the two downstairs bedrooms. I'll use the bathroom in the loft, and you can use the one down here."

Vrog got up, and as he swayed on his feet, he shot a hand out to lean on her shoulder. "I'm a little lightheaded."

"I took too much from you." Wrapping an arm around his middle, she led him to the bedroom. "It's not safe for you to climb the stairs. Use this shower, and I'll use the one in the loft."

He shook his head. "You didn't take too much. It's just the drugging effect of your bite. Stay here. I'll go up."

She didn't know a bite had such an effect. Would she feel the same when Vrog bit her? Her core tightened at the thought, but she refused to get distracted.

Vrog was lightheaded, and it didn't matter whether it was from blood loss or from being high. She couldn't leave him alone.

"Not happening." Aliya didn't remove her arm from his waist. "In fact, I'm going to stay here and help you wash. I don't want you falling and banging your head."

He grinned. "You just want to see me naked."

Yep, he really was drunk.

"I do," she admitted as she walked him into the shower and set him down on the bench.

His arms hanging at his sides, he made no move to undress. "I need a few moments."

Letting out a breath, she kneeled at his feet and removed his shoes and socks. "You can't even take off your clothes, and you think that you can climb those narrow stairs?"

"You don't have to do this."

"I want to." She rose to her feet, unbuckled his belt, and lowered the zipper. "Are you going to lift your bottom, or do I need to do it for you?"

"I'll do it." He managed to lift an inch, but it was enough for her to tug his jeans down.

As his shaft sprang free, fully erect and huge, Aliya had to bite her lip to stop herself from gasping. She'd never seen a man's anatomy up close, and it was much bigger than she'd imagined. Was that supposed to fit inside her?

"I'm sorry about the mess." Vrog smiled apologetically. "You really shouldn't be doing this. You're a virgin."

She chewed on her lower lip. "Are you bigger than most males?"

He grinned. "I'm taller than most humans, and I'm proportionate all over."

That made sense.

What didn't make sense was her fascination with his anatomy and her desire to taste what had come out of it. Was she depraved?

When his shaft twitched under her gaze and grew even bigger, she pried her eyes away from it. "What's happening?"

"He enjoys the attention."

She chuckled and tugged his T-shirt up. "Does he have a name?"

"He's nameless, but feel free to give him any name you like." He lifted his arms and let her pull the T-shirt off.

Vrog's chest was a work of art, all smooth, lean muscles that looked as if they'd been lovingly sculpted by the hand of an exceptionally talented artist.

"You must work out a lot." Unable to resist, she put her hands on his chest and smoothed them down to his abs. "You are beautifully built."

"Thank you." His arms shot around her, and he drew her to him. "You are overdressed." He smashed his lips over hers.

Vrog

rog hadn't planned on going any further than kissing, but Aliya wasn't acting like a blushing virgin, and he felt emboldened.

But as his drunkenness started to abate, he remembered the way her eyes had widened at the sight of his arousal, and it hadn't been all about desire. She'd looked concerned, and when she'd asked him whether he was bigger than most, it hadn't been meant as a compliment.

Letting go of her mouth, he released his hold on her. "You'd better go before this gets out of hand."

She hesitated for a moment, her eyes roaming over his naked flesh, and the scent of her desire flaring. "I'm not sure that I want to go."

"You're not ready for more."

"Says who?" She took a step back and looked at him. "Can I wash you?"

"You can do with me as you please."

She smiled. "Okay then."

Her hands were surprisingly steady as she pulled her hoodie over her head and tossed it outside the shower to join the garments she'd removed from him. "I've never undressed in front of a man before." She reached for the hem of her T-shirt. "I'm a little nervous."

"You're gorgeous, Aliya." Vrog folded his arms over his chest to keep from reaching for her.

It was her show, and he would be damned if he interfered.

As she tugged the T-shirt up, he held his breath, but she wasn't naked underneath. She had a sexy red bra on, and instead of taking it off, she pushed her leggings down, revealing matching red panties.

"You are so beautiful," he murmured.

"Thank you." She reached for the handheld and turned the water on.

"Aren't you going to take the rest off?"

"No." She checked the temperature before aiming the spray at his arm. "Is that okay?"

"Perfect."

That was disappointing, but he wasn't complaining. Aliya was running the show, and if she wanted to leave her bra and panties on, then she wasn't ready for more.

As he hissed when she aimed the spray at his groin, she immediately moved it aside. "Did I hurt you?"

"I'm just sensitive there right now."

Eyeing his erection, she chewed on her lower lip. "I'm not good at this." She handed him the showerhead. "Maybe I should just watch."

"I can work with that." He stood up and offered her the bench. "But after I'm done, I'm washing you."

Her cheeks reddened, but she didn't say no and leaned her back against the tiled wall.

He took the bar of soap and started lathering his chest, his abs, and then he was down to his groin, palming his erection.

A hiss left his throat.

If he kept going, he would come again, and he didn't know whether Aliya was up for that, although given her rapt attention to his ministrations, she might.

"Tell me what you want me to do, Aliya." He kept pumping up and down slowly. "Do you want to see me come again?"

She nodded.

"Take off your panties and play with yourself while I do that."

"Play?"

"Have you never pleasured yourself with your fingers?"

She shook her head.

"Why not?"

"I didn't know that was something women did. My roommates tried to convince me of the merits of a battery-operated-boyfriend, but I told them that I wasn't interested in a mannequin as a boyfriend. That's just silly."

"I bet they laughed."

"They laughed so hard that they were out of breath and clutching their sides, but they never explained what was so funny."

"Perhaps one day I'll show you what a battery-operated-boyfriend is, but right now, I want to teach you how to pleasure yourself.

She smiled. "Always the teacher."

Vrog put the showerhead back in its cradle and knelt in front of Aliya. "May I?" He hooked his thumbs on both sides of her panties.

Her eyes wide like saucers, she nodded.

Slowly, he dragged her panties down her thighs, and as the scent of her arousal flared, he inhaled the intoxicating smell, and his head spun again. Perhaps she'd taken too much of his blood because he'd never reacted like that to a female.

Aliya was hairless, and given how smooth everything was, it hadn't been thanks to a razor or waxing. Apparently,

Kra-ell females had that in common with their immortal cousins. He still remembered Stella's smooth flesh from all those years ago.

Dipping down, Vrog pressed a soft kiss to the top of Aliya's mound before looking up at her beautiful face. "I think it's about time for you to be introduced to the pleasures your body is capable of feeling. Would you allow me to take off your bra?"

It was one of those overly padded numbers that made it impossible to see what her breasts looked like under it.

She shook her head. "There isn't much to see." She lifted her hands and covered the cups.

He placed his hands over hers. "You are perfect, Aliya. In every way." He gave her a reassuring smile. "Big is not always better."

She huffed out a nervous laugh. "Do you hear that a lot from the ladies you bed?"

"I'm not sure what you mean by that, but no."

"You're big."

"Yes, you said that before."

"Did it scare off some of your partners?"

Vrog had never encountered a female who looked at his shaft with concern before, but Aliya had apparently never seen an adult male naked.

He stifled a chuckle. "I'm not that big." He winked. "I'm just the right size." He reached behind her to unclasp her bra. "Let me see you."

Reluctantly, she let the bra straps slide down her arms, and the entire contraption fell forward. Her breasts were indeed very small, just two gentle slopes, but they were nonetheless perfectly shaped and topped by sizable, stiff nipples.

"Beautiful." He leaned forward and pressed a kiss to one and then the next. "I want to lick and suck on these sweet berries. But first, I need to give you a thorough soaping." He took the container of body wash off the shelf and squirted a generous amount into his hands.

Aliya sucked in a breath as his palms made contact with her breasts, and as he gently massaged, she dropped her head back against the tile and closed her eyes.

"Look at you." He took the handheld and rinsed the soap off her breasts, letting the soapy water sluice down to the V between her legs.

Damn, he wanted to be that water, to touch her softness with his fingers, his tongue, and finally his erection, but this wasn't about what he wanted. This was Aliya's introduction to the pleasures her body was capable of, and she couldn't have found a better teacher than him.

She followed his gaze down and parted her legs just an inch, letting the water penetrate her between her thighs.

With a groan, Vrog went down on his knees again and took one turgid nipple between his lips.

As he gently sucked on it, Aliya moaned and arched into his mouth, and as he switched to her other nipple, she threaded her fingers into his hair and held him to her. "This feels so good."

He flicked his tongue over one berry while circling the other with his thumb. "I'm just getting started."

Aliya

⚬~⚬

Vrog had just started?

Already Aliya was on fire, her toes curling on the shower floor.

Why were they still in the shower, though?

They could be in a bed—

Did she want him to take her to bed?

Hell, yeah.

After tonight she would be a virgin no more, and she would have zero regrets. She still wasn't a hundred percent sure that Vrog was the one for her, but he was getting close. Yvonne had said that if a male checked most of Aliya's boxes, which meant that he matched most of the things she wanted in a partner, then she should look no further.

Vrog was doing a great job checking those boxes and some that she hadn't known she had. The things he was doing to her with his fingers, his lips, and his tongue were pure magic. She couldn't wait for him to touch her where she ached for him the most.

Letting go of her nipple, he kissed a trail down her belly until he reached the top of her mound and then looked up into her eyes. "Will you allow me to kiss you here?" He applied light pressure on her knees, pushing them apart.

She wanted him to do more than kiss her there, but he was the teacher, and she trusted him to give her what she needed.

"Yes." She parted her legs, letting him see all of her. "Kiss me there."

He put his palms on the inside of her thighs, spreading her even wider before pressing his lips to the throbbing bundle of nerves at their apex.

Aliya cried out, and as he flicked his tongue over the same sensitive spot, a coil tightened inside of her, readying her for the climax she'd heard so much about but had never experienced.

"Vrog," she murmured. "Please. I need more."

"I know." He brushed a finger over her wet folds, coating it, and as his tongue circled the bundle of nerves, he pushed the tip of it inside of her.

Aliya's eyes rolled back in her head. "I'm dying."

He chuckled against her lower lips. "You are being reborn."

She wanted to tell him that he was being arrogant, but as he pushed his long finger all the way in and at the same time sucked on that most sensitive place at the top of her slit, stars exploded behind her closed lids.

As the coil snapped, sending her shooting up to the sky, Aliya heard herself scream, but with the blood roaring in her ears muting everything, it sounded as if it was coming from a great distance.

Vrog kept licking and sucking, pulling every last thread of pleasure out of her until she pushed on his head to make him stop.

Panting, Aliya looked into Vrog's glowing eyes and cupped his cheeks. "Take me to bed, my teacher." She leaned down and kissed his lush lips, tasting herself on them.

For a long moment they just kissed, pouring their nascent feelings for each other into the kiss, and then Vrog's arms shot around her, and she was lifted off the bench and carried into the bedroom.

After gently laying her on the bed, he stood by the side of it and looked at her as if he didn't know what to do next.

His eyes were glowing, his erection was jutting straight out of his hips, and his fangs were fully elongated, so despite her inexperience, Aliya had a good idea about what he needed.

"Come to me." She opened her arms and spread her legs. "And take from me."

"Are you sure? We don't have to do it tonight." He put his hand on his shaft and squeezed. "I can climax just from looking at you."

"I want that erection inside my core, and I want your fangs at my throat. Nothing less than that will satisfy me."

Vrog

~~~

There wasn't even a smidgen of hesitation in Aliya's tone. The lady knew what she wanted, and Vrog was more than ready to oblige, but he had to pace himself.

Despite her bravado, and despite having climaxed like a firecracker just moments ago, Aliya was still incredibly tight, and he needed to take care with her.

Surging over her, he braced his weight on his forearms and took her lips in a scorching kiss. Where their bodies were touching, his shaft had aligned itself at her entrance, and as he kissed her, he pushed forward with just the tip.

Aliya spread her thighs even wider and arched up, taking another inch into her, but Vrog wasn't allowing her to take more. Pulling out, he pushed back again with just that one inch and kept kissing her.

Wrapping her arms around him, she sank her fingers into his ass, her nails digging in to hold him in place. The sting spurred him on, and when she tilted her pelvis up and took a little more of him, he felt powerless to resist.

If Aliya were a human, he would have already encountered her hymen, but other than tightness, he hadn't felt anything that would indicate that there was a barrier of any sort.

Perhaps Kra-ell females didn't have it.

Letting go of his mouth, Aliya hissed, "You're killing me, Vrog."

"Patience, love. You're very tight, and I don't want to hurt you."

She gave him a smile that was all about seduction and female power. "You can't hurt me. You were made for me."

Hell, if those weren't the sexiest words he'd ever heard.

Still, she was inexperienced and didn't know her own limits. He couldn't just ram into her. But he could go a little faster for the sake of both their sanities.

Focusing on her face, he pushed in another inch, and when her expression remained all about pleasure, he withdrew and pushed a little deeper.

This time she winced.

He stilled. "Did I hurt you?"

She shook her head and tilted her pelvis up, but he knew she was lying and held back.

"Give it a few more seconds." He rested his forehead against hers. "Don't rush me. It takes everything I have to hold back and make this as pleasurable for you as a first time can be."

A tear slid down the corner of her eye. "I don't deserve your kindness."

"Yes, you do." He took her mouth and kissed her long and hard, distracting her until he felt it was safe to push a little further.

The moment he let go of her mouth, she smiled up at him, looking wicked with her fangs fully elongated and her eyes blazing red. "Take from me." She turned her head to the side, elongating her neck.

The naughty girl hoped to snap his resistance with her offer, and she almost succeeded.

He managed to hold back just long enough to lick her neck in preparation for his bite, and then it was game over. With a roar, he pushed all the way inside her and struck her neck at the same time.

The taste of her blood was exquisite, the best he'd ever taken, and as his release exploded out of him, Aliya's sheath contracted around his shaft, and she cried out, a powerful climax rocking her body.

When the storm receded, he retracted his fangs, closed the puncture wounds with a couple of swipes of his tongue, and then lifted his head to look at Aliya.

Her eyes were closed, but the blissful expression on her face was all he needed to know that he hadn't hurt her.

Bracing on his forearms, he kissed her lips lightly. "Are you okay?"

Aliya opened her eyes, and her smile widened. "I'm wonderful." She lifted her head and kissed him. "You were right. The Mother must have created us for each other because we fit together perfectly."

Aliya

It was still dark outside when Aliya woke up in Vrog's arms. They were both naked, the soft down blanket tangled between their legs, and the scent of their lovemaking permeating the bedroom.

Lovemaking, not sex.

He'd been so gentle with her, so considerate. It had been a very human joining, and it had been wonderful.

Aliya had no regrets, no misgivings, her fantasies about a Kra-ell violent coupling gone and buried, never to be resurrected. That lifestyle was not for her, and she was done feeling guilty for not living up to the Kra-ell standards. She and Vrog had found their own music to dance to, their own moves, and it had been spectacular.

Burrowing closer, she stuck her nose in the crook of Vrog's neck and inhaled his masculine scent. He was warm, his arm around her strong and sure. She could get used to waking up next to him in bed every morning.

How could the Kra-ell females live without this intimacy? This closeness?

Didn't they know what they were missing?

Would her roommates mind if he spent the nights with her? If they did, she was sure that Wendy and Vlad would welcome her back into their home now that she and Vrog were a couple.

Were they, though?

Yeah, they were.

The Mother had created them for one another, which Aliya should have realized weeks ago instead of indulging in fantasies of having a harem like a proper Kra-ell female. She was a hybrid, and evidently more human than Kra-ell.

"Good morning, love," Vrog murmured.

It was the second time he'd called her love, and each time her heart leaped at the term of endearment, captured it, and stored it in the same place as her other cherished moments.

"It's still dark outside." She lifted her head and kissed the underside of his jaw.

"I know." His hand on her back started a slow trek down to her butt and rested there. "How are you feeling?" He opened his eyes and smiled at her.

"Wonderful. And you?"

"I've never been better." He pressed his lips to hers in a soft kiss. "We forgot to let your roommates know that you are not coming home until Monday. They must be worried about you."

She chuckled. "They're probably not home yet. They went hunting last night."

He arched a brow. "Hunting for what?"

"Sex. They call going to clubs hunting because that's how they get human partners. They hadn't been for a long while because they were having fun with Kalugal's men, but Bernice missed the club scene, so they started going again."

He tightened his hold on her ass. "I'm glad that you didn't partake in their games. Does that make me a bad Kra-ell?"

"The worst." She wound her arms around his neck and kissed him. "But perfect for me because I'm the worst Kra-ell female. I don't want a harem of males, and I want to make love and not just have sex, and I want to go to sleep with my male every night and wake up next to him each morning."

"That's what I want too. Am I your male, though?"

"You'd better believe it." She mock glared at him. "You belong to me and no one else. I don't want you to even look at another female." She laughed. "I'm so bad, and I love it. Jealousy is so un-Kra-ell, but I don't care. The Mother brought us together for a reason. Maybe we are supposed to start a new breed of Kra-ell?"

Vrog sighed. "It's not possible to start a new tribe with just two members."

"From what I've heard, Emmett bonded with Eleanor, so he's like us. Vlad, Mey, and Jin are one-quarter Kra-ell, and they bonded with immortals as well. That makes five of us."

"We might find more." He turned to his back and pulled her on top of him. "Mey and Jin are probably not the only Kra-ell descendants who were put in orphanages. We could search for others in the Beijing area and the Mosuo territory."

She smiled down at him. "What would we look for? Tall, skinny people with eyes that are too big for their faces?"

"That's a start. And those who have paranormal abilities and a penchant for blood."

Darlene

"Are you sure that you don't want to come with us?" Geraldine walked over to Darlene and sat next to her on the couch. "It's such a beautiful day. It would be a shame to waste it watching television."

"I want to catch up on my soap operas. During the week, I'm too pooped at the end of the day to stay awake, and I fall asleep five minutes into the show."

Organizing William's domain was a daunting undertaking. She had been working twelve-hour days and had hardly made a dent in the mess. Then it was off to the gym for weight training with Kri and Ronja and some cardio. When Darlene got home, she barely had the energy to get into the shower, wash the day off, and climb into bed.

"Shai and I are going to drive down to the beach and have cocktails in a restaurant that has a balcony right over the water."

"Enjoy. I want to veg."

Geraldine cast her a look that was half disapproving and half pitying, and for a moment, Darlene felt like the little girl who'd disappointed her mother. But even though abandoning her hadn't been Geraldine's choice, she had lost the right to reproach her daughter when she'd disappeared all those years ago.

"Well, enjoy your vegging. We are probably going to go somewhere for dinner, but there are leftovers in the fridge from yesterday that you can warm up."

"I know how to take care of myself. You don't need to fuss over me. Have fun."

"We will." Shai wrapped his arm around Geraldine's shoulders and walked her out the door.

She really needed to move out of their house and find a place to stay. Maybe one of the immortal females needed a new roommate.

According to Cassandra many of the clan females were shacking up with Kalugal's men, but there were no truelove matches, so those pairings were fluid.

Darlene envied the ease with which the clan females hooked up with whomever they wanted, and she envied even more the ease with which they ended those relationships, while she couldn't even bring herself to call Leo.

"You're such a damn coward." She pushed off the couch and padded barefoot to her bedroom.

Edna had informed her that Leo had been served with the divorce papers two days ago, but the attorney hadn't heard back from him yet.

That wasn't surprising.

Knowing her husband, he'd torn the papers to shreds without even reading them.

She'd left him everything—the house, the money, their retirement accounts. He had no reason not to sign them other than to spite her.

Snatching the phone off the charger, she went back to the living room and put it down on the coffee table.

If she was going to talk to Leo, she needed to load up on liquid courage. It was going to be a tough conversation, and she knew that he would throw nasty accusations at her just to hurt her, or maybe because he really believed that she'd left him for another man.

Taking the wine bottle with her, she went back to the couch and sat down.

Two glasses of wine later, Darlene was still not ready to make the call, but if she had another glass her mind would get too clouded, and she might blurt out something she wasn't supposed to despite the compulsion that had been placed on her.

With trembling hands, she typed Leo's number and waited.

When he didn't pick up right away, she was tempted to hang up, but he answered after the third ring.

"Hello?"

"Hi, Leo. It's Darlene."

"You slimy cunt. Who are you screwing?"

Well, that was a promising start.

She closed her eyes, inhaled, and let the breath out slowly. "I'm not screwing anyone," she said in a calm tone, for once not letting him rile her. "But even if I was, it's irrelevant. Did you read through the divorce papers? I left everything to you. All you need to do is sign in front of a notary, mail them back, and it's over. We don't have to make a huge fight out of it."

For a long moment, she only heard him breathing.

"Can we meet somewhere and talk about it?" Leo's tone changed from accusing to pleading. "If you're not screwing anyone, why are you leaving me?"

He sounded hurt, and for a moment Darlene felt guilty, but then she remembered why she was doing this. Leo had betrayed Roni, and she could never forgive him for that, but she couldn't say it over the phone. His line was tapped, and she'd better not mention Roni at all. Besides, there were plenty of other reasons, and she should have divorced him a long time ago.

"There is nothing to talk about. I'm tired of the fights, the putdowns, the name-calling, and all the crap you've put me through. You don't love me, not even a little, and I can't go on like that. I can't keep catering to your moods, staying away from people because you can't stand it when I befriend anyone, and tiptoeing around you while feeling guilty for never being good enough. I'm sick and tired of living my life as if I don't matter and only you do. I deserve better."

"How long did it take you to prepare that speech?"

The venom in his voice was like acid in her veins.

"Years," she hissed. "But I was too much of a coward to actually do something about it."

"Because you found someone who was willing to screw you? Where the hell are you?"

Shouting a string of curses in her head, she somehow managed to keep from hurling them at him. She wasn't going to stoop to his level.

"I got a well-paying job which I enjoy doing. That was what gave me the courage to finally leave you. I don't need alimony from you, I'm not going to fight you over money, and we don't have young children to argue over either." She closed her eyes and decided it was time to tell him. "In fact, *we* don't share children at all. Your suspicions were right. Roni is not your son."

"I knew it! You're a damn whore, Darlene. You've always been loose."

Gritting her teeth, she said, "We were separated when I had a fling with Roni's father, and you weren't being celibate either. That was the only time I've ever been unfaithful to you, and it doesn't count because you walked out on me. I never cheated on you while we were together, and I don't intend to start now, so sign the damn papers and set me free."

"Fine." He hung up.

Slumping back against the couch cushions, Darlene closed her eyes and let out a breath. She was exhausted, but she also felt a huge weight lift off her chest. She'd said her piece, and Leo agreed to sign the papers.

He might still give her a hard time, but after she revealed the truth about Roni, there was no way he would want her back. He had no ammunition against her, nothing to exert pressure on her, and now that she'd talked to him, she didn't need to see him ever again.

Mia

At seven in the morning sharp, Mia opened the door and let Margo in. "You are incredible." She pulled her bestie into her arms. "I can't believe you are doing this for me."

Margo was not a morning person, so for her to wake up an hour early to help Mia get ready for the meeting was truly going above and beyond.

"You're welcome, but we need to get on with it. My boss hates tardiness, and she'll be on my case all week if I show up late on Monday."

Margo was late for work nearly every day, but Mia wasn't going to point that out.

"Where is Tom?" Margo asked as Mia opened the door to her room.

"He's in his house. I told him that you were coming to do my hair and makeup, so he escaped to prepare for the meeting where he could have some peace and quiet, but he'll be back for breakfast, or he'll have to deal with my grandmother."

Margo put her bag on the bed and pulled out her super-duper expensive hair styler. The contraption was a hairdryer and brush combined into one, and the brushes were interchangeable. Margo claimed that it was worth the exorbitant price she'd paid for it, but Mia doubted it. She'd seen similar devices for a fraction of the price.

Pulling out her desk chair, she sat down. "Let's see if this thing is really worth the money you shelled out for it. It cost as much as a new tablet."

Margo brushed her fingers through Mia's damp hair, parting it into four sections and securing them with pins. "You realize that budget concerns no longer apply to you. Just ask Tom to get you one of these, and you'll be able to produce salon-style results at home." She turned the hairbrush on and started working on the first section.

"He's buying Perfect Match for me. I can't ask him for anything more, and I don't want to."

Margo laughed. "A few hundred dollars is nothing to him. How much is he paying for Perfect Match?"

The amount was so fantastical that Mia didn't want to repeat it. Besides, maybe she wasn't supposed to discuss the deal with others. Not that Margo would share the details if she asked her not to, but it was a good excuse to avoid repeating that absurd amount.

Her friends might start treating her and Tom differently when they realized that he wasn't just rich, but probably one of the richest people in the world.

Mia shook her head, earning a glare from Margo. "I keep thinking that I'm still inside the virtual fantasy. Things like this don't happen in real life, and especially not to someone like me."

Margo paused with her brush. "Maybe fate had a reason to send Tom your way. It made him aware of what the technology of Perfect Match can do for people with mobility issues, and when he fell in love with you, it became personal to him. He felt it in here." Margo tapped her chest. "It was no longer just a curiosity or an intellectual observation. He felt your pain."

Mia shook her head at her friend. "It would be so nice if things worked like that, but they don't. Fate, or whoever is looking over us, doesn't take pity on those it has wronged or just overlooked, and it doesn't send a billion-aire to level the playing field. Life is random, and so many suffer while pretending that they are okay or hiding. I was young and naive before the event, and I believed that life was fair, but it isn't, and nearly all of us are carrying pain either from our own injuries or those of people we care for."

Margo shrugged. "Believe what you want, but that's what I think." She started working on the next section of hair.

"I just got incredibly lucky," Mia said. "Or what's more likely, I'm still inside the virtual adventure, and I will wake up soon."

Smirking, Margo put the brush away. "Keep thinking that none of this is real while you are at the meeting. It will make things less stressful for you." She sprayed Mia's hair with one of the products she'd brought with her. "Although if this is your virtual fantasy, what am I doing in it?"

"You're my best friend. I want you with me wherever I go, even inside the virtual world."

"Right." Margo made a face. "I don't remember you mentioning Frankie or me when you filled in the questionnaire."

"There was no section about best friends, but when Tom takes over the company, I will make sure that it's added."

As Margo was putting the finishing touches on Mia's makeup, the door opened and Toven walked in wearing gray slacks, a white dress shirt, and a charcoal jacket, but no tie.

The man was so gorgeous that it was difficult not to stare at him, and Mia didn't blame Margo for gawking even though she'd seen him plenty of times before.

"Hi, Margo." Toven looked Mia over and smiled like a hungry wolf. "Is it going to take much longer?"

"Nope. I'm done." Margo managed to tear her eyes away from him. "Mia just needs to get dressed."

"Good, because we really have to leave right away. Gabriel just texted me the address, and I checked how long it would take us to get there given the traffic conditions. We are not going to make it on time."

Mia pushed to her feet. "You should call Gabriel and tell him that we are running late."

Toven shook his head. "I'll call him when we are halfway there, and I have a better estimate of our time of arrival." He raked his eyes over her. "By the way, you look beautiful." He gave Margo the thumbs up. "Thanks for doing this for Mia."

"That's what best friends are for." She glanced at her watch and winced. "I need to get out of here as well, or I'm going to be late." She collected her arsenal of beautifying tools and dropped them into her bag. "Best of luck." She threw them both air kisses and rushed out the door.

Standing next to the closet with the suit hanger in hand, Mia waited for Toven to leave, but he didn't move. "Your grandmother is packing you a sandwich to go."

She chuckled. "As if I would dare eat anything and stain my clothes on the way to the most important meeting I've ever attended."

"Rosalyn thought of everything. She packed you an apron."

Her grandmother was the best.

"I don't think I'll be able to eat anything anyway. My stomach is in knots." She gave him a small smile. "I need to get dressed." She took the suit and ducked into the bathroom.

Mia hadn't missed the disappointed expression on Toven's face, and she felt like a coward for not undressing in front of him, but she could only handle one thing at a time, and right now it was taking all her resolve not to puke her guts out from stress.

Kian

❧

"I've never been to this building before." Syssi looked around the sprawling lobby. "It's nicer than the one across from the Keep."

"I agree." Anandur winked at the receptionist and adjusted the lapels of his suit jacket while Brundar walked over to the woman to give her instructions regarding their guests.

The redhead was hiding an arsenal of weapons under his jacket, which was entirely unnecessary, but he'd insisted and even convinced Brundar to do the same. One would think that they were going to a meeting with a mafia boss and his army of goons instead of two engineers and one eccentric billionaire.

Kian circled an arm around Syssi's waist. "We have many office buildings throughout the downtown area, but this is the only one that has a top-floor restaurant. After the meeting, we can have lunch there."

"I can't stay for lunch." Andrew pressed the button for the elevator. "I told my boss that I had a dentist appointment and would come in late."

As the elevator doors opened and the five of them walked in, Kian leveled his eyes at his brother-in-law. "I've said it before, and I'm saying it again. You should quit that job and come work for the clan."

Andrew smiled. "I don't want to. I like my job. Especially now that I don't really need it to make a living."

Syssi cast him an incredulous look. "You said that you hated being shackled to a desk."

"I've changed my mind since then. I love having access to classified information I'd never have been privy to while working in the field. Besides, I might be a clan member, but I'm also a proud citizen of this great nation of ours, and it's my honor and duty to protect it from terrorists and other foreign threats."

"Good one, Andrew." Anandur chuckled. "After a speech like that, even Kian can't bribe you to quit your job."

"Or guilt me into it." Andrew's grin was all about the satisfaction of shutting Kian up.

As they entered the office Kian used for important meetings with humans and sat around the conference table, he glanced at his watch to check the time. "We have ten minutes until our guests arrive." He turned to Anandur. "Is the restaurant open already?"

"It's open. Do you want me to get everyone coffees?"

"They are supposed to have room service. Call them and have them deliver a couple of carafes and eight cups."

Anandur pulled out his phone. "Do you also want something to nosh on?"

"Cookies," Syssi said. "That should be enough. We don't want to fill up if we are going to lunch after the meeting." She made a pouty face. "I miss Allegra already. I might not make it through lunch."

"She's fine." Kian patted her hand. "With Alena and my mother fussing over her, she's as happy as can be, and she won't even miss us." He took Syssi's hand. "I like having you all to myself for a couple of hours."

"You are not with Allegra twenty-four-seven like I am, so it's easier for you to be away from her."

Kian was saved from coming up with a retort by the ringing of Anandur's phone.

"It's the receptionist." He accepted the call. "Yes, send them up, please." He ended the call and put his phone on the table. "It's Gabriel and Hunter, and they are right on time."

Silent as always, Brundar checked the security camera feed from the lobby and nodded to Anandur, confirming their identity.

When a couple of minutes later a knock sounded at the door, Anandur pulled it open. "Good morning, gentlemen."

When the two partners walked in, Kian rose to his feet. "Good morning." He offered Hunter his hand.

"This is a very good morning indeed." Hunter grinned as he shook Kian's hand. "I've never imagined that I would one day receive an offer of twenty-five billion dollars for the company I founded with Gabriel."

"Hartford is running late," Gabriel said as he shook Kian's hand. "He's stuck in traffic."

"Where does he live?" Syssi asked.

"Not too far from his girlfriend would be my guess." Hunter shook her hand. "The guy has it bad. Originally, he wanted to buy the company just so she could enjoy virtual adventures, and the idea to make the service more accessible and affordable to people with disabilities came later."

"I think it's admirable," Syssi said.

"Hello, beautiful lady." Gabriel leaned down and kissed her cheek. "I don't know what it is about virtual fantasies that attracts gorgeous people." He pulled out a chair and waved a hand at their group as he sat down. "You, your hubby, and even your bodyguards look like movie stars." He glanced at Andrew. "You're the only normal-looking one."

"Thanks." Andrew leaned back in his chair. "I'll take it as a compliment."

"You're welcome."

"Hartford looks like a male model," Hunter said. "Life is unfair. Someone so rich shouldn't be so good-looking."

As Anandur's phone rang again, Brundar lifted his own phone to check the camera feed and frowned. "He has the girl with him, but she's walking just fine."

"She wears prostheses," Gabriel explained. "My wife says that it takes a formidable will for a double above-the-knee amputee to learn to walk with prostheses."

"I bet," Syssi said. "Is Hartford as good-looking as Hunter says?"

Brundar shrugged. "I only saw his back, and he looks in good shape."

Kian pushed to his feet. "He probably brought her with him to manipulate us into selling, but his tactics are not going to work on me. Once the issue with the insurance is solved, she'll be able to enjoy as many adventures as he's willing to pay for."

When the knock came, Anandur opened the door and gasped.

Alarmed, Brundar pulled out a couple of throwing knives, and Kian jumped to his feet, standing in front of Syssi and blocking her with his body.

Taking a step back, Anandur pulled the door fully open and lifted his hand to signal Brundar to stand down. "No danger here. I think. But you are in for one hell of a surprise."

Puzzled, Kian waited for the Guardian to move out of the way so he could assess the situation, and when Anandur did just that, Kian understood what the Guardian had meant.

Walking up to the couple, he smiled at the petite brunette and offered her his hand. "Hello, Mia."

"Hi." She lifted her small hand and gripped his with surprising strength. "And you are?"

He turned to the man standing next to her. "Hello, Toven. I am Kian, son of Annani, grandson of Ahn."

Toven

᠎

T oven stared at the man who called himself Kian. Could he really be Annani and Khiann's son?

Annani could have been pregnant when Mortdh murdered Khiann. Toven remembered her sneaking away from the assembly. He'd thought that she'd been overwhelmed with grief and couldn't stand being there any longer than necessary, but since he'd snuck away as well, he didn't know whether she'd returned. She might have escaped, which made perfect sense if she'd been carrying Khiann's baby.

Mortdh had been amassing an army to the north, and she must have realized that if he did attack he could win, and finding her pregnant, he would kill her.

"Do you know each other?" Mia asked, breaking the spell.

Kian smiled. "Toven and I are distant relatives."

"I thought that everyone was dead." Toven couldn't take his eyes away from the miracle standing in front of him.

"Evidently, some survived. We thought that you were dead too."

"How did you know who I was?"

Annani's son glanced at Mia before returning his gaze to Toven. "Perhaps you and I should step outside. Our family's history is complicated."

"Who is Annani?" Mia tugged on his hand.

"She's a distant relative, and she was my brother's betrothed."

"I should have guessed that you were related," Gabriel said. "How many people can look like that? He waved a hand at them. "You two look like statues of mythological gods."

The guy didn't know how right he was.

Ignoring Gabriel, Kian glanced at Mia again. "I guess she doesn't know who you are."

Toven shook his head. "Who I am is not who I was."

Mia squeezed his hand to get his attention. "What is he talking about?"

Toven didn't move his eyes away from Annani's son. "He's talking about our family's dirty laundry that shouldn't be aired in public."

"Is this about the fortune you inherited?"

Kian lifted a brow. "Is there something you need to tell me, Toven?"

Annani's son was treading on dangerous ground, and if he wanted to play, Toven was ready to take him on, but the sound of Mia's heartbeat accelerating doused his aggression as effectively as a bucket of ice water.

He and Kian needed to talk in private, but he had to defuse the tension first.

"Where are my manners." Smiling, he offered Kian his hand. "It was quite a shock to discover that my entire family didn't perish. Let's start over. I go by Tom Hartford these days, and I'm delighted to meet you." He wrapped his arm around Mia's shoulders. "This is my fiancée, Mia Berkovich, and we've kept her standing for far too long." He shifted his eyes to the pretty blond woman looking at him as if he was an apparition. "You must be Kian's lovely wife."

The redhead and the blond looked like bodyguards, and he had a feeling that they were both immortal, as were Kian's wife and the male sitting next to her. How could so many have survived the attack, and he hadn't known?

Maybe the survivors were from Mortdh's compound.

There was only one weapon that could have caused such destruction, and only one god who could have wielded it. Mortdh was the only one who had the means and had been either crazy enough to go on a suicide mission, or not smart enough to realize that the weapon needed to be launched from a considerable distance, and that necessitated a rocket.

Mortdh hadn't owned one, none of them had.

All the rockets from antiquity had either been used or no longer functioned, so the only way to use the bomb was to drop it from an aircraft, and that was a suicide mission. Mortdh had never been a scholar, and he probably hadn't known that the blast would kill him. Even if he'd somehow managed to escape the blast itself, he could have never escaped the toxic wind.

Devastated and feeling ill from grief and the effects of the toxicity, Toven had immediately boarded his aircraft and flown back to where he'd come from, and he hadn't returned for millennia.

"Seeing you standing at the door was quite a shock for me as well." Kian raked his fingers through his longish hair. "This is Syssi, my wife."

She rose to her feet and offered Mia her hand. "I apologize for sitting there like a doofus and staring. This was one hell of a surprise."

Mia chuckled. "I'll say. I thought that the negotiations would be stressful. Now I'm starting to think that my anxiety was prophetic."

Syssi tilted her head. "Do you get glimpses of the future?"

"Not really." Mia looked at Toven. "I never even dreamt of meeting a man like Toven."

Syssi snorted. "You don't know the half of it." She cast an accusing look at him, but then something she saw made her expression soften. "Hi, Toven." She offered him her hand. "I'm so glad we found you. Welcome back to the family."

Kian

They needed to get rid of Gabriel and Hunter, but that wouldn't solve their problem. Mia didn't know who Toven was, and they couldn't just send her home with one of the Guardians.

Besides, she was their insurance policy.

Toven probably wouldn't dare do anything in front of her, so they were safe from his compulsion.

Once Syssi was done introducing Andrew, Brundar, and Anandur to Toven and Mia, Kian turned to Gabriel. "I apologize for wasting your time, but finding a distant relative, who I was convinced was dead, is too big of a revelation for me to continue business as usual. We will have to reconvene at another time." He turned to Toven. "Do you agree?"

"Yes. Of course." Toven smiled at the founders, who were regarding them both suspiciously. "I hope we didn't inconvenience you too much."

"Don't worry about it." Gabriel rose to his feet. "Watching the drama unfold was entertaining."

Hunter seemed less agreeable as he leveled his gaze at Toven and then shifted it to Kian. "Whatever you decide between you, just be mindful of what you promised us."

"Don't worry." Kian offered him his hand. "Toven and I are not even going to talk about the deal. And if we do, you have my word that I will not do anything before discussing it with you. Perfect Match is your baby. Syssi and I are just its godparents."

When Hunter still didn't look convinced, Toven clapped him on the back. "Trust me, Hunter. I have only your best interests at heart. Neither Kian nor I would ever cheat you out of anything."

There had been a subtle note of compulsion in his tone, and it had done the job.

Hunter unclenched his jaw. "I don't know why, but I trust you. Call us when you're ready to have another meeting."

"I will."

Once those two had left and Anandur closed the door behind them, Kian still didn't know what to do with Mia.

Sitting next to Syssi and looking anxious, she darted her gaze between them and Toven. The girl was not well, and he didn't want to cause her unnecessary stress.

"What's going on with that coffee I ordered?" Anandur broke the long moment of awkward silence. "Are they flying the beans in from Colombia?" He pulled out his phone.

Syssi released a long breath and smiled brightly at Mia. "Are you hungry?"

The girl put a hand on her belly. "How did you know that I didn't have breakfast?"

"I didn't. But I could use a bite to eat, and there is a great restaurant on the top floor of this office building. We can go there and leave these two here to reconnect. Once they are done, they can join us at the restaurant."

Looking unsure, Mia cast a questioning look at Toven, who in turn looked at Kian. "Do I have your word that Mia is safe with Syssi?"

"My family owns this office building, and the security is top notch. No harm will come to her while she's our guest."

Toven offered Mia a hand up, and then pulled her into his arms. "I promise to tell you everything later."

She looked at him with so much trust and love in her eyes that even Kian, with his limited emotional intelligence, couldn't remain indifferent.

"I love you." She cupped his cheek, and when he leaned into her hand, she kissed his lips. "Come find me when you're done."

"I won't be long."

Anandur got up. "I will join the ladies."

Syssi shook her head. "Stay here with the boys. You heard Kian. It's a secure building, and we are safe here."

"Boss?" Anandur asked.

As if Kian would dare contradict Syssi. Besides, she was right. If not for his mother, the brothers wouldn't even be there. He didn't need bodyguards whenever he left the village.

"They'll be fine. It's not like Doomers are lurking in our building."

"Who or what are Doomers?" Toven asked.

"Your brother's followers and my clan's enemies."

Toven arched a brow. "Unless I'm mistaken, Mortdh is dead."

The guy couldn't possibly be that clueless.

"Mortdh is indeed dead, but he has a greater following today than he had back then. I'll tell you all about it later."

Mia

"Don't worry," Syssi said as she and Mia entered the elevator. "Toven is a valued member of our family, and we are overjoyed to find him alive and well." She entered the numbers seven and two for the top floor. "But boys will be boys, and even brothers get into pissing contests."

As the elevator lurched up, Mia leaned against the wall for stability. "I wouldn't know. I'm an only child."

Syssi's eyes clouded with unshed tears. "I had two, but I lost my younger brother. You met my older brother earlier."

"I'm so sorry." Mia put her hand on Syssi's arm.

"It happened a long time ago." She heaved a sigh. "He died in a motorcycle accident."

As the elevator doors opened and they stepped out into the restaurant's lobby, the hostess smiled at them. "Welcome to the Seventy-Second. Do you have a reservation?"

"We don't," Syssi said. "Do you have a private room available?"

The hostess arched a brow. "For the two of you?"

"We will be joined later by five more guests, but it will take a while. In the meantime, we can enjoy the view over a cup of coffee and a couple of appetizers to tide us over until the rest of our party arrives."

"I'll see what I can do about the private room. What name would you like to put the reservation under?"

"McLean."

The woman's eyes widened. "As in Onegus McLean? The owner of the building?"

"Onegus is not the sole owner. He manages our family's assets."

The hostess's entire attitude changed. "I'll get the room ready for your party right away." Her snooty expression was gone, and she was suddenly eager to please. "Would you like to wait for them in the private room, or enjoy the view next to the window?"

Syssi turned to Mia. "What's your preference? If you suffer from a fear of heights, the window might not be a good idea."

"I don't have a problem with heights, and a table over-looking the view sounds great."

Syssi was friendly and seemed harmless, but after the weirdness in the office a few floors down, Mia didn't want to be alone with the woman. Public places were always safer.

Despite Syssi's reassurances, Mia had sensed the men's hostile undercurrents, and it wasn't just simple male posturing over who had bigger muscles, or in this case, deeper pockets. In the muscle department, Kian might have an advantage over Toven, but she doubted his pockets were as deep.

Once they were seated at a cozy table for two overlooking the cityscape, a waiter rushed over with two menus.

"Welcome to the Seventy-Second. Would you like coffee or tea while you look over the breakfast offerings?"

"I would like a cappuccino, please," Syssi said.

"Do you have herbal tea?" Mia asked.

"Of course. I'll bring you a selection of teas to choose from."

"We would also like a breadbasket," Syssi said. "My friend and I are famished."

"Right away, ma'am." The waiter pivoted on his heel and scurried away.

Syssi chuckled. "I wonder if he would be as accommo-dating if I hadn't mentioned Onegus McLean."

"Is that your last name?"

"Onegus McLean is the public face of our family."

They were a very secretive family, but given that most of them had perished, maybe there was a good reason for that.

The enormous amount of money at Toven's disposal was too fantastical for even the most powerful drug lord in the world, and Mia couldn't think of another illegal activity that could be that profitable. Maybe they dealt in weapons?

This was a great opportunity to find out. As her friends had pointed out, with her innocent-looking face and her disability, no one suspected Mia of cunning or subterfuge. Syssi's guard was down, and she might reveal things to Mia that she wouldn't have revealed to anyone else.

"Is all this secrecy connected to what happened to the rest of the family?"

Syssi nodded. "In a way."

"What happened to them?"

Syssi shifted in her chair and then smiled broadly at the waiter who brought their chosen hot beverages and a basket of bread.

"Just in time. Thank you." She pulled the cappuccino toward her and dropped two cubes of sugar into it.

Mia looked over the selection of herbal teas and chose a packet of ginger with lemon. "Thanks."

"You're welcome." The guy took the box back. "Have you decided on what you want to order?"

Mia hadn't even looked at the menu yet. "We need a little more time."

"No problem. I'll be back in a few minutes."

Dunking the teabag in the hot water, Mia regarded Syssi from under her lashes. "Can you tell me what happened to them, or is it a secret?"

"It's not my tale to tell. You should ask Toven."

"I don't think he knows."

"I don't know the details either. All I can tell you is that it was a terrorist attack. A bomb went off in the family's compound, killing everyone who was there. Luckily, Kian's mother was away, and apparently so was Toven."

That was an odd answer.

"Where was Kian?"

"Oh, he was away as well." Syssi lifted the cup and took a sip.

"What about the others? Where were you and your brothers and the two guards?"

"Kian and I weren't married then." Syssi plastered a fake smile on her face. "It was a long time ago."

Obviously, the woman was not telling her the truth. What the heck was Toven's family involved in?

Maybe they were a terrorist organization? Was there a lot of money in that?

Her grandfather said that to understand what was going on, all you needed to do was to follow the money. Every organization needed funding, and the motives of those providing the funds were usually about making more money or gaining more influence, which in turn made them more money. The problem was that the general public wasn't privy to that information, and if they didn't know where the funds came from, how was an ordinary person supposed to follow the money?

Kian

Kian knew that he was taking a risk talking with Toven without safety measures. He was a god, and he was a powerful compeller. Compared to him, Kalugal was probably an amateur.

On the other hand, he had the element of shock on his side. He at least had known that the god was alive and had been searching for him. Toven had thought that he was the only survivor.

"Let's sit down." Kian motioned to the conference table. "We ordered coffee, and it should get here shortly."

Toven shook his head. "I would have preferred something with a little more kick than coffee."

"I hear you."

As Kian pulled out a chair for the god, he saw from the corner of his eye Anandur putting an earpiece in first one ear and then the other.

Why he'd brought the earpieces to the meeting was just as unclear as his insistence on being armed as if he and Brundar were going to war, but whatever the reason, Kian was going to give him a raise just for that.

He wasn't the only one who'd noticed, though.

Toven had as well. "Take the transmitters out," he commanded, imbuing his tone with so much compulsion that Kian felt a strong urge to walk over to Anandur and take the earpieces out himself. Thankfully, the command hadn't been directed at him, and Anandur was protected.

"Those are not transmitters. The earpieces are designed to block compulsion, which is why Anandur didn't respond to your command. His job is to protect me, and to do so, he needs to be immune to your tricks." Kian pointed to the chair again. "Please, sit down. You have nothing to fear from my men or me."

"Are you a compeller?"

Toven must have been too agitated to notice that Kian had pulled out a chair for him and walked around to the other side of the conference table. He sat down across from him.

"I'm not," Kian said.

Toven's eyes were full of suspicion. "Compulsion is a rare trait even for gods, so for you to have your men carry protection against it implies that more of us survived. Since you are not a compeller, and you wouldn't need protection from Annani, who else is still alive?"

Was Toven under the impression that Kian was a god?

Didn't gods know to differentiate between immortals and gods? Perhaps for the time being, he should perpetuate the misconception.

"Areana also survived, but we only found out about it recently."

Toven's expression brightened. "That's wonderful news. Where has she been hiding?"

"Hiding is not the right term. Imprisoned is more accurate, although she doesn't view it as such."

"What do you mean? Who can hold a goddess captive?"

"A very powerful immortal. She's mated to Navuh, your nephew."

That statement didn't have the shocking effect Kian had hoped for.

Toven only shook his head. "How did I miss all this?"

"Good question." Kian leaned back. "And an even better one is how did you escape the bombing?"

"I wasn't there. I got fed up with the endless discussions and decided that I'd had enough. I flew to what's now called South America. I'd been exploring that region for centuries."

"When did you learn about the disaster?"

"I came back and found desolation. I didn't stay to catch my death as well." He sighed. "I assumed that all the gods were dead, and the grief alone was enough to destroy me. I don't think I ever recovered." He looked at Kian. "I guess your mother was pregnant with you when she escaped. Where did she go?"

Kian didn't correct him. "She fled to the far north. She found a home among the northern tribes, pretending to be one of their deities."

Toven smiled. "Annani always had a penchant for drama, which was part of her charm. I hope she hasn't changed much from when I knew her as a young woman."

Kian chuckled. "She hasn't."

Toven's eyes started glowing with excitement. "I would like to see her. Can you take me to her?"

"That depends. First, I need to ascertain that you're not a threat to her."

"Why would I be? We were friends." He narrowed his eyes at Kian. "Do you think that I'm like my murderous brother?"

"I know that you're not. My mother always spoke fondly of you, and she loved your father. You must have taken after Ekin, while Mortdh took after his mother."

"He did." Toven leaned back in his chair and crossed his arms over his chest. "I didn't know her, but I heard that she was a power-hungry manipulator, and Mortdh detested her even though he was just like her. Regrettably, our father wasn't very discriminating in his choice of bed partners. If the lady was agreeable, he never said no."

Kian nodded. "That's what my mother said about him as well. He was a character, that's for sure, and he was brilliant. He also championed humanity and moderated Ahn's rigidity and ruthlessness."

A cloud passed across Toven's eyes. "Ekin was an idealist, and he imparted his ideals to me. I also believed that Ahn was too harsh and too controlling, and that Ekin's way was better, but I learned the hard way that Ahn's rigid rules were necessary. My father's soft ways would have never worked on their own. Humans behaved themselves because Ahn had put the fear of the gods in their hearts." He tilted his head. "Annani never got the chance to practice her leadership skills during the time of the gods. I wonder whether she became more like her father or like mine. How did your mother manage to control those northerners?"

"Annani is not ruthless, but rather cunning and creative. That being said, she's also a natural leader and a powerful goddess. I guess she took the best qualities from Ahn and Ekin and blended them to create a leadership style of her own."

Syssi

yssi felt bad even though she hadn't really lied to Mia. Mortdh's bombing of the gods' assembly could be classified as a terrorist attack. He hadn't moved against an army. He'd murdered civilians.

After the waiter took their order, Mia folded her napkin over her knees. "I still don't understand how it's possible that Toven didn't know about the attack. An event like that must have made the news. Do you think that he chose to suppress it?" She refolded the napkin. "Or maybe he knew but he didn't want to tell me because he didn't want to upset me."

Both options were unlikely. Even though news didn't travel as quickly back in the gods' era, Toven must have found out what had happened, but since he hadn't told Mia that he was a god, he couldn't tell her about the demise of the other gods either.

"Perhaps he just can't talk about it." Syssi pulled a slice of baguette out of the breadbasket. "Maybe after talking it out with Kian, he will be able to open up to you about it."

Mia nodded. "Makes sense."

"Let's talk about more pleasant things. How did you like your virtual adventure?"

Mia's eyes brightened. "I loved it. The world-building was so incredible that Toven decided to base his next book on that environment." She scrunched her nose. "I didn't consider it before, but would he be in violation of copyright laws if he does that? The environments are the property of Perfect Match."

"They are, but since each variation is significantly different than the original because they are based on the participants' input, it might be argued that they are the actual creators. Which environment did you choose?"

"Toven created a custom one for us, or rather had a guy named Brian adapt elements from several scenarios to create what Toven wanted." She smiled. "All I wanted was to be a fairy in a fae world."

"I wonder who Brian is." Syssi searched her memory for the programmers she'd met while designing environments for the adventures, but she didn't remember a Brian. Maybe he was a new hire. "But that's not important. Tell me more about that world."

"It was five hundred years in the future, and the human population had shrunk to fifty million people worldwide. It wasn't because of a nuclear war or pollution or any of the other doomsday scenarios, though. It was because of a very gradual but steady decline in birth rates. Things just fell apart. Factories stopped manufacturing goods and crumbled to dust, roads deteriorated until they were unsafe to travel, and the remaining human population went back to living like it had in the Middle Ages. They became farmers and traveled by horse and carriage, but unlike their ancestors, they knew about all the wonderful technology that had been lost."

Chills ran up Syssi's arms. Was that a glimpse of a possible future? Perhaps the Fates were trying to tell them something?

"What you're describing doesn't sound very exciting."

"I'm just getting to the good parts." Mia leaned back as their waiter put the appetizers they'd ordered on the table.

"Enjoy." He refilled their glasses with water.

"Thank you." Mia gave him a sweet smile.

She was adorable, a perfect combination of vulnerable and strong, feminine and sweet, but with an iron core. No wonder Toven had fallen head over heels in love with her. She was the kind of girl strong men found irresistible.

When the waiter left, Syssi took one avocado egg roll from the platter and put it on her plate. "I'm dying to hear the rest of it, but if you want to dig in first, I'll wait."

"I'm almost done." Mia took a sip of water. "The interesting part was the gods' return. They came under the guise of saving humanity from extinction. They offered to extend the human life span to three hundred years on average, and they did that for free, but they also offered genetic enhancements in exchange for goods and services. Toven had wings, and I had pointy fairy ears."

"Was he a winged god?"

Syssi could understand why Toven designed his adventure to include gods. Any anomalies in his actions could be explained in the context of that fantasy world.

"No, he was an enhanced human. The gods didn't have wings." Mia frowned. "Come to think of it, that's strange. If they could give wings to humans, they should have given themselves wings as well."

"It was a fantasy." Syssi scooped another appetizer onto her plate. "Things didn't have to make sense. That being said though, I tried to make the ones I designed logical. Even a world with magic has to follow that world's rules. Otherwise, suspension of disbelief is difficult."

Mia's eyes widened. "You actually designed those environments? Are you a programmer?"

"I'm an architect with a rich imagination. I came up with the concepts, drew some sketches to illustrate what I meant, and wrote a bunch of scenarios. The programmers took it from there."

"That sounds like so much fun." Mia lifted an egg roll and bit off a chunk.

"It was, and I enjoyed doing that tremendously, but once my daughter was born, I had to take a break. I keep coming up with ideas though, and I write them down to develop later." She sighed. "But I have to go back to work soon, so I don't know when I'll get to that."

"Architecture is a creative occupation. It should also be enjoyable."

"It is, but I don't work as an architect. I work in research, which I also enjoy."

"What kind of research?" Mia asked.

"Neuroscience."

"Oh, wow. You must be very smart to do all those things. When did you have time to study architecture and neuro-science?"

Syssi debated whether she should mention the paranormal aspect of Amanda's research.

People usually reacted dismissively when she brought it up, but she had a feeling that Mia was a Dormant and might have a paranormal talent. Toven had turned from a cold bastard who hadn't wanted a relationship with his own son to a love-crazed boyfriend who was willing to do anything to make his woman happy.

Things like that didn't happen in the human world, and she suspected the Fates had manipulated events again.

Besides, she really liked Mia, and the feeling was mutual. They were at ease with each other like old friends who'd known each other for years.

"I didn't study neuroscience. I was drawn to it because I wanted answers for my ability to predict the future, so I volunteered to be a test subject and stayed on as a research assistant."

"That's so interesting." Mia's doubtful tone betrayed her thoughts, and then she stuffed a whole egg roll into her mouth, so she didn't have to say anything more.

Syssi sighed. Regrettably, Mia's reaction was predictable. She thought that Syssi was a nutcase.

"Do you have any paranormal talents?" she asked.

Mia shook her head and picked up a napkin to dab her lips. "Unless stubbornness counts as a paranormal talent, I don't have any. What kind of predictions can you make?"

Smirking, Syssi reached into her purse and pulled out her wallet. "Did you ever play heads or tails?" She pulled a quarter out of her purse.

"Of course." Mia looked at the quarter suspiciously.

Syssi handed it to her. "Toss it."

"Okay." Mia flipped it expertly, and when it landed on the table, she slammed her hand over it. "Heads or tails?"

"Tails."

She lifted her hand. "Correct."

"Keep flipping."

After the seventh correct guess, Mia no longer looked doubtful. "How do you do that?"

"I just know. Keep going, so you won't think it's a fluke."

Mia tossed it five more times, and Syssi guessed each one correctly. It was unusual even for her to make twelve correct predictions in a row.

"Toss them a few more times. This is a new record for me."

Mia chuckled. "It must be my magnetic personality."

When Syssi predicted the next ten tosses correctly, they were both astonished.

"I think I know what your talent is." Syssi regarded Mia with even more appreciation than she'd had originally. "You are an enhancer."

Mia

An enhancer? What the heck was Syssi talking about?

The woman was a darling, and she was incredibly accomplished, but she was a little nuts. A lot of smart people were eccentric. Syssi had seemed so normal, though, so friendly. Mia had felt as if she'd found a kindred spirit. Not that they were alike in any way, but she was comfortable with Syssi in the same way she was with Frankie and Margo. The difference was that she'd just met Syssi, and she'd known Margo and Frankie since the three of them were little girls.

The coin must have been rigged. Or maybe it was a fluke?

No, that wasn't possible. No one could predict twenty-two tosses in a row correctly.

Snatching up the quarter, she examined both sides. "How did you do that?"

"I'm sort of a seer." Syssi grimaced. "Most of my predictions are too vague to be useful, and usually grim, but one way or another, they come true. Coin tosses and cards guesses are nifty parlor tricks, but they are not very useful either."

Mia snorted. "I bet you could make a killing in a casino."

"Maybe I could with you by my side. I've never had a straight run like this, so it must be because of you. I would love for you to come to the lab so Amanda and I could run tests on you, or rather your influence on others."

"I'm sure that it's not me, but I don't mind visiting your lab and trying out my mysterious powers." She wiggled her fingers.

"I'm so excited." Syssi pulled her phone out of her purse. "I need to tell Amanda about you."

"Who is Amanda?"

"She's the professor I work for, and she's also on maternity leave." Syssi lifted her head and smiled. "We both have little girls. My Allegra is almost four months old, and Amanda's little Evie was born two weeks ago."

"Congratulations."

"Thank you."

Syssi looked so thrilled to be a mother that Mia's gut clenched with regret. She would never experience the joys of motherhood the way a birth mother would.

Thanks to the new medication, she felt much stronger now and less fearful of pregnancy, but she still had a genetically inherited heart defect, and she wasn't going to pass that on to her children. The only way she was going to be a mother was if she and Toven adopted a child.

Syssi finished typing and sent the text, and then started typing again.

"Who are you messaging now?" Mia asked.

"Kian." Syssi lifted her head and cast Mia an apologetic look. "He's not involved in the research, but this is so exciting that I have to share it with him."

The woman was definitely nuts. Her husband had just discovered a relative who he'd believed was dead, and she was bothering him with nonsense while he was reconnecting with Toven.

"You might be getting excited over nothing."

Shaking her head, Syssi continued typing on her phone. "This is my job, Mia. I've dealt with paranormal talents for years, and I know what to expect. From all our test subjects, I'm the best at those kinds of predictions, and I've never done so well." She finished the text and sent it. "I usually get the first six to eight correct, and then my brain gets tired and needs to rest before attempting it again. It's worked the same for all the other paranormals I've tested. They've all had diminishing results."

"Did you ever test an enhancer?"

Syssi shook her head. "You're the first one."

"So how do you know such a talent even exists?"

"I don't, which is why I'm so excited and why I want to test you. If you're for real, it would be an amazing discovery."

A shiver ran down Mia's back. "I don't want to become a lab rat."

"You won't." Syssi reached for her hand. "We wouldn't even document testing you."

Mia frowned. "I don't get it. I might not know much about science, but isn't the whole purpose of research discovering new things and publishing them in science magazines?"

"Normally, yes. But things are a little murky in paranormal research. No one takes it seriously, and we can't even publish papers about the research we do. If Amanda didn't have private funding, the university would have never approved her side gig."

Now the picture was becoming clearer.

Syssi was a crazy genius, and she funded paranormal research to feed her own obsession with the subject. No one in the scientific community was interested in her paranormal gig, so even if Mia was an enhancer, no one was going to take it seriously and come after her so-called talent.

"That's good to know. I feel less anxious about visiting your lab now. It might be fun." She took a sip of water.

"But if you and Amanda are both on maternity leave, who is going to test me?"

"We have post-docs working in the lab, but I want to test you myself." Syssi smiled. "You've given me an incentive to go back to work."

Toven

While Kian had spun tales of his mother's adventures, the coffee had arrived, and as they took a short break for it to be served and the waitress to leave, Toven pictured the young Annani braving the savage frozen north while taking care of a baby.

She'd always been a powerhouse, but what he'd loved about her the most was her joyfulness, her zest for life, and her tenacity. No matter what obstacles Annani had to overcome, she never quit until she got what she wanted.

It was no wonder that she had persevered while he'd allowed himself to wither and fade until he'd become a ghost of a god.

"I guess it was easier for Annani to overcome her grief because she had you." He put his coffee cup on the table. "She wasn't alone." Toven looked at the guards. "Are they your sons or grandsons?"

The redhead snorted, the blond's stoic expression didn't change, and the male sitting next to Kian chuckled under his breath.

"I have a confession to make," Kian said. "I'm not a god, and I'm surprised that you couldn't tell the difference between a demigod and a full-blooded god."

Gods varied in power, and some immortals were as powerful as or more so than some of the weaker gods. So even though Kian didn't feel as powerful as Annani, it hadn't occurred to Toven that he wasn't a full-blooded god. But if he wasn't Khiann's son, then whose?

Probably some random mortal Annani had found among the northern savages.

"Given your name, I was sure that you were Khiann's son. I assumed that Annani had been pregnant with his child when she fled."

Kian shook his head. "She wasn't. My mother mourned her mate's death for many years before deciding that it was her duty to continue the gods' work of helping humanity to become a just and civilized society. But since she couldn't do it alone, she took human lovers, and over the millennia, she had five children. I was the second born. My elder sister Alena is the many times great-grandmother of Anandur and Brundar, but we don't know who Syssi and Andrew's progenitor was."

"Maybe we are Toven's descendants?" Andrew suggested. "We should have Bridget test it."

Toven flinched. "I have only one son."

"That's what you think," Andrew said. "We know of at least one more of your children."

Toven felt as if the man had kicked him in the gut. "Do you know Orlando?"

"He goes by Orion these days," Kian said. "And we know him very well. He's mated to my sister Alena, and they are expecting a child. You are going to be a granddaddy for the third time."

He had another child and two grandchildren?

Toven swallowed. He wanted to know how they had found Orlando, or how he had found them, but that could wait. He needed to know who his other child was.

"Who's the other one?"

"You have a daughter. Her name is Geraldine, and she has two daughters. One of them has a son, so you are also a great granddaddy. There might be many more."

"Impossible. How do you know that Geraldine is my daughter?"

Kian leaned closer. "Do you remember the journal Orlando, aka Orion, swiped from your desk in Paris?"

Toven nodded. "I thought that he wanted a memento of me."

"He had a more practical use for it. Orion tracked the females you listed in your journal, and he found one who had given birth to a daughter nine months after she hooked up with you. She'd given up the child for adop-

214

tion, but he managed to find her. The story gets complicated, and I don't want to get into the details, but she found her way to our clan first, and when he came looking for her, he found us as well."

"I have a daughter," Toven murmured. "Two granddaughters and a great-grandson." He looked at Kian. "When can I see them?"

Kian was about to answer when his phone pinged with an incoming message.

"Excuse me for a moment." He pulled it out and frowned as he read the message. "That can wait. We have a more urgent matter to discuss."

That sounded ominous. "What happened?" Toven asked.

"It's more about what might happen." Kian put the phone on the table and then raked his fingers through his hair. "I need to ask you a very personal question. Did you and Mia have sex, and if you did, did you use condoms?"

Of all the random things to ask. "I don't see how it's any of your business, and if you're worried that I got her pregnant, I didn't."

"That's not what I'm worried about. The text was from Syssi. She has reason to suspect that Mia is a Dormant. If you had sex with her without a condom, you might have already induced her transition, and with her heart condition, that might be extremely dangerous to her."

Toven hadn't heard the term Dormant in over five thousand years. Dormants were the children of immortal females with human men, and since all the immortals had perished along with the gods, the only way Mia could be a Dormant would be if she was Annani's descendant, but then Kian would have known about her, and she would have been induced at puberty like all children born to immortal mothers were.

"The only way Mia could be a Dormant is if she's one of yours, but that's not possible. Her mother wasn't an immortal. She died as a young woman, leaving Mia in her grandparents' care." He narrowed his eyes at Kian. "Are your people being selective about which children get induced and which do not?"

In the time of the gods, every child born to an immortal mother had been induced regardless of their status or any other factor. It had been their right, and for the inducers, it was considered a privilege and an honor to facilitate the transition. No Dormant child had been left behind.

Kian looked as if Toven had greatly offended him. "We would never discriminate against any child. All our children get induced. Mia is not one of ours."

Kian

༄

Kian shouldn't have been surprised at how little Toven knew about Dormants. Even Bridget hadn't known what to expect when they'd found Syssi and Michael, the first adult Dormants they'd discovered.

Michael's transition had been easy, but Syssi's hadn't, and if not for his mother's intervention she might not have made it.

At the thought, a cold shiver ran down Kian's spine. He couldn't imagine living without her. Ending his own life would have seemed like an easy way out, but he had an entire clan that depended on him and checking out was not an option.

"What's wrong?" Toven asked. "I don't like the scent coming off you."

"Syssi was a Dormant. She was a healthy young woman, and yet her transition didn't go smoothly. She barely made it."

Toven's eyes softened. "I get it. You can't imagine life without her. It's the same for me with Mia, but for better or worse, she's not a Dormant."

"There is a lot you don't know about Dormants." Kian refilled his cup, buying himself time to formulate his explanation. "Adult Dormants are different from early teens Dormants. We've been blessed with a good number of them since Syssi was first discovered by my sister, and we've learned a few things over the past four and a half years. One had cancer, others were too old, but thankfully, everyone has made it."

With assistance, which Toven might be aware of. According to his mother, the healing properties of gods' blood had been a well-guarded secret, but as Ekin's son, Toven must have known about it.

"That's good to hear, and I'm happy for them, but even though I wish you were right about Mia, I don't see how it's possible. How do you determine whether someone has the godly genes? Do you take a blood or tissue sample and have it analyzed?"

Kian chuckled. "I wish it was that simple. We don't know enough to identify the code of godly genes. Our methods are not an exact science, and a lot of it is speculation, but in your and Mia's case, it's quite obvious."

Toven frowned. "How so?"

"Orion described you as a cold, jaded male who didn't care about anything or anyone. You're no longer that male, and the catalyst for the change must have been Mia. Didn't you wonder why you were so taken with her?"

Toven nodded. "The thought that she was my truelove mate crossed my mind, but I dismissed it because she's human, and gods can only bond with other gods and on rare occasions immortals."

"That should have clued you in. We've noticed that immortals and Dormants feel a special affinity to one another, the same way immortals who are not enemies feel a special connection. An instant rapport is one possible indication that the person is a Dormant. The other indicator is a paranormal ability, but plenty of our transitioned Dormants have none."

"Mia doesn't have any paranormal abilities." Toven crossed his arms over his chest. "I would have known if she had."

Smiling, Kian pulled out his phone. "According to my wife, Mia is an enhancer. We've never encountered such a talent, and I didn't even know that enhancing others' paranormal abilities was possible, but Syssi has convincing evidence." He went on to explain Syssi's coin-tossing experiment.

"It could have been a fluke."

"Maybe. But given Mia's condition and the fact that you could have unwittingly induced her transition, you need to suspend your disbelief and accept that I might be right. If she starts transitioning, her life will be in danger, and you can't take her to a human hospital. She needs to be cared for by a doctor who knows what's going on and who has helped many other Dormants transition success-fully. Bridget is our most experienced physician, and Mia's best hope."

Toven eyed him with a frown. "You can give me the phone number of that doctor, and if Mia starts transi-tioning, I'll immediately take her to her or ask the doctor to come to us."

Kian shook his head. "We have all the necessary medical equipment in our clinic, and Mia needs to be right next to it until it is safe to assume that she's not transitioning. Our hidden village is more than an hour's drive away from here, and even longer than that from Mia's home. You can't take the risk. If I were you, I would take her to the village straight from here. I can send someone to collect your belongings."

Letting out a breath, Toven uncrossed his arms. "I can't just spring all of that on her out of the blue. Her heart can't take it. She doesn't even know that I'm immortal."

"Then it's about time that you told her. Besides, we have two Perfect Match machines in the village, so you don't have to buy the entire company to enjoy them. You two can have fun while you wait."

Toven groaned. "It's not that simple. Mia's grandparents will worry about her, and they have the right to know what's going on. If anything is." He pinched his forehead between his thumb and finger. "It just doesn't seem likely."

Kian let out an exasperated sigh. "Look, Mia might not be transitioning, and if you keep her safe by using a condom from now on, and she doesn't start transitioning in the next couple of days, it might be safe for her to go home. I don't know why you are being so stubborn about it. You can just call her grandparents and tell them that the owners of Perfect Match invited you to spend a few days with them at their secluded mountain mansion."

"But if she starts transitioning, I will need to bring them to be with her. That's non-negotiable."

It was absurd that Toven thought that he was in a position to negotiate. Kian was doing him a favor, not the other way around. And it was ironic that the man who'd turned his own son away was worried about his girlfriend's grandparents.

Orion would be pissed, and rightfully so.

"The only way I'll allow Mia's grandparents into our village is if you compel them to keep our existence a secret."

"Of course."

"Are you sure that you can compel them? Some people are immune."

Toven nodded. "I'm sure. I've compelled them before, so I know that they are not immune."

"Then it's settled. You and Mia are coming home with us."

"Not so fast." Toven shook his head. "I need a few moments to think."

Toven

Toven poured himself another cup of coffee while thinking about what Kian had said, and even more so about the things he hadn't said.

Was it safe for him to just take the guy's word that he meant Mia and him no harm? What if he was laying a trap for them?

Making him frantic over Mia's supposedly impending transition was a good strategy to scare Toven into forgetting about his own safety and going blindly where Kian led him.

Lifting the cup, he regarded Annani's son, searching his expression for clues. "This village of yours, is it home only to immortals, or do you employ humans?"

"We don't have humans in the village, but we have two Dormants who are not ready to be induced yet."

"We had one more." Andrew sighed. "A human who wasn't a Dormant. My wife and I are also transitioned

Dormants, and when we moved here, we had to take her ailing stepfather with us. He suffered from dementia, so secrecy wasn't a problem. He passed away a year ago."

Toven dipped his head. "My condolences."

"Thank you."

If that had been meant to distract him from asking more questions, it hadn't worked. "How many people live in the village?"

"A few hundred," Kian said. "Why all the questions?"

Apparently, Annani's daughters and granddaughters had been busy. If her people found the first Dormant about four and a half years ago, then all those immortals were the descendants of Annani.

"I can't take Mia to a place I know nothing about. I might be walking into a trap."

Kian snorted. "You're a god. You can seize the minds of everyone living in the village. I'm the one who's taking a risk by inviting you."

Toven shrugged. "You have Annani. She was powerful as a girl. I can only imagine how powerful she is five thousand years later."

"If you wish, I can put Orion on the line. He was suspicious of us as well, but Geraldine assuaged his fears."

"I can't be sure that they are not being coerced. What I can be sure of is that neither of them has any fondness for me. I turned my back on Orion, and I didn't know that

Geraldine existed. But if Orion found her by investigating the women in my journal, then I could have done the same, but it didn't even occur to me. My children have no reason to stand in my corner."

Letting out a breath, Kian pulled out his phone. "I guess the only one you'll believe is my mother. I wanted to tell her about you in person, but you leave me no choice."

Toven lifted his hand. "You can put the phone down. I don't trust Annani either. She might be a completely different person now. Fates know that I am."

"How can I convince you then?"

"Tell me why it's so important to you to get Mia and me into your village."

"Because she could die, and if she does, you will find a way to end your life as well, and I don't want that to happen if I can help it. But if you choose to believe that I'm a cold bastard who only cares about his own interests, then perhaps I should approach it from another angle. You must realize how valuable you are to my people. Having a powerful god amongst us will make our community stronger and my mother happier. Mia and you joining our clan is a win-win for everyone. You get to be with your children and grandchildren, Mia gets access to the best and only medical care available to transitioning Dormants, and I get a powerful ally. There is no downside for either of us unless you are a selfish jerk, which you were, but I believe that Mia has cured you of that."

Toven wasn't the best at sniffing out lies, but he was good enough, and Kian seemed sincere. Still, he didn't understand the urgency and wasn't willing to be bullied into dropping everything and going straight to the village. If need be, he would get Mia another dose of his blood to tide her over until they got her to the clinic.

"If memory serves me right, a fever is the first sign of transition in females, and it takes between several hours to a couple of days for the other symptoms to manifest. Is it different for adult Dormants?"

"It's not."

"Then I see no reason to rush to the village. Mia was feeling great this morning, and if anything has changed, your wife would have let us know." He pulled out his phone. "After lunch, I'll take Mia home and tell her the truth. If she gets even a little warmer, I'll call you, and we will make arrangements to get her to the clinic. Can I have your phone number?"

"Of course. And I would like to have yours as well."

Once they were done exchanging numbers, Toven pushed to his feet. "We should join the ladies."

Syssi's brother rose to his feet and offered Toven his hand. "I need to leave. It was interesting meeting you, and I hope to see you in the village. Welcome back to the family."

"Thank you." Toven shook the guy's hand. "It was nice to meet you."

After Andrew left, Kian turned to Toven. "Before we join the ladies, there is one more thing you should consider. If Mia transitions, she might regrow her legs. I'm not sure if it's possible after so long, and Bridget will have a more educated opinion, but it's something you should discuss with Mia. The process is long and painful."

Toven nodded. "I'm more concerned about her heart, so I didn't even think about the possibility of her regrowing her legs." He shook his head. "I don't know if I should tell her about it and raise her hopes for nothing. If she turns out not to be a Dormant, or she can't transition because of her heart, she will be crushed."

Kian put a hand on his back. "Mia is a survivor. She's stronger than you give her credit for."

Mia

As Kian, Toven, and Kian's two guards joined them at the table, Mia searched Toven's expression for clues as to how the talk with Kian had gone, but he wasn't easy to read even after all the time they'd been together.

It might not have been long in terms of the number of days that had passed since they'd first met in the virtual world, but given that they'd been spending the majority of their time together, it was a lot. Toven was very guarded, but Mia had learned to read his little tells, like the almost imperceptible tightening of his lips when he got impatient or worried, or the glow in his eyes when he was excited or aroused.

Now he seemed troubled, preoccupied, but also excited.

As the hostess rushed over to lead them to the private room Syssi had reserved, Toven took her hand and gave it a gentle squeeze. "How are you holding up?"

"I'm fine. You're the one who's discovered surviving family members."

His hand on hers tightened. "What did Syssi tell you?"

The question was asked so quietly that Mia could barely hear him, but somehow, Syssi did and turned around. "I told Mia about the terrorist attack on the family compound, and that everyone was presumed dead. I don't have all the details."

As a silent communication passed between Toven and Syssi, Mia was certain that they were hiding something from her.

Whatever.

They were entitled to their family secrets. It also must be a painful subject for them, and they might not have wanted to ruin their happy reunion by dredging up the disturbing memories.

Except, the only one who looked happy about it was Syssi. The men were still in their posturing mode, looking awkward and tense.

After the waitress had taken their orders and they were left alone in the private room, Syssi lifted her glass of water. "I propose a toast. To family lost and found, and to future cooperation."

"Don't we need wine to make a toast?" Toven asked.

"It's too early for wine." Syssi waited patiently until he lifted his glass and clinked it with hers.

"To family and cooperation," Toven repeated.

As everyone followed their lead, Syssi grinned happily. "Now that the cards are on the table, we should discuss Toven's idea for Perfect Match as a joint venture and not as a sale or a purchase."

"Hunter and Gabriel are not going to be happy," Toven said. "I sold them on the idea of having their financial future and that of their children and grandchildren secured for life."

"We can still do that," Kian said. "You can buy them out, and we can become partners. Naturally, they will stay on as paid directors, but we will own most of the company between us."

Toven shook his head. "I will not enter a deal where I'm not the majority shareholder. I want to make the decisions."

As the discussion about Perfect Match continued, Mia pulled out her phone and texted her grandmother. With all the excitement, she'd forgotten to let her know that they were not going to be back for lunch.

"How about we own it equally?" Syssi offered.

"I promised Hunter and Gabriel that they could retain some of the shares. If you and I have equal shares and disagree, then they will have the power to decide."

"That's easily solved," Kian said. "There are different kinds of shares, and they can get the non-voting type.

That way, no decision can be taken and implemented without both you and Syssi agreeing."

"That might be a solution, but before we move forward with that arrangement in mind, we need to come up with a vision for the company's future that we both can live with."

"Your vision is too grandiose," Kian said. "You might have the money to finance it and treat it as a philanthropic endeavor, but we don't. We already finance a charity project of our own, and it's a huge drain on our resources."

"What's your charity?" Mia asked.

"We rescue trafficking victims and rehabilitate them," Syssi said.

"Thank you. I'm so glad that someone is doing something about that. I don't know why the government is not addressing the problem. If I were in charge, I would create a special task force to fight that despicable trade on all fronts and in full force."

"That's because you're not a politician," Toven said. "In a democracy, elected officials only care about getting elected again, and trafficking victims are not going to bring them votes. That's why the homeless situation is not getting taken care of either."

Mia frowned. "That sounds so cynical. I would like to think that at least some of the people we vote for actually care."

Toven smiled at her as if she were a naive child. "Don't listen to what they say. Look at what they do or don't do. Rhetoric is easy."

Sticking her chin out, she crossed her arms over her chest. "Maybe they can't do anything about it. Perhaps those problems are too complicated and pervasive to solve."

"It's a matter of prioritizing," Kian said. "To politicians, those who don't vote are not as important as those who do."

Toven

How had the conversation gotten sidetracked into human politics? They had more important things to talk about, and they were riling Mia unnecessarily over irrelevant things.

Even with Toven and Annani's powers combined, they couldn't affect government policy. Not in democracies where the real power belonged to the bureaucracy and not the elected figurehead.

Things had been easier in the days of kings and queens when influencing one individual could have been enough to turn the tide. Even today, it was possible in places where tyrants ruled. But Toven had failed to do good even when the conditions had been favorable, and he was never going to attempt large-scale changes again.

"Let's talk about the coin tosses." He turned to Syssi. "Twenty-two correct guesses in a row is unprecedented. Maybe your real paranormal talent is telekinesis, and you flipped the coin with your mind?"

Syssi shook her head. "I'm a paranormal phenomenon researcher. If I had telekinesis, I would have known that. Besides, neither I nor the professor I work for have ever encountered that talent. I'm not saying that it doesn't exist, but if it does, it's very rare."

Mia chuckled. "Not to mention that telekinesis is as bizarre if not more so than Syssi predicting the future and me enhancing her performance."

"Actually," the redheaded Guardian said, "an enhancer is not such a farfetched scenario. You know how professional gamblers sometimes have a lucky charm lady with them? Maybe those ladies contribute their positive aura to the gambler's performance."

Mia pursed her lips. "That's an interesting hypothesis, but we are just speculating. We will know more when I go to Syssi's lab and try my witchy powers on some of the other paranormal talents."

"I can see how your ability could be very useful," Kian said. "You could enhance someone's telepathic ability or fortify another's remote viewing."

The redhead smirked. "You know what would be even more useful? Someone who could nullify a paranormal talent, especially if they could do it remotely."

As the discussion continued, Toven withdrew from it to gather his thoughts.

He'd run out of time and excuses, and later today he would have to tell Mia everything, including that she was possibly a Dormant and had the potential to turn immortal, which might also mean regrowing her legs.

His blood would probably keep her alive and help her survive the transition, but he needed to talk to the village doctor to make sure.

It should be Mia's decision whether she wanted to take a risk and let him induce her, but it might be too late for that, and if she didn't make it, he would never forgive himself for not figuring out what she was before it was too late.

Except, he hadn't known that a damn condom was needed to prevent her from transitioning. If Mia didn't kick him out after his confession, he was going to drive to the nearest pharmacy and load up on protection.

It hadn't even occurred to him that she might be a Dormant, but it should have. He'd been cognizant of his inexplicable attraction to her, even contemplating that if she weren't human, she could have been his truelove mate. Not that she was lacking in any way, but he had never felt like that about any female. Not even his wife, whom he'd loved.

There was no denying that he'd bonded with Mia, and that was the strongest indicator that she was a Dormant.

The affinity Kian had talked about was pretty evident as well.

Observing Mia with Syssi and Kian, and even with the two guards, Toven could see that in action. She'd been terrified of this meeting, but despite the shocking news, the blond guard who had the vibe of a coldhearted assassin, the redhead who looked like he could wrestle a bear and win, and Kian's intense personality, she seemed totally at ease with all of them.

Toven wondered about the human who had sired Kian, contributing genetic material that produced an immortal who had the vibe of a god. Annani must have chosen her lovers carefully, ensuring that only the best fathered her five children.

She had been blessed by the Fates because conceiving five times was unheard of for a goddess. For a male god, siring two children was considered very lucky as well, but not as rare.

Could he sire one more child with Mia?

How the hell was he going to tell her that he already had two children?

If she didn't kick him out for endangering her life with his venom, she would do so after hearing that he'd turned his back on his son and hadn't tried to find out whether any of the females he'd been intimate with had conceived.

Fates, how was he going to do all that without causing her distress? If she was healthy, he would have given her a couple of drinks to relax, but that wasn't an option. He would have to thrall her to keep her calm.

So far, she'd been doing great, and he could hear her heart beating nice and steady despite all the excitement, so maybe she could take what he needed to tell her without him having to thrall her.

Vrog

"I thought that I would find you here." Vlad hung his satchel on the back of the chair and sat down. "I didn't see you this morning. How was your weekend with Aliya?"

"Great." Vrog smiled. "We came back early in the morning, but you were already gone." He turned to look at Aliya, who was talking to a customer at the counter. "Poor Aliya is exhausted. I suggested that she take a day off, but she wouldn't hear of it."

They'd hardly spent any time sleeping, making love so many times that he'd lost count.

Vlad followed his gaze. "She looks happy."

"You think so? She's always friendly with the customers."

"That's not the same as happy. She's practically glowing." Vlad turned to look at the papers strewn over the table. "What are you working on?"

"Kian tasked me with establishing a school for the clan's children. I'm making lists of items I need to research for what I envision." He started collecting the pages and putting them in a neat pile. "But the truth is that I'm having a difficult time concentrating. Thoughts about my future with Aliya keep intruding."

Leaning back in his chair, Vlad crossed his arms over his chest. "Isn't it too early to be making plans for the future?"

"It is, but I want us to move in together. I can ask Kian to give us a house, and I know he will gladly do that, but I don't know how to broach the subject with Aliya."

Vlad lifted a brow. "Does that mean you've decided to stay here for good?"

"If things with Aliya work out, then yes." Vrog tapped the stack of papers. "I'm excited about this new project. I'm on borrowed time with my school in China. At some point, I will have to start wearing makeup to make myself look older, and that's just a temporary solution. My best option is to sell the school and start a new one."

"That's music to my ears." Vlad grinned. "I like having you here, and so does Wendy. We are a family."

Vrog swallowed the lump that formed in his throat. "The Mother blessed me with the best son any father could hope for, and the best future daughter-in-law. And she also blessed me with a perfect mate. I don't know what I did to deserve such incredible gifts."

"You're a good man, Vrog." Vlad uncrossed his arms and put a hand on his shoulder. "But don't expect me to start calling you Dad."

"Of course not. I haven't earned the honor."

"It's not that. I don't blame you for not being there when I was growing up, but I can't regard you as a father figure, and we are just getting to know each other."

Perhaps one day that would change, and Vlad would be able to call him Father, but for now, Vrog was grateful for what they had.

"Hello, my love." Wendy leaned to kiss Vlad's cheek. "How was work?"

"Same as usual." He twisted around to pull a paper bag out of his satchel. "I brought you chocolate chip muffins."

She winced. "You're so sweet, but I can't eat them. I gained two pounds over the last week, and if I keep going like that, I'm not going to fit into my wedding dress."

"About that." Vlad ran his fingers through his long, stick-straight hair. "Did you hear about the cruise ship Kian bought for the clan?"

"He did?"

"Yeah. Jackson told me about it. Apparently, plans are being made to have Alena's wedding on the ship, and the celebration will last an entire week. I thought that maybe you would like to have our wedding during the cruise as well. The entire clan will be there, and Annani will preside over the ceremony."

"That's a great idea. When is Alena planning to get married?"

"In three months, more or less. Kian still needs to renovate the ship."

Letting out a sigh, Wendy opened the bag and pulled out a muffin. "That means postponing our wedding again." She took a bite out of it. "Besides, what if Alena wants the entire week to be just about her and Orion? She might not want to share the spotlight with us."

"I think she would. Maybe other couples will decide to get married as well, and each day there could be a different wedding."

"Sounds like great fun to me," Vrog said. "Maybe Aliya would want to seize the opportunity and marry me on the cruise ship as well."

Wendy clapped her hands. "I love it." She waved to get Aliya's attention. "Can you come over here for a moment?"

Vrog blanched. "I was just joking. Please don't tell her what I said."

"Why not? She's been gushing all morning about how wonderful you are and how stupid she was to wait so long to realize that. There is a good chance she'll say yes."

That was good to hear, but all he wanted for now was for Aliya to move in with him.

"What's going on?" Aliya pulled out a chair next to Vrog and leaned to kiss his cheek. "Are we planning a party?"

"Yes." Wendy grinned at her. "Kian bought a cruise ship for Alena's wedding. It's going to be a week-long celebration, and Vlad and I are thinking about postponing our wedding and having it on that cruise as well."

"That sounds amazing. I've never been on a cruise ship."

"Neither have I," Wendy said. "The ship will be ready in about three months, which gives you plenty of time to decide if you want to marry Vrog, but since there are only six nights on a seven-day cruise, you might want to reserve a spot before they are all gone."

"That's a good idea. Who do I need to talk to?"

Vrog gaped at her. "For starters, me. You didn't ask me if I wanted to marry you."

"You don't?"

"Of course, I do."

"Then what are you making a fuss about?"

He shook his head. "First, we need to move in together. What if you find me annoying and change your mind about wanting to be with me?"

She hadn't even told him that she loved him yet, and he hadn't said the words either. Love between partners wasn't part of the Kra-ell way of life, but since they were apparently doing everything like humans, declaring their love for each other was an important step in their relationship.

Unless for Aliya, it was what humans called a marriage of convenience. He was the only one who could potentially give her a long-lived child, and she must have realized that during the time she'd been undecided.

Aliya laughed. "Relax. I was just teasing." Rising to her feet, she moved over, planted herself on his lap, and wrapped her arms around his neck. "The Mother brought us together for a reason, but I agree that we need to spend more time with each other and solidify our love before we stand holding hands before the Clan Mother and have her join us in a ceremony. I've never even planned to have one, but when Wendy suggested it, I thought we should reserve a spot just in case we want to, and if we discover that we can't stand each other, we can always cancel."

"A clan wedding is not like getting married in the human world," Wendy said. "There are no contractual ramifications."

Vrog didn't care whether there were or not. He was still stuck on Aliya saying that they needed to work on solidifying their love.

Kian

Everyone was deep in thought as they made their way to the valet station. Kian waited until they were seated in his SUV with the doors closed before commenting on what they'd learned. "I need to summon a family meeting. I kept thinking about who I should tell first, my mother or Orion and Geraldine, and I realized that the best way would be to tell them together."

"I keep thinking about Mia's talent," Syssi said. "I can't wait to get her into the lab and test it. Amanda can't wait either. I texted her about it, and she flipped." She smiled at Kian. "I guess that both of us will be returning to work sooner rather than later."

Kian didn't like that one bit, but he knew better than to voice his objections. He had security cameras installed all over the basement level of the lab, and when Amanda and Syssi were at work, he had a couple of Guardians parked outside the university. If anything looked even slightly suspicious, they could get to them in moments.

"Is Amanda's office ready?" he asked.

"I don't think so, but since Allegra and Evie are still so small, they don't need much. A mat on the floor and a baby gym will be enough for Allegra, and Evie is still a newborn. We can get a double stroller and have the nanny take them on walks around the university grounds."

"Do you have a nanny lined up?" Kian asked.

"Not yet, but we can bring someone from the village until we find a suitable human. I'm going to ask Margaret."

Kian grimaced. "Are you sure she's your best candidate? She doesn't have the best track record as a mother."

Syssi waved a dismissive hand. "You can't hold her past against her. She's a different person now."

"Still, I would prefer Vivian. We know that she's a good mother."

"I can ask her," Syssi agreed. "But I don't know if she can. She volunteers in the halfway house, and she takes care of Parker and Magnus."

"Give it a try. Maybe she misses cuddling a baby. I would be much more comfortable knowing that Vivian is taking care of Allegra and not Margaret."

"Am I the only one who thinks that Toven is a strange god?" Anandur asked. "When I'm near Annani, I can feel the power radiating from her, but I don't feel anything from him, even though he's supposed to be as powerful as her. My immortal alarm didn't go off when he entered the room. If we didn't know what he looked like, we wouldn't have known that he wasn't human."

"True," Kian agreed. "Maybe he's learned to suppress his godliness so well that it comes instinctively to him, and he doesn't know how to turn it back on anymore."

"Maybe spending some time with Annani will do him good," Syssi said. "She can recharge him." She mimicked plugging a cord into an electrical socket.

Kian sighed. "I had hoped that when we found Toven, the two of them could get together, not as truelove mates, but at least as companions. Annani is going to be lonely without Alena."

"What about Ronja and Merlin?" Anandur asked. "They could move into the sanctuary and keep her company."

"Ronja won't go anywhere until Lisa is in college," Syssi said. "I think the best solution is for Annani to move into the village. She can be with her children, and when she needs time away, she can take any of the single clan members as her companion and go traveling."

"I offered," Kian said. "She's not ready to make that decision."

"She might be now after staying in the village for so long." Syssi twirled a lock of hair around her finger. "It's good that she has her own house in the village now. I think it makes it easier for her to be away from the sanctuary for longer periods of time."

"If she moves into the village, we will need to put someone in charge of the sanctuary. I'll ask Alena to make a list of possible candidates." Kian pulled out his phone. "Dinner at our house at six?"

Syssi nodded. "I'll let Okidu know. What are you going to tell the family? They are going to wonder why we are inviting them for dinner on a Monday."

"I'll say that we have good news to share."

Anandur chuckled. "Everyone will think that you are pregnant again."

"I wish." Kian smiled at Syssi. "Are you ready for another one?"

She pursed her lips. "I would rather wait a little longer, but if the Fates were to bless us with another child today, I would be overjoyed."

"Me too." He took her hand and lifted it to his lips. "My love for you and for Allegra is boundless. But like the universe, it will expand to encompass another child."

"Oh, stop it." Anandur pretended to wipe tears from his eyes. "You're making me cry, and that's dangerous because I'm driving, and my ruined mascara is running into my eyes."

Next to him, Brundar shook his head.

"Don't shake your head at me," Anandur admonished. "I want to see you keeping your stoic expression once you and Callie are blessed with a child."

Kian snorted. "Yeah. I would like to see that as well. The mighty Brundar going ga-ga and goo-goo."

"Dream on," Brundar murmured under his breath.

Mia

~~~~~

Toven had been deep in thought the entire drive back home, and Mia had kept quiet so as not to disturb him.

She had a thousand questions she wanted to ask him, but they could wait until he sorted himself out.

Toven should be overjoyed to find out that his entire family had not perished in that terrorist attack, but it had also been a shock.

Besides, God knows what he and Kian had talked about when they were alone. Perhaps old pain had resurfaced along with the reminiscing, or maybe they'd been planning retribution against those terrorists, and the dark thoughts were still circling in Toven's mind.

"Are you okay?" Mia asked. "It has been quite a day."

"It has." He cast her a smile, but his eyes were clouded. "You handled the meeting exceptionally well. I don't know why you were so scared of it."

She shrugged. "I can handle family drama, but not business negotiations. I expected technical discussions and talk about stock options, future expansion, insurance problems, and other things that I don't know much about." She took a deep breath. "But most of all, I dreaded the pitying looks. Thankfully, there were none, and Syssi was nice and friendly and not at all condescending even though she must be a genius to do all the things she does."

Toven's eyes cleared as his interest was sparked. "Like what?"

"She's an architect who works in a neuroscience lab and designs environments for Perfect Match. She's also a new mom. Kian and Syssi have a little baby girl named Allegra. Syssi showed me pictures of her, and she is adorable. She has her daddy's intense gaze and her mother's pretty face."

Mia tried to keep the longing from her tone, but as usual, Toven saw right through it.

"You can be a mother, you know. I will hire a live-in nanny to help with the baby at night and another one to help during the day. You will never be left alone to take care of her."

"That still doesn't solve the problem of my crappy genetics."

Toven snorted. "Your genetics are not at all crappy, and our child will not inherit your heart condition."

Mia shifted in her seat as much as she could so she could face him. "You say it with such conviction that I'm tempted to believe you. But our child will have a fifty-fifty chance of inheriting my problem."

"They will have zero chance of that. My genetics will ensure that."

Mia had not found Toven prone to boasting, even though, in her opinion, he had every right to do so. He was gorgeous and rich and the dream guy every woman fantasized about, but he wasn't a god.

"That's a somewhat arrogant statement, don't you think?"

"No, I don't." Toven pulled up to the curb and turned off the engine.

The construction crew's truck was on the driveway, and given the whizzing noise coming from the house, they were operating a water saw to cut tile.

"I will explain everything shortly, but first, I need to get rid of the workers. I need privacy for what I'm about to tell you."

That sounded ominous, and Mia swallowed. "You have to give me a clue. Is it good or bad?"

"I think it's good. But you might not agree." He opened the door and walked around to help her out of the car.

In the house, he left her in the living room and went to talk with the crew.

The sawing noise cut off immediately, and a few moments later, the workers were on their way out.

The crew's boss stopped to talk to Toven. "We didn't clean up. If you let us stay for another twenty minutes, I'll get the guys to clear out the debris and vacuum the place."

"That's okay, Bobby. You can come back tomorrow and continue the work." Toven pulled out his wallet and handed the guy money. "Take your guys out for drinks, and you can add the lost work hours to your bill."

"Thanks." Bobby pocketed the money. "We will be here tomorrow at seven in the morning, and I'm not going to charge you extra for it. The tip you gave me is more than generous."

When they were all gone and silence stretched between her and Toven, he walked over to the couch, sat down, and took her hand.

"What I'm going to tell you will require suspension of disbelief. I want you to keep an open mind and wait for me to provide proof before dismissing what I'm telling you."

Toven was a storyteller, and he was probably exaggerating. As sordid or notorious as his family's history was, she wasn't so naive as to not believe it.

As the saying went—life was stranger than fiction.

"With such a dramatic preamble, I can't wait to hear it."

Toven nodded. "For starters, I'm not human."

Was that his attempt to make light of what was to follow?

Mia laughed. "Of course not. I knew that you were an alien all along."

"I'm serious. I'm not mortal, Mia. I'm a god."

Toven

Mia pulled her hand out of Toven's and lifted both in the air. "I've never known you to have an ego that matched your looks and wealth, but maybe you've just been hiding your god complex well." She leaned closer and looked into his eyes. "That being said, I have noticed that your eyes glow from the inside sometimes. I thought it was some anomaly or a reflection, but if you are not human, that would explain it."

She was taking it better than Toven had expected, and her heart wasn't racing.

"So, which god are you?"

He had a feeling that she was just humoring him. She either thought that he was playing a game with her, or that he was crazy.

For now, he should downplay his role in the gods' pantheon and the many names he'd been called by different cultures.

"Naturally, I'm not really a deity, I'm flesh and blood, but my people were called gods by the ancient humans."

"How can you be immortal if you're flesh and blood?"

"My body doesn't age, and it has a rapid healing ability. I can be killed, mostly by another god, but it would be very difficult for a human to end my life. I can just seize their minds and freeze them in place."

"What if they ambush you while you're asleep?"

He cast her a smile. "Why? Are you plotting my demise?"

"Gods forbid." She put her hand over her chest. "But since you're obviously building another adventure for us, I used what I learned about the gods from the previous one. You told me that Had-dar slept in an impenetrable underground chamber."

Now her calm response made sense.

Mia thought that he was testing a storyline on her. Perhaps he could use it to his advantage.

"That's what many of the gods used to do, but I never liked living underground, and I had other methods of protecting myself." He smiled at her reassuringly. "I added the gods to our adventure as a safety precaution. In case my avatar let something slip, it wouldn't have been out of place in a world ruled by gods."

Mia frowned. "Why does that make sense to me?" She shook her head. "You asked me to suspend disbelief until you could show me proof. I need to see it."

"There are several ways to prove it, but I chose the one I think will be the least scary for you. I'll let you make a small cut in the palm of my hand and watch as it immediately closes."

He rose to his feet, went over to the kitchen, and returned with a knife and a dishtowel.

Sitting back next to Mia, he spread the towel over his trousers and handed her the knife.

Mia shook her head. "I can't cut you. You do it."

"Then you'll think it was a trick. You must be the one to do it." He put his hand palm up on the towel. "Don't worry. Even if you stab it right through, it will heal before your very eyes."

"What about an antiseptic?"

"I don't need it. My body eliminates bacteria and viruses."

Heaving a sigh, she took his hand in her small one, turned it palm up, and then dipped her head and kissed it. "That's for the boo-boo I'm going to make."

He leaned and kissed her lips. "You're so sweet."

"I'm nuts. That's what I am for starting to believe you. Can you grow wings?"

Toven laughed. "Stop stalling and just do it."

"Fine." She picked up the knife and pressed the tip to his palm too lightly to break the skin.

"Push harder."

Mia chuckled. "That's my line." She gave the knife a little push, and this time it did the job.

"Don't look away," he commanded as she lifted her head to look at his face.

"It disappeared," Mia whispered. "It didn't take even a second." She brushed her thumb over the spot where the cut was, smearing the few drops of blood around.

Toven lifted the kitchen towel and cleaned his hand. "Is that proof enough? Or do I have to provide more?"

"What else have you got?"

"You can go to the bedroom and whisper something. I'll hear it. I can lift the refrigerator with hardly any effort. And I have fangs. Other than that, I can enter your mind and make you see, hear, and smell anything I want. I can also plant fake memories and make you believe they are real, and I can suppress memories, making you forget them."

She was still staring at his hand. "If you can manipulate my mind, you could've made me see your hand healing right away. Maybe it's still bleeding all over your pants, but my brain is ignoring it."

"Look at me, Mia."

When she lifted her head and looked into his eyes, he knew that she believed him but was desperately trying to hang on to a more rational explanation.

"Why tell me this now? Is it Kian's doing? Is he a god too? What happened that made you tell me?"

He clasped her hand. "I wanted to tell you so many times, but I was afraid of what it might do to your heart. I hoped to have more virtual adventures with you like those we had, and to wait until you were so used to a world with gods in it that you would accept me with no trepidation, or as little as possible. But the Fates twisted my arm, and I'm forced into presenting you with your options with no proper preparation."

Mia

"My options? What do you mean? Do you have to leave me?"

"Never." Toven lifted her hand to his lips. "I'll try to make it as succinct as I can. What I learned earlier today was that you might be a carrier of immortal genes, which we call a Dormant. I truly believed that apart from me all the gods and immortals perished in a bombing five thousand years ago, but I was wrong. Kian's mother survived, and so did her half-sister. Some of the immortals survived as well. They must have been away from the immediate blast area and went into hiding, and you might be one of their descendants. If you are a carrier of the immortal genes, I can induce your transition into immortality. In fact, I might have unwittingly done so already. On the one hand, it puts you in grave danger, but on the other hand, it could mean a complete cure for you, including new legs and immortality."

If Toven's delivery hadn't been so serious and grave, Mia might have thought that he was playing a cruel joke on her, or that he was trying out a new book idea. But even though she found everything he'd told her fantastical, she'd promised him to suspend her disbelief and hear him out.

But what the freaking hell? He was over five thousand years old? She'd noticed that Toven often sounded older than he looked, but this was on a whole different level.

Then again, if she was still inside a virtual fantasy, which was the only thing that actually made sense, then anything was possible. Somehow she'd retained her own identity in the virtual world, and that was why she was aware of how unrealistic everything was.

"How old are you?"

"Nearly seven thousand years old."

"Oh, wow. Talk about an age difference."

He smiled. "It doesn't bother me. Does it bother you?"

She tilted her head and regarded his gorgeous face. Did it matter how long he'd lived if he looked only a few years older than her?

Besides, she was going to wake up soon, so there was no harm in her playing along.

"You know what? It doesn't, and as much of a shock as it is to learn that I'm dating a being as old as human civilization, it's even more of a shock to learn that I can turn immortal and regrow my legs."

"That's right." He seemed so pleased that she was accepting everything he was telling her.

Heck, she wanted to believe that it was real, and she had no way of knowing whether it was or not. Pinching herself would hurt in the virtual world just as much as in the real one, and the same was true for Toven's demonstration. It was an unsettling thought. How could she possibly know? What proof could convince her?

Why fight it, though?

She was living a dream, and it didn't matter if it was all in her head or happening in reality. She was happy, and it felt real. So what if she was stuck forever inside this fantasy?

Mia had no problem with that. Still, even a fantasy world needed to make sense.

"How come you didn't know any of that before meeting Kian?"

"I didn't know that there were any Dormants in the human population. I hadn't encountered any during my travels, and I traveled extensively."

"What makes you think that I am a Dormant?"

"Several things. One is the almost instant bond between us. It's very rare and unique to gods and immortals to be blessed with a truelove mate. When that happens, the attraction is immediate and undeniable, and the bond formed is unbreakable. That's how I feel about you. Do you feel it too?"

Mia nodded. "I'm obsessed with you. From the very start, I felt like we'd known each other on some subconscious level, and that we belonged together." She smiled. "When you first told me that you were buying our neighbor's house, I thought that you were nuts, but in just days, I was thankful for it. I need to be with you, and every separation, even for a few hours, is difficult. But I thought that it was normal because I was in love."

Leaning closer, he took her lips in a soft kiss. "I'm so in love with you, my Mia, and I hate being away from you."

"I'm glad that I'm not the only one who's nuts, but given that I'm starting to believe that I'm sitting on a couch with a god, that's debatable." She laughed. "I'm probably still inside the virtual fantasy, but I don't mind being stuck in there with you." She leaned and kissed him on the lips. "Best fantasy ever."

Looking amused, he cupped her cheek. "I assure you that we are not inside a virtual adventure and that all of this is real. Would it make it easier for you to suspend disbelief if you thought of me as a member of a divergent species instead of a god?"

"Yes. A lot. But you are still freaking ancient."

"I can't do anything about that." He let out a breath. "Let's get back to the other indicators of dormancy. I didn't know this until today, but there is a special affinity between Dormants, immortals, and gods." He chuckled. "I'll rephrase. The special affinity all of those who are not entirely human feel for one another."

Mia wrinkled her nose. "That doesn't work. It makes me think of cyborgs. What else?"

"The third indicator is a paranormal ability, which Syssi believes you have. Frankly I've never heard of an enhancer, but since she's a researcher in the field, I'll take her word for it."

"Yeah. That was kind of far-fetched, but we will know more once she tests me in her lab to see if I have the same effect on other paranormal talents."

As Mia began to accept that she was not inside a fantasy, the excitement and anxiety was making her warm and sweaty. She withdrew her hand from Toven's to take her jacket off. "You said that you might have unwittingly induced my transition. How?"

"That's also something I learned today. Back in the days of the gods, Dormants were induced at the age of thirteen." For a moment, he looked uncomfortable. "Do you remember that I had fangs in our adventure?"

"How could I forget?"

"That was another feature I included to address my unique needs. I have fangs that elongate when I'm aroused or in response to aggression. I also have venom glands, and my venom has euphoric and aphrodisiac effects, which you have experienced. It also has healing properties, which you have benefited from."

She lifted a hand to her neck. "I didn't dream it. You bit me."

He nodded. "The venom also serves as a catalyst to induce transition, and for a young female Dormant, that's enough. But for an adult female, insemination is needed as well. So, if I didn't induce you already, we can prevent induction by using condoms until you decide whether you want to attempt it or not."

Toven

Mia shook her head. "What is there to decide? If I could get a complete cure for my heart, regrow my legs, and become immortal, why wouldn't I do it?"

"Because it's a difficult process, and your heart might not take it. We need to talk to a doctor who has experience with transitioning Dormants. They have one in their hidden village, and Kian has urged me to get you there as soon as possible. In case your transition is imminent, you need to be supervised by a physician who knows what's going on and how to help you. Kian said that Dr. Bridget has supervised all of their transitioning Dormants, and she hasn't lost one yet." Toven rubbed the back of his neck. "I'm confusing you by not presenting things in the right order."

"No, I get it." Mia closed her eyes for a moment. "I want to talk to that doctor. Will she know if my transition is about to start?"

"I'm not sure," Toven admitted. "The first sign is usually fever, so the moment your temperature rises even by a fraction, I'm rushing you over there, and all the other issues we need to address will have to wait."

"What other issues?"

"Your grandparents and what we are going to tell them. If we go to the village to talk to the doctor and stay a couple of days until we are sure that you are not transitioning, we can come up with a good story. We could tell them that the silent partners invited us to spend time with them in their mountain cabin or on their yacht. But if you start transitioning, we can't keep it from them. They need to know what's going on." He swallowed. "I don't want to even think about it, but if you didn't make it, and I prevented them from being with you, I would never forgive myself."

"Will Kian allow them in?"

"He said he would, but he conditioned it on compelling them into keeping the village and its residents a secret."

"What do you mean by compelling?"

"There are two ways in which a god or an immortal can manipulate a human's mind. One is thralling, which is reaching into the human mind and either planting or removing memories. Some are better than others at that, and the level of control is usually connected to how pure their blood is. There is a hierarchy. Nearly every god can thrall immortals and humans, and nearly every immortal can thrall humans but not other immortals and definitely not gods. The other way of mind manipulation is compulsion, which is a much rarer talent. Only a few gods had the ability, and it was particularly strong in my family. I learned today that some immortals have the ability as well."

She narrowed her eyes at him. "Did you ever compel me?"

"Yes. When you asked too many questions I couldn't answer, I compelled you to talk about something else. I also thralled you several times to forget that I bit you."

He'd also thralled her into deeper sleep to give her his blood, but he couldn't tell her about that. The gods hadn't even talked about the power of their blood amongst themselves, and there was a good reason for that. If word got out, they would have been drained to the last drop.

Even gods were not invincible.

She lifted her hand and rubbed the spot on her neck. "You didn't do a very good job with that. I dreamt about you biting me."

He smiled. "I didn't thrall you every time I bit you. Sometimes, I didn't have to because you didn't remember it after coming down from the clouds of euphoria. But I'm going to compel you to keep this conversation a secret. You can't tell anyone anything I tell you about gods, immortals, and Dormants."

Her eyes widened. "I felt it. You used compulsion in your last sentence." She waved a hand. "There was a different timbre to your voice, like a very subtle vibration."

"That's very astute of you. Most people can't tell the difference."

"But if I can't talk about it with anyone, how am I going to discuss it with you?"

"Good point. You are allowed to talk about gods, immortals, and Dormants with me."

"How about the people in the village? I need to talk to the doctor."

He laughed. "You are so clever, my Mia. You are also allowed to talk freely about anything you wish with anyone in Kian's village."

"Are Hunter and Gabriel immortals?"

"They are not."

"Yeah. That makes sense since they were dismissed. So, how is it going to work? Did Kian give you the directions to his secret village?"

Toven shook his head. "He gave me his phone number. He'll send a car to pick us up."

"Do you know how many Dormants their doctor has helped transition?"

"I don't. Kian said that not all of them were healthy, and some barely made it, but so far they haven't lost anyone, which gives me hope."

"Me too." She let out a breath. "There is so much I want to ask you that I don't know where to start, but maybe I should save my questions for when we are in the village.

How long before we know whether I'm already transitioning?"

"Two days at most, and as I said, we are using condoms from now until we have all the facts and decide what we want to do."

"Right." She grimaced. "It's going to be awful, but I guess there is no way around it. I'd rather transition when I'm ready and prepared. Unless there is another way to prevent my induction?"

"If there was, I'm sure Kian would have told me. I can't refrain from biting you, not indefinitely anyway, but I can live with condoms."

"That's kind of ironic, don't you think?" She put a hand on his arm. "You don't need to use protection to prevent an unwanted pregnancy, but you need it to prevent an unwanted transition."

Toven grimaced. "About that. There is one more big shocker I need to reveal. I have a son and a daughter. I knew about the son, but I didn't know about the daughter. I also discovered that I have two granddaughters, a great-grandson, and one more on the way."

Mia

No wonder Toven had been so shaken after talking with Kian. It hadn't been only about discovering that not everyone in his family had died, but also about his children and grandchildren.

She could understand him not telling her about the son he knew about. It would have been difficult to explain a son that was most likely older than her.

"How old are your children?"

"Orlando is about five centuries old, and Geraldine is less than one century old. Throughout my very long life, I was convinced that I was infertile, and ever since my people were gone and I had only human lovers, I never stayed anywhere long enough to find out whether any of them had conceived. I met Orlando by pure chance on a street in Paris, and the only reason we recognized each other was that we look so much alike."

"You must have been overjoyed to find out that you had a son."

"I wasn't. We were like a mirror image of one another, and it was difficult enough to hide in the modern world without having a doppelgänger."

That was such a cold thing to say.

"What did you do?"

"I told him that we couldn't be seen together for safety reasons, and that was that. I haven't seen him since. He stole one of my journals and used it to track down the women I'd been with over the last century, and that's how he found Geraldine."

Mia shook her head. "I don't even want to get into why you kept information about your lovers in journals, or how many of those journals you have. That's just creepy. But I can't believe that you told your son to get lost. You find out that you have a son after thousands of years of being convinced that you can't have children, and you dismiss him?"

"It wasn't one of my proudest moments, but I did it for his safety as much as for my own."

"You could have found a solution. You could have talked on the phone or sent each other letters. As far as the two of you knew, you were the only immortals on the planet."

"Precisely why it was so dangerous for us to keep in touch. Believe me, I agonized about my decision for years, but if I were in the same situation again, I wouldn't act differently. Orlando was a grown man who knew how to take care of himself. He didn't need me."

Mia couldn't believe how callous Toven could be. Did she even know the man she'd fallen in love with?

First of all, he wasn't a man. He was a god. And secondly, he had no idea what a real family was.

She'd been blinded by his looks and by everything he had done for her, but the truth was that she'd felt he was different all along but had chosen to ignore it.

"Am I not dangerous to you as well? Why turn your back on your own son but let me into your life? That doesn't make any sense."

"Logic had nothing to do with it. I fell in love with you."

"But you didn't fall in love with your son?"

"I did not."

"Unbelievable," Mia murmured under her breath.

Apparently she had a lot to learn about the man she loved, and maybe she could teach him a thing or two about what it meant to be a family.

"Can we put the issue of my children aside for a moment?" Toven took her hand. "Right now, we need to decide when we are leaving for the village and what we are telling your grandparents. Time is not on our side."

"Are your children in Kian's village?"

"Yes. And so are my grandchildren and my great-grandson."

"Good, so we will get to meet them when we get there. If I don't develop a fever tonight, I prefer to leave tomorrow morning. That way, I can tell my grandparents that we were invited to spend a few days with Kian and Syssi, and it won't even be a lie. Just not the entire truth."

Mia had a feeling that from now on most of what she was going to tell her grandparents and her friends would be half-truths. She didn't like that, but there wasn't much she could do about it if she moved with Toven into the immortals' village, and even if she didn't.

If she turned immortal and regrew her legs, she would have to do a lot of lying, or Toven would have to compel her grandparents, Frankie and Margo to guard her secret.

The other option was to get everyone she loved to move into that village with her. Her grandparents wouldn't mind severing their ties to the mortal world, but her friends would, so that was a no-go.

Besides, she was getting ahead of herself.

What if she wasn't a Dormant after all? And even if she was, perhaps the doctor might tell her that she couldn't transition because of her heart.

"We should tell my grandparents about the invitation to spend time with Syssi and Kian right now. They are probably wondering why we didn't stop by their place straight after the meeting."

He nodded. "Will it be okay with you if I don't join you? I have an errand to run."

"What errand?"

He smiled sheepishly. "I need to buy condoms."

The condoms were probably an excuse, but Mia had no problem with that. She wasn't the only one who was still reeling from the day's discoveries. Toven had received some earthshaking news as well, and he needed some time alone to process everything.

She leaned over and kissed his cheek. "Take your time but be back for dinner."

Toven

~~~~

Toven's mind was in turmoil.

Mia thought that he was a monster for turning his back on Orlando, and yet she hadn't pushed him away. Instead, she'd gotten that determined look on her beautiful pixie face, which told him that she would do her best to fix things between him and his son.

It was just one more thing to love about her.

Mia never shied away from a challenge, but she never rushed into anything either. She would assess the situation, decide on a course of action, and then gently steer everyone in the right direction.

What had he done to deserve a mate like her?

Mia might think that she was lacking somehow because of her physical disability, but the truth was that his emotional handicap was much more difficult for her to deal with than her mobility issues had ever been for him.

Hers might still be fixable, while his was probably beyond repair.

After driving aimlessly for several minutes, Toven pulled out his phone and dialed Kian's number.

"Hello, Toven," the guy answered right away. "Is Mia okay?"

"She is, thank you for asking. We had the talk, and she decided that unless she gets a fever tonight, tomorrow morning is good enough."

"I'll send a car. Does she still live with her grandparents?"

There was no need to mention the house Toven had bought next door, although Kian had probably found out about it already. In the hours since they had parted ways after the meeting, he had most likely compiled a file about Mia.

"Yes, she does. Do you need the address?"

"I do. Can you text it to me?"

He was sure that Kian had it. They were both pretending that the guy hadn't investigated the hell out of both of them.

"I will do that as soon as we hang up. What time should I expect the car?"

"Is ten o'clock in the morning good?"

"Excellent." He hesitated to ask the question that was burning in his chest, but he had to know. "Did you tell Orlando that you found me?"

"Not yet, but I'm about to. I called a family meeting to inform everyone, including my mother. Why?"

"I just wondered what his reaction was. We didn't part on good terms."

"I know. He told us about it."

"I did it to protect us both."

"Yeah, I get that, but you could have handled it better. Don't sweat it, though. The good thing about family is that they have no choice but to forgive you."

Toven snorted. "That's so untrue. Mortdh was my brother, and I hope he burns in hell for all eternity. How's that for forgiveness?"

"That's an extreme case, but I'm with you on that one. Still, your jerky behavior toward Orion could be excused, and if you grovel a little, I'm sure he'll forgive you."

"I'm not going to grovel, but I'm going to suggest a fresh start. I hope he accepts it."

"He will. He's a good man." Kian chuckled. "If he wasn't, I wouldn't have approved his and Alena's mating. Not that she asked my permission, but naturally she wanted my blessing."

"You sound like a male who knows how to deal with family. I might need your advice."

Kian laughed. "I'm the last one you should ask for advice on such matters. I suggest that you talk with Syssi. Everything I know, I've learned from her."

Toven could believe it.

The impression he'd gotten from Kian was that the guy was a straight shooter, but he was too intense, too direct, and his diplomacy left a lot to be desired. His wife, on the other hand, put everyone around her at ease.

"Can I ask you for one more favor?"

"Sure."

"When Mia and I arrive at the village, and after we talk to the doctor, can you organize a get-together with my children and grandchildren? Or perhaps I should ask that favor from Syssi."

"Don't worry. We will roll out the welcome wagon for you and your lady. I just hope she doesn't start transitioning before tomorrow."

"Yeah, me too. Thank you, Kian. I appreciate everything you're doing for us."

"That's what family is for, and for better or worse, you're family. You're my sister's father-in-law, and soon, you and my mother will welcome a new grandchild together."

"Indeed. And isn't that just extraordinary?"

"It definitely is. I'll see you and Mia tomorrow, Toven." Kian ended the call.

After dropping the phone on the passenger seat, Toven rubbed his chest. His heart ached with all that he had lost and all that he could still have.

He'd lost so many years of his children and grandchildren's lives, but it wasn't too late for a new start, provided that Mia made it through the transition.

Maybe it wasn't a good idea for him to reconnect with his children before she transitioned successfully.

If she didn't, Toven would find a way to end his life as well, and to Orlando, that would be like another slap in the face. Geraldine, her daughters, and his grandkid didn't know him, but it was true for them as well.

Perhaps he should keep his distance until he knew for sure that he wasn't going anywhere.

Mia

W hile Toven shopped for condoms and sorted out his thoughts and feelings about the events of the day, Mia had time to come to terms with what she'd learned.

She could accept Toven's insane age and his alien-ness, and even the possibility of becoming immortal, but his relationship with his son bothered her, and she wondered how the daughter he didn't know about would react to him.

Perhaps it was easier for her to focus on those family issues because they belonged in the world she was familiar with. The rest of Toven's fantastic story belonged in an alien world where the mythological gods were real, some of them were still around, and their immortal descendants lived in a hidden village that was driving distance from her home.

As for herself, she was excited by all the possibilities Toven had presented her with, but not without reservations. Immortality was great, but would it be so without her friends?

Mia had come to terms with her grandparents not being around in a couple of decades from now, but she'd been looking forward to spending many more years with Frankie and Margo, including their future husbands and children. Would she be able to see them grow old while she didn't?

It was a painful thought, but on the other hand, she had eternity with Toven to look forward to. There were still so many questions that she needed to ask him. If he managed to give her a child, would it be a god or a demigod? And would it mean that their children would not inherit her heart problem even if she didn't transition?

Somehow, regrowing her legs was the least of what mattered to her.

Four years ago, that would have overshadowed everything else, but she'd learned to live with it, and it wasn't the end of the world. Her heart condition was more debilitating and limiting than her compromised mobility.

"Hello, family." Margo walked in with Frankie in tow. "I hoped you'd call me right after the meeting." She kissed Mia on the cheek. "Was it too overwhelming to talk about?"

"Yeah." Just not for the reasons Margo imagined.

"I'll tell you about it over dinner. I didn't even tell my grandparents yet because I want to do it in one shot."

She also needed Toven to hear her tell it so he wouldn't say something that would contradict her version.

Thankfully, she didn't have to wait long.

The doorbell rang a few moments later, and as Frankie opened the door, Toven walked in with a bouquet of flowers in his hand.

"Am I late?" He strode into the kitchen and handed the flowers to her grandmother.

"You're just on time." She took them from him. "What's the occasion?"

He cast a smile at Mia. "I was in a celebratory mood."

"Did they agree to sell?" Mia's grandfather asked.

"Let's sit down to dinner first." Her grandmother shooed Toven out of the kitchen. "The soup is getting cold."

When they were all seated, and the tureen had been passed around, Margo waved her spoon at Toven. "So, are you the new owner of Perfect Match?"

"Not yet." He gave her a small smile. "We are still negotiating. The silent partners' preference is to do a joint venture with me, and I might just take them up on it. They like my vision for the company, and they are willing to work with me to achieve it." He looked at Mia. "They invited Mia and me to spend a few days with them, and I hope we will have a working blueprint by the end of it."

Her grandmother frowned. "When are you going?"

"Tomorrow." Mia smiled apologetically. "They suggested it during the meeting, but Toven and I needed to go home and discuss it before taking them up on their offer. It was so sudden."

"Why not wait for the weekend?" her grandfather asked.

Mia shrugged. "Who knows with those eccentric billionaires?" She winked at Toven. "They are used to having things done on their schedule. Besides, I'm done with the illustrations, so it works for me. I could use a luxurious vacation with a nice couple."

"I bet." Frankie sighed. "Where are they taking you?"

"I don't know, but they promised that Toven and I would love it."

She was getting better at giving vague answers that saved her from having to lie. It still felt bad, though.

Frankie scooped up the last of her soup and then took a slice of bread to wipe the bowl clean. "So what happens if you decide to do a joint venture with the silent partners? Are you going to buy the founders out?"

"That's one of the options," Toven said.

"What I want to know..." Margo pushed her empty bowl aside. "Is whether Frankie and I are going to get free tokens."

"You are," Toven reassured them. "I'll put you on the research team, and your job will be evaluating the different adventures and giving them scores. You can have as many as you want."

Her friends exchanged happy grins and high-fived each other, and then Frankie turned to Toven. "I don't want to be greedy, and I'm more than happy with enjoying virtual adventures and evaluating them for free, but could it be a paying gig? I'd quit my job in a heartbeat to do this for a living."

Margo lifted her hand. "Count me in. I have a thing for geeky smart guys, and that place must be full of them."

"Sure thing." Toven grinned back. "As soon as I have a say in it, you're hired."

"Yay!" Frankie clapped her hands. "I can't wait to tell my boss that I'm quitting."

Mia's heart did a happy flip.

She finally had a way to pay her friends back for all the support they'd given her, and she could stay close to them even if she moved into the immortal village.

"Can I have a job at Perfect Match too?" Mia batted her eyelashes at Toven. "Not just as a tester and evaluator, though. Syssi told me that she designed some of the environments, and I would love to try my hand at it too."

Smiling, Toven leaned over and kissed her cheek. "You, my love, are going to be a shareholder in the company. You can do whatever you please."

Mia's enthusiasm sobered a little. "Do you intend to buy the shares in my name, or is this a marriage proposal?"

He frowned at her. "I thought that the proposal was already accepted. Did I misunderstand?"

Mia's grandmother cleared her throat. "Perhaps we should give Mia and Toven a few minutes of privacy to sort things out."

"It's okay, Grandma. We are not fighting. I was just joking about the proposal. I told Toven that we needed to live together for at least a year before getting married."

"You said six months," Toven corrected.

"I agreed to six months, but then you decided to buy Perfect Match."

"What difference does that make?"

The guy was seven thousand years old, supposedly brilliant, and yet he couldn't read between the lines?

Mia rolled her eyes. "Do I really need to explain?"

Understanding finally dawning, he smiled. "How about we split the difference between six and twelve and make it nine months of living together before we get married."

Margo stared at Toven and then at Mia. "Is there something the two of you are trying to hint at?"

Mia's eyes widened. "I'm not pregnant."

"That's a shame." Margo pouted. "The two of you will have gorgeous babies."

Annani

As Annani's family assembled around Kian and Syssi's dining table, the most popular topic of conversation was guessing what Kian's good news was.

Annani was wondering the same thing, but she was not as excited as the younger members of her family to find out. As long as the news was good, she was fine waiting for Kian to make his announcement.

So far he had been sitting at the head of the table with Allegra cradled in his arms, making silly faces at her and talking in baby talk, which was very entertaining. Annani could watch her son with her granddaughter all day long.

"What do you think this is about?" Jacki took a seat on Alena's other side.

"No clue," her daughter said. "Kian is adamant about keeping up the suspense until everyone gets here."

"It must be something big if he gathered the entire family." Amanda glanced at Syssi. "I bet it has something to do with the new talent you found."

Syssi shrugged. "I don't want to spoil Kian's surprise. You'll have to be patient."

When everyone was seated, Kian handed Allegra to Syssi and rose to his feet.

"I'm not one for much preamble, so I'll get right to it. We found Toven."

"What?" Orion exclaimed. "How? And where is he?"

Annani's heart soared with happiness. She did not care about the details. She just wanted to see him.

"That's a slightly longer story." Kian sat back down. "A week ago on Monday, I got a call from our partners at Perfect Match that someone was interested in buying the company. I didn't take it seriously, but when the founders asked for twenty-five billion dollars, and the buyer not only agreed but provided proof of funds, Syssi and I were intrigued. The story was that he found his perfect match, but she had a congenital heart problem, and after their session had to be terminated because of it, she was denied access to the studios. She's also a double amputee, so the virtual fantasy world allows her to enjoy things she can't in real life. Long story short, Toven decided to buy the company so they could continue enjoying the virtual world together."

"That's sweet," Amanda said. "A little nuts, but sweet."

Orion huffed out a breath. "Are you sure it's him? He doesn't sound like the man I met in Paris. That guy was dead on the inside."

"We met him along with his mate this morning," Kian continued. "Naturally, we all recognized him right away because he looks so much like you, and I called him by his real name to make sure that it was him. He confirmed, and we pretended to be long lost relatives without mentioning anything about gods and immortals."

"Because of the Perfect Match people?" Alena asked.

Kian nodded. "And also because he hadn't told Mia anything yet."

"How did he manage to keep it a secret from her?" Annani frowned. "How long have they been together?"

"Too long for him to keep thralling her, but since he's also a compeller, I assume that he alternated his methods."

A prickle of unease rushed down Annani's spine. "Toven probably does not know that repeated thralling can cause brain damage to humans. I hope Mia is okay."

"She's more than okay," Syssi said. "She's lovely and bright and has a unique paranormal talent." She explained her coin-tossing experiment and what she thought Mia's influence on the results had been. "I can't wait to get her into the lab." She grinned at Amanda.

"You might have to conduct the experiments in the village," Kian said. "Toven never suspected that she was a Dormant, and they didn't use protection. She might be transitioning tonight, but I hope she won't start until tomorrow morning when they get to the village. She needs to talk to Bridget about her options."

Amanda clapped her hands. "We need to prepare a welcome party at the pavilion. I don't have time to prepare a banner, but I can send Onidu to get balloons."

"I'm not going to be there to welcome him with smiles and open arms." Orion bristled. "He doesn't deserve it. Not from me."

Annani could not blame him for being angry. Toven had treated him deplorably.

"I suggest that we skip the welcome party this time," she said. "Toven and Mia already know Syssi and Kian, and they should be the only ones to greet them at the pavilion. The rest of us can wait here." She smiled at Syssi. "I would have offered my house, but yours is bigger."

"What if Mia is not a Dormant?" Alena asked. "Her supposed paranormal talent hasn't been tested yet, so the only indicator is Toven falling so madly in love with her."

"I'm sure she is," Syssi said. "We can invite Lisa to test her Dormant detecting powers, but it will have to wait for when she's back from school. She lost too many school days during Ronja's transition, and she can't afford to lose any more."

"If you don't mind," Kalugal said. "Jacki and I would love to greet my great-uncle in the pavilion."

Kian nodded. "I'm sending Okidu to pick them up at ten o'clock in the morning, so they will get here about eleven-thirty. Right on time for a family lunch."

Kalugal leaned back and wrapped his arm around Jacki's shoulders. "I think my long-lost relative merits a day off work."

Jacki dutifully nodded. "I agree."

"Fine," Kian grumbled. "But I know what you are after. Toven probably knows where the gods came from, and he might even know something about the Kra-ell."

Kalugal shrugged. "Naturally, I'm curious about what my great-uncle knows, but that's not the only reason I want to greet him. Family is important to me."

"It's up to you, but I agree with my mother that only Syssi and I should greet Toven and Mia at the pavilion. I don't know enough about Mia's condition, but if her heart is fragile, too much excitement is not good for her. We shouldn't overwhelm her."

Kalugal sighed. "You're right. I wouldn't want to cause the lady undue excitement. Jacki and I will wait here."

"Thank you." Kian looked at Amanda. "For the same reason, I also suggest that you tone down their reception. No one should jump up from behind furniture and yell surprise."

Amanda rolled her eyes. "What about balloons? Can we at least have that?"

"Balloons should be fine. Allegra likes them."

Toven

As a limousine pulled up in front of Mia's grandparents' house, she gave each a hug and a kiss.

"Call as soon as you get to wherever you're going," Rosalyn said. "Didn't they give you some indication of where it is they are taking you?"

"Only that it's about an hour and a half drive from here, so it's not too far away."

Toven put Mia's suitcase on top of her wheelchair and wheeled both toward the door. "We are only going away for two or three days." He smiled at Curtis.

Or so he hoped. As much as he wanted Mia to turn immortal, he was terrified of her entering transition.

He opened the door. "I'd better get these into the trunk."

As soon as he stepped out, the limousine driver opened the door, and as he rounded the vehicle, Toven's face split in a grin.

"Okidu? Is that you?"

"Master Toven." The Odu rushed over with a face-splitting grin of his own.

Without giving it much thought, Toven embraced the Odu and clapped him on the back. "You have no idea how happy I am to see you." He lowered his voice. "I go by Tom now."

"Of course, Master Tom. My mistake." The Odu winked as he took the wheelchair and the luggage from him.

A lot must have changed in the thousands of years since Toven had last seen Okidu. He'd perfected mimicking human expressions, and evidently, he had also developed a sense of humor.

Shaking his head, Toven went back into the house to get his carry-on and to say his goodbyes, and with that done, he led Mia to the limousine.

"Good morning, Mistress Mia." Okidu bowed and opened the back door for her. "I am Okidu, Master Kian's and Mistress Syssi's butler, chauffeur, cook, cleaning person, and all-around helpful fellow."

"They are very fortunate to have you." She offered him her hand. "Are there more like you who Tom and I can hire?"

He made a sad face. "All seven of us are employed at the moment. I do not see that changing any time soon."

"Seven?"

"I'll explain on the way." Toven helped Mia get in and then followed her inside.

When Okidu closed the door behind them and then got behind the wheel, Mia lowered the window and waved at her grandparents, who were standing just outside their front door and waving.

"They are acting as if I am leaving for a long trip and not just a couple of days." Mia waved some more and sent them air kisses.

"When was the last time you were away from your grandparents for more than a few hours?"

When Okidu pulled out into the street, Mia raised the window back up and sighed. "A couple of overnight school trips, but that was a very long time ago."

He wrapped his arm around her. "That's going to change now that we are together. I'll take you all around the world."

She winced. "Only after my transition is complete and I have my legs back. I have no desire to travel the world in a wheelchair."

Toven's heart squeezed. Mia was talking about regrowing her legs as if it was a done deal, but they still needed to talk to the clan doctor and find out if it was even in the cards.

Plastering a smile on his face, he dipped his head and whispered in her ear, "So, do you want me to tell you about Okidu and his six brothers?"

"Oh, so that's what he meant by seven of us. He's one of seven brothers, and they are all butlers?"

"That's right, but that's not the most fascinating thing about him." Toven paused for effect. "Okidu is a cyborg, and so are his brothers. They were an engagement present to Annani from her beloved." He smiled at the Odu, who was peeking at them through the rearview mirror. "But Okidu was always my favorite."

"Thank you, Master Tom. But please, do not say that in front of my brothers. They will be jealous."

"I won't, but you can call me Toven now. Mistress Mia knows me by my real name."

"Very well, Master Toven."

Gaping at him, Mia said. "So let me get it straight. Okidu is several thousand years old, and you have known him from before the catastrophe. If the gods knew how to build cyborgs, how come there is nothing mentioned about them in mythology?"

"First of all, there are plenty of mentions in the Sumerian and Assyrian mythologies. You just need to pay attention to the details. And secondly, the gods didn't know how to build the Odus. The technology was lost. Okidu and his brothers are precious relics."

"Oh." She glanced at the Odu. "I'm so sorry to hear that."

"No need to be saddened, mistress." Okidu smiled in the mirror. "All will be resolved in time."

That was an odd comment, but Toven still remembered that the Odus hadn't always made sense. They stored in their brains everything they ever heard, but they often used the information inaccurately.

About an hour into the drive, the limousine's windows turned opaque, and Okidu took his hands off the steering wheel.

"What's going on?" Toven asked. "Is this a self-driving limo?"

"Yes, it is, master." Okidu turned around to face them. "It is a safety precaution to keep the village's location a secret. Not even the clan members residing within know its precise location. All their cars are equipped with these special windows that turn opaque when the vehicle nears the village, and it switches to self-driving mode."

"That's amazing," Mia said. "I feel like we are in a science fiction movie."

Toven concentrated on the sensory input he could still collect. If he needed to find his way in and out of the village without the help of a specially designed vehicle, he wouldn't be totally clueless.

A few minutes later the limo entered a tunnel, drove through it for about four minutes, and then stopped. When the vehicle lurched up, it was clear that they were in a lift.

"Are we going up?" Mia asked.

"Indeed we are," Okidu said. "The tunnel goes through the belly of the mountain, and then the elevator takes the vehicle up to the village parking structure, which is still located underground. From there, we will take another elevator to the surface. That is the only way in and out of the village, so if we are ever attacked, we can prevent our enemies from gaining access by collapsing the tunnel."

"What about food and water?" Toven asked.

"Oh, we have our own water supply and stores of food that can last us a decade."

"Who are your enemies?" Mia asked. "Humans?"

"Among others." Okidu smiled apologetically. "But you should ask Master Toven these questions. I am just a simple butler, and my knowledge is limited."

Toven knew that to be complete nonsense, but it was a diplomatic way for Okidu to redirect Mia's questions to him.

"Well?" She arched a brow.

"Frankly, I'm not sure. My time with Kian was spent on him explaining adult Dormants to me and what it meant for you. We didn't have time to go over the entire history since his mother and I escaped death and headed in different directions."

Mia

~~~

This day was shaping up to be like a virtual adventure. Except, Mia's imagination would never have come up with a scenario like this.

She was in a limousine driven by a cyborg butler; well, at the moment, the limo was in an elevator after driving itself through a tunnel, and she was about to visit a secret village inhabited by a goddess and her immortal descendants.

When the car lift stopped, and its door opened, the windows became clear again, and Okidu took over the wheel, guiding it into a parking spot.

"Welcome to the village, Master Toven and Mistress Mia." He turned the engine off, got out, and rushed over to open the passenger door for them.

He refused to let Toven help him get their things from the trunk, carrying everything, including her folded wheelchair as if it weighed nothing.

If she didn't fully believe that he was a cyborg up until then, that alone was enough to convince her. Okidu looked like a stocky middle-aged human, and there was no way he could have carried the combined weight of everything she'd brought with her with such ease.

They entered another elevator, and as it stopped several floors higher, its door opened to a beautiful glass pavilion where Kian and Syssi were waiting for them.

"Good morning." Syssi pulled her into a quick hug. "Do you feel like Alice in Wonderland?"

"Yeah." Mia chuckled. "But instead of falling down the rabbit hole, I took a ride in a limo driven by a cyborg."

Syssi frowned. "Okidu is not a cyborg, but I guess that's the term you are most familiar with."

"That's what Toven said."

"I didn't want to call Okidu a robot." Toven's eyes darted around as he shook hands with Kian. "I hoped Orion would be here to greet us."

"Orion is waiting in our house with the rest of the family." Kian put a hand on Toven's shoulder. "We decided that it was better not to overwhelm Mia with a large crowd right as she stepped out of the elevator."

Mia had a feeling that Kian was being diplomatic, and Orion's absence wasn't about her fragile heart. It was probably his lack of eagerness to welcome the father who'd treated him deplorably.

"Orion needs time to adjust." She smiled at Toven. "An apology might soften him up."

"I'm not going to apologize." Toven wrapped his arm around her shoulders. "But I'll try to explain and make it up to him."

A large golf cart waited for them as they walked out the sliding doors of the pavilion, and after Okidu loaded their luggage, they all got in and the butler took the wheel.

"Golf carts are the only mode of transportation in the village," Syssi explained. "Originally the village was small, and it took ten minutes at most to get from any house to the village square. But we've added three new areas, and now the distances are longer. Still, most people walk, and the golf carts are used mainly to transport purchases, groceries, and guests."

Mia looked around the lush greenery and the village square. "I guess you don't have a need to accommodate people with disabilities."

"Actually, we had a few cases of people recovering from injuries who needed help getting from place to place."

"Doesn't everyone heal instantly?"

Syssi smiled. "I wish. Small cuts and bruises do, but some injuries take even Immortals weeks to heal. Some take months."

As Okidu pulled out into the path, Syssi leaned over and patted his shoulder. "Please drive slowly, Okidu. I want to give Toven and Mia a tour."

"As you wish, mistress."

"This is the village square." She pointed. "That's our office building, next to it is the café, which is the central hub of the village's social life. The next building over is the clinic, and over there is the playground, the ponds, and the lawn where we hold outdoor events." As the cart continued down the path, the public area gave way to residential homes. They weren't big or fancy and seemed to share similar layouts, but they looked inviting, and the architectural details and the different front yards made each one unique.

"This is what we call phase one of the village. Kian and I used to live right over there up until a few weeks ago." Syssi pointed at one of the houses they'd passed. "But now we live in phase three, which is a little farther away." She smiled apologetically. "Initially, we didn't want a house that was bigger or fancier than all the others in the village, but as the family kept growing, and hosting dinners became impossible with the space we had, we decided to build a larger home in the new phase."

"Who is going to be there?" Toven asked.

"Annani, Orion and his mate Alena." Syssi counted on her fingers. "Geraldine and her mate Shai, your grand-daughter Cassandra and her mate Onegus, your other granddaughter Darlene, who's currently unmated, your great-grandson Roni and his mate Sylvia, your great-nephew Kalugal and his wife Jacki, Kian's other sister Amanda, her mate Dalhu, their baby daughter Evie, and our daughter Allegra." She turned to Kian. "Am I forgetting anyone?"

"Bridget," Kian said.

"Right, the doctor is coming to talk with Mia."

Mia didn't know who she was more excited to meet, the goddess or the doctor. It was good that the new medication was regulating her heart, or all that excitement would have been too much for her.

Was it the medication, though? Or was it Toven's venom that was responsible for her miraculous improvement?

Lifting her hand to the spot where he'd bitten her last night, she stifled a moan. It had been incredible, and this time, Mia remembered every delicious moment of it.

Reaching for Toven's hand, she cast him a sidelong glance, expecting one of his soft smiles, but his jaw was set, his shoulders stiff, and he looked like someone preparing for war instead of meeting his family.

"It's going to be okay," she whispered. "Naturally, there will be a few awkward moments, but once that's out of the way, things will just fall into place like pieces of a puzzle."

He gave her a tight smile. "I hope you're right."

"She is," Kian said. "My mother wouldn't have it any other way, and she's the boss."

Toven

As Okidu parked the golf cart in front of Kian's house, Toven's pulse started racing with excitement tinged with trepidation. He was about to meet his family, old and new, and he knew that his welcome would be a mixed bag.

Annani would be happy to see him, he had no doubt of that, and perhaps the daughter he hadn't known about would welcome him as well, but he braced himself for rejection from Orlando.

"It's going to be okay." Mia squeezed his hand as they walked up to the front door. "If Orion gives you the stink eye, just keep smiling, pull him into a hug, and say that you're sorry. What is he going to do? Tell you to get lost?"

Toven chuckled. "That's exactly what he'll say, but I'll follow your advice. Thank you."

She fisted her hand. "If he gets nasty, he will have to deal with me, and despite my deceptively sweet appearance, I can be vicious when I need to."

In front of them, Syssi chuckled. "I doubt that, but kudos to you for protecting your mate."

As Kian pushed the door open, someone shouted welcome, and was soon joined by more voices and some clapping.

Kian groaned. "I told them not to do that." He looked at Mia. "I hope they didn't startle you."

"Not at all." She grinned up at Toven. "You see? They are excited to meet you."

He lifted her hand to his lips and kissed it. "Maybe it's you they are happy to see?"

"They don't know me."

Toven wanted nothing more than to stay out on Kian's front steps and keep talking with Mia, but it was time to enter the lion's den.

"Let's go." He tugged on her hand and led her inside.

"Toven!" Annani beamed at him as she floated toward them, looking just as he'd remembered her—tiny, beautiful, and with an incredible mane of fiery red hair.

"Annani." Toven let go of Mia's hand to embrace her. "I thought that I'd lost you forever." Tears prickled at the back of his eyes as he held her to him tightly.

She held on with as much force, sniffling delicately against his chest. "You are a sight for sore eyes." Chuckling, she let go of him and took a step back. "Although I have had the privilege to look my fill upon the face of your son, who is your spitting image."

She turned around and waved in Orlando's direction.

The look in his son's eyes was a mixture of anger and hurt, and as Toven braced for the rejection he knew was coming, he decided to follow Mia's advice.

He didn't wait for Orlando to come to him. Instead, he walked over to his son and pulled the reluctant male into his arms. "I'm sorry. I thought that I was doing the right thing, but I was wrong. I could have handled it much better."

The tight muscles in Orlando's back relaxed a fraction, and he even returned the embrace. "My mate tells me that forgiveness benefits the forgiver more than it does the forgiven, so I decided to forgive you." He pulled out of Toven's arms. "Let's start from the beginning." He offered Toven his hand. "Hi, my name is Orion."

"I'm Toven." As he shook his son's hand, he glanced at the tall blond woman standing a step behind him and smiling broadly. "And you must be the lovely Alena." He released Orion's hand, and offered his to Kian's sister.

She took it, but instead of shaking it, she pulled him into a tight embrace. "You need to get used to this, Toven. We are a family of huggers."

Gently holding on to her, he chuckled. "I've been well trained over the past several weeks." He released her and walked to where Mia was being introduced by Syssi and Kian to other members of their extended family.

"This is Mia, my fiancée. Her family and friends are big-time huggers as well."

"Hello, Mia." Alena wrapped her arms around her. "Welcome to our family."

"Thank you, but don't I need to transition first to become a member?"

Alena's smile wilted. "Yes. Generally, that's the rule. But I strongly believe that you will. The Fates have brought you and Toven together for a reason, and it wasn't to play cruel tricks on either of you." She lifted her eyes to Toven. "You've suffered for thousands of years, walking the Earth alone, believing that everyone you cared for was gone. Mia is your reward." She returned her gaze to Mia. "And you, my dear, have suffered enough and overcome enough adversity to earn the greatest boon—a truelove mate."

Chuckling nervously, Mia cast a quick glance at Annani. "That sounds lovely, and I don't want to sound like a heretic, but things are seldom fair in the real world, and my suffering is inconsequential in comparison to that of others."

"Oh, my dear Mia." Annani laughed, the sound sending goosebumps over Toven's skin. He'd never thought he would hear a goddess's lovely laugh again, but here he was, in the presence of Ahn's daughter, the rightful heir to the gods' throne.

"The Fates must love your humility and compassion. I have no doubt that they chose you for Toven after much deliberation, and they could not have chosen a better mate."

Mia

"Thank you." Mia bowed her head. "This is very kind of you to say."

"It is the truth." The goddess threaded her arm through Mia's and led her to the dining room. "We can finish the introductions and the stories over lunch. I am famished."

Mia had a feeling the goddess was somehow aware of how difficult it was for her to remain standing for long periods of time, and she appreciated the thoughtfulness.

She was also overwhelmed, shell-shocked, and dizzy, but not so much that she hadn't noticed how different Annani was from Toven.

The goddess was glowing. It wasn't just her eyes, which actually weren't glowing that much at all, but her very skin. Wherever she wasn't covered, which was mainly her face, her chest, and her arms, she emitted a subtle glow.

Mia had never seen Toven glow, and she wondered whether it was something unique to female gods or was Annani more powerful. She certainly felt like she was. The air around her was practically crackling with energy, but it wasn't unpleasant. On the contrary, it was soothing, nurturing, and Mia had a feeling that being around Annani was beneficial on some level. Like going to a mineral spa or something of that nature.

As soon as they entered the sprawling dining room, another butler who looked like Okidu's twin brother bowed to the goddess and pulled out a chair for her at the head of the table.

"Thank you." Annani smiled at him before taking the seat with a fluid grace that defied gravity.

"Sit next to me." She motioned for Mia to take the seat to her left.

The butler immediately pulled out a chair for her as well, and as Toven entered with Kian and Syssi, Annani repeated her request for him to sit to her right.

"I cannot wait to hear what you have been up to throughout all these years." Annani put her hand over Toven's.

"Same here." He looked at her fondly. "I shouldn't be surprised that you managed to achieve so much more than I did, and not for lack of trying. I failed time and again."

The goddess nodded. "I failed many times, but I just kept going for the simple reason that I could not give up. It was my duty to continue the work of our people." She smiled. "I also thought that I was the only one left."

"We have so many things to talk about." Toven looked at the pretty brunette, who was the daughter he hadn't known he had. "But that can wait for another time. Right now, I would like to get to know my family better, and I will start with my lovely daughter. What can you tell me about yourself, Geraldine?"

Pushing a lock of hair behind her ear, she glanced at her mate. "Where should I start? Should I tell Toven about Sabina?"

Toven frowned. "Who's Sabina?"

"She is me before my memory loss." Geraldine rubbed her fingers over her temple. "In my other life, I was named Sabina, I was married to a human named Rudolf, and I had a daughter named Darlene." She looked at the aforementioned daughter and smiled. "Orion found me while I was still Sabina, and we met on several occasions. He always made me forget that we did, though."

"How?" Toven asked. "You are a demigoddess. He shouldn't have been able to thrall you."

"Well, he did. I'm not a powerful immortal, or at least I don't think I am. Shai thinks that I learned to suppress my abilities to blend in better, and I did such a good job of it that I can no longer summon them." She sighed. "Anyway, my husband saw me with Orion and thought that I had a lover. We fought a lot about that, and one of those times we were on the beach. I got mad and took a swim to blow off some steam, but I must have swum too far, and I got hit by a boat. If I weren't immortal, I would have died from that injury." She looked at the doctor who sat on the other side of the table. "Bridget says that even an immortal would have died after losing half her brain matter, but since I was a demigoddess, I was able to regenerate quickly enough to survive. The problem was that my memories were gone along with my brain matter, and I had no recollection of my life prior to the accident. I did not know that I was married or that I had a daughter. Long story short, Orion found me, put me in a rehabilitation clinic, where I relearned to speak and take care of myself, and he kept helping me when I was released, but he never told me about my prior life."

Toven frowned at his son. "Why did you keep it from her?"

"Because she wasn't aging, and sooner or later, she would have had to fake her own death anyway. I figured it was a good opportunity for a clean exit." He looked at Darlene. "Darlene had a very difficult time forgiving me, but eventually, we made our peace with one another."

"Not entirely," Darlene said. "I'm still angry at you for the years I could have had with my mother. She could have dragged it out for much longer. If she had waited with faking her death until I finished college and got married, things would have been much easier for me." She looked at Geraldine. "And for you."

The irony of that story wasn't lost on Mia. Orion had made a judgment call that had negatively impacted the lives of Geraldine, her husband, and her daughter. He could've come up with a better plan, but at the time, that had seemed to him like the best course of action.

Toven had done the same thing with him. He'd figured that it was safer for them to keep their distance, but if he'd given it more thought, he also could have come up with a better plan.

Annani

Annani waited patiently for Geraldine and Cassandra to tell Toven the rest of their story of how they had found their way to the clan, and how they had trapped Orion.

In the meantime, lunch had been served and consumed, and when the table was cleared and coffee and tea were served, their stories finally drew to an end.

On the other side of the table, she could see Kalugal bristling with impatience, as he waited for his turn to engage Toven in conversation, but he would have to wait a little longer.

As soon as there was a moment of silence around the table, Annani leaned over to Mia. "I heard that you and Toven met in a Perfect Match virtual fantasy, and that your session had to be terminated due to a health problem."

Mia nodded. "I specified in the questionnaire that I can only handle a mild level of excitement, and I even had a doctor supervise my session just in case something went wrong. It was fantastic the first time around, but during our second session, Toven took it a little further than what I was comfortable with."

"I bet." Amanda snorted.

Mia's cheeks reddened. "What I meant was that he scared me senseless, and my heart couldn't handle the stress. The doctor terminated the session, and I was rushed to the hospital. Realizing that something went wrong, Toven got my information out of them and tracked me down." She turned to Toven and smiled. "Now I know how you did that. You compelled or thralled them to release the information to you."

"Guilty as charged. I was frantic with worry."

"I can imagine," Annani said. "How long were you hospitalized?"

"I was released after several hours of observation. The next day, Toven showed up on my doorstep, looking like the god he is, while I was an absolute mess, but he didn't run off like I expected him to. He stayed, and when Perfect Match refused to let me participate in any more adventures, he decided to buy the company, so we could have as many virtual adventures together as we wished. Somewhere along the way, we fell in love, and then Kian and Syssi found us when we came to negotiate the purchase."

"That must have been a stressful event as well. How did your heart handle that?"

"Surprisingly well, but then my health has improved dramatically since I've started a new medication. Toven found a Swiss clinic that specializes in congenital heart problems, and he took me there. They gave me medication that is only available in Europe, and it has been a game-changer for me. I don't remember feeling this well since even before the event. I have energy to spare."

Annani arched a brow. "The event? Do you mean what happened during your virtual session?"

Mia shook her head. "I mean the heart failure that cost me my legs. I knew that something wasn't right with me even before that, but I blamed stress and lack of sleep for the way I felt. Then one day I collapsed, and I almost died. They had to amputate my legs to save my life."

"That must have been horrible." Annani patted Mia's arm. "I am glad that you feel so much better now."

"I do." Mia smiled at Toven. "Before yesterday, I didn't know that Toven was biting me and injecting me with his venom, but I'm sure that it has something to do with my feeling of well-being as well. Or maybe it's just his love."

"Love is a powerful remedy," Annani said.

And so was a god's blood. Did Toven know about that? Had he been injecting Mia with more than his venom?

"The venom's effect is temporary." Alena regarded Toven with suspicion in her eyes, probably having the same thoughts. "It's a short-term booster, and it can heal minor abrasions, but it can't heal a heart problem. The credit belongs to the medication you're taking."

As Toven shifted his gaze to avoid Alena's penetrating look, Annani was convinced that she was right. Hopefully, he had kept at least that part a secret from Mia. She needed a private moment with him so she could warn him about sharing that information.

Pushing to her feet, Annani smiled at Mia. "I need to borrow your mate for a few moments."

Mia looked surprised, but she nodded. "Of course."

Annani put her hand on Toven's shoulder. "Come. I need a word with you, goddess to god."

He cast a worried look at Mia, but it was not as if he could refuse the invitation. "Are you going to be alright without me for a few moments?"

"I'll be fine. I'm sure that you and Annani have a lot of family matters to discuss."

Toven

~~~~~~~~~~~~

Toven had no idea what Annani needed to talk to him about privately. Was it about his missing glow? Or did she want to ask questions about Mortdh?

Maybe she thought that his brother had given him a warning, and that was why he'd escaped the bombing. If he were in her shoes, that scenario would have occurred to him as well, but she couldn't be more mistaken.

Toven had expected his brother to attack the gods' stronghold with the army he'd assembled. He'd never expected Mortdh to go on a suicide mission with the most destructive weapon in his arsenal. Hell, he hadn't even known that Mortdh had it.

His brother had been an insane megalomaniac, but he hadn't been suicidal, and he hadn't been stupid. He should have known that he couldn't outrun the toxic wind resulting from the blast, and that he would be killed along with his victims. Toven had even considered a malfunction, but why would Mortdh have the weapon on his two-person aircraft in the first place?

The small flying machine hadn't been designed for that.

There was no way to know what had happened, and after five thousand years, it was time to put the speculations to rest and just chalk it up to Mortdh's insanity. Perhaps his brother's mental health had deteriorated during the years he'd built his stronghold in the north. Toven had made an effort to have as little contact as possible with Mortdh.

"We can talk in here." Annani opened the door to a room with a large desk, several bookcases, and a comfortable-looking couch. "This is Kian's home office." She sat on the couch and patted the spot next to her. "Close the door and join me."

He did as she asked. "What did you want to talk to me about?"

"I will get straight to the point." Annani adjusted the skirt of her gown, so the folds cascaded evenly to the floor. "Did you give Mia your blood to make her better?"

He nodded.

"Does she know?"

He shook his head.

"Excellent. Do not share this secret with anyone."

"How did you know?"

Annani smiled. "I figured out that her miraculous improvement could not be the result of some new drug or your venom. Besides, I would have done the same. In fact, I have been doing it for a very long time, and the only ones who know about it are Alena and Kian. Not even their mates are privy to the information for their own safety. You know what would happen if knowledge of the power of our blood got out."

"I do, but if we are already talking about it, our blood is not the cure-all it was rumored to be. While Mia was being tested and treated in the Swiss clinic, I visited the adjacent hospital. I found an elderly human with a failing heart and gave him a small transfusion. He was on his death bed and unconscious, but after the transfusion, he woke up and seemed to improve for a few hours. But it did not last. I kept giving him infusions every other day, and when he didn't improve enough, I started doing it daily, but he died anyway."

"Interesting." Annani shifted to face him. "I have mostly used my blood to facilitate transition in our little girls and to help older Dormants transition, but there was one instance when I used it to cure a Dormant male's cancer. Why do you think it worked for him but not for your patient?"

"How old was he and how sick?"

"He was in his mid-forties, and he was just in the beginning stages of cancer. He was undergoing chemotherapy, but he stopped because it was affecting his focus. By the way, he is Bridget's mate, and she does not know about my help." She smirked. "Kian and I pulled a Mission-Impossible-style operation to cure Turner and then to

318

help him through his transition without Bridget being any the wiser."

"Doesn't she suspect anything?"

Annani shrugged. "She might, and one of our other doctors suspects it as well, but they do not know for sure, and that is good enough. I am not afraid of my people betraying the information voluntarily. I am worried about it getting tortured out of them."

"By whom?"

She waved a hand. "Humans looking for a miracle cure or the fountain of youth, or the Doomers."

"Kian mentioned them. He said that they were Mortdh's followers, but he didn't elaborate. Who is their leader?"

Kalugal had introduced himself as Navuh and Areana's son, so if Navuh's son was a resident of the village, Navuh must be on friendly terms with the clan. Maybe one of Mortdh's other sons was leading those Doomers? But as far as Toven knew, Navuh had been the most powerful of his brother's children.

Annani sighed. "There is so much you still do not know. Your brother's son Navuh not only survived but thrived. He inherited a few immortal females and several Dormants from Mortdh, and he used them to breed an army of immortal warriors. He has been a thorn in my side throughout history. I do not know whether he is motivated by his hatred of me or by his wish to rule over everyone in the world, but he has successfully thwarted my efforts to bring democracy to all of humanity over and over again. If not for him, the world would have been a much better place today."

"Or not." Toven grimaced. "Humans needed time to mature from their savage ways. You might have failed regardless of Navuh. But if Kalugal is Navuh's son, what is he doing here?"

"Kalugal fled his father's oppressive control during WWII, taking a unit of warriors with him. The story of how we found him and how he ended up in our village is fascinating, but perhaps he should be the one to tell it."

Toven nodded. "I would also like to hear how Areana ended up being mated to Navuh and turned against you."

"She did not turn against me. He keeps her isolated in his harem, and she does not know what is happening in the world."

"Why aren't you trying to rescue her?"

Annani sighed. "That's a long story for another time." She took his hand and cradled it between her tiny child-like hands. "I am so happy that you finally found your way to us. With our powers combined, there is so much more we can do."

He hated to disappoint her, but he lacked her enthusiasm, and he was done trying to save the world. "Right now, I'm interested in one thing, and that's to help Mia transition successfully. I've been experimenting with how much of my blood I was giving her, but since you have much more experience with that, perhaps you can tell me what the optimal dosage is?"

She let go of his hand, lifted her little finger, and put the fingers of her other hand on the first knuckle. "About this much."

"For everyone? Or should I change it according to weight or age?"

Annani tilted her head. "Who else do you intend to give your blood to?"

"Mia's grandparents, and perhaps her two best friends as well. She loves them dearly, and I've grown very fond of them as well. I want to keep them alive and healthy for as long as I can."

"Oh, Toven." Annani leaned closer and wrapped her arms around him. "That is so wonderfully loving of you. But after you help Mia and all is well with her, you must join my efforts. We can do so much good for the world."

Extracting himself from her arms, he smiled. "I heard that your son is waging war on trafficking. I'm willing to help with that, but don't ask me to help you change the world. It's a losing battle that I've grown disillusioned with, and I can't stomach any more failure. From now on, my efforts will be focused on making small, manageable improvements."

She looked at him with so much compassion in her eyes that it made him uncomfortable. "Is that why you lost your glow?"

He shrugged. "The glow was a painful reminder of all that I have lost, and I've been suppressing it for so long that I don't know how to bring it back. Not that I want to. I prefer to pass for a human."

"I understand." Annani rose to her feet but motioned for him to remain seated. "You and Mia need to talk to Bridget, and it is not the kind of conversation that should be had in front of others. I will ask them to join you in here."

"Thank you."

"You are most welcome." She stopped in front of him and leaned to kiss his cheek. "Having you here in my son's home makes me giddy with joy. I hope you will stay in our village."

Mia

No one seemed to think that it was strange for Annani to take Toven aside and talk to him privately while her family remained in the dining room. The conversation around the table continued as if the two hadn't left, with Syssi telling everyone her theory about Mia's possible paranormal talent.

"I wish we had a telepath with us," Amanda said. "We could have tested you right now."

Cassandra chuckled. "I'm not going anywhere near you. I have trouble controlling my so-called paranormal talent without any enhancement."

"What's your talent?" Mia asked.

"I blow things up."

Mia turned to Syssi. "You said that you hadn't encountered telekinesis. Doesn't blowing things up with your mind count?"

"Telekinesis is defined as the ability to move objects. Cassandra doesn't do that. She blasts them with her mental energy and they explode, which can qualify as movement, so perhaps you are right."

"What's your talent?" Mia asked Kian.

"I don't have any."

"That's not true," Syssi said. "Your business acumen might be your paranormal talent."

He shrugged. "Perhaps. But it's not as exciting as what Cassandra can do."

"Hello, family." Annani floated into the living room without Toven. "I left Toven in Kian's office and promised to send Mia and Bridget to him."

"Thank you." The doctor rose to her feet. "Are you ready, Mia?"

"Yes." She lifted Toven's satchel that he'd left hanging on the back of his chair. "I have my medical record here." She hefted it over her shoulder.

Cassandra's mate rose to his feet. "Let me carry it for you. It looks heavy."

It was, but she could manage a few feet. "I've got it. Stay and enjoy time with your family."

After a moment of hesitation, he sat back down.

"This way." The doctor motioned for her to follow.

The door to the office was open, and as they walked in, Toven rose to his feet. "Thank you for giving us this consultation, Doctor Bridget."

"That's my job." The doctor pulled out one of the chairs facing the desk and turned it around to face the couch. "Please, sit down and tell me what you know so far so I won't waste time on unnecessary explanations."

"Just assume that we don't know anything about Dormants and transitions," Toven said. "What I know is irrelevant because it's five thousand years old, and I was never interested in what actually happened to the young Dormants as they transitioned. Mia knows a lot more than I do about human medicine, but she just learned about the world of gods and immortals yesterday, and everything is new to her."

"Got it." The doctor looked at the satchel Mia had put on the floor. "I'll start with the basics, then you can ask me questions, and after we are done, I will look over the medical file."

"How do I know if I'm a Dormant?" Mia asked. "There must be a test to determine that."

"There isn't. Not yet. Once we decipher the immortal code and find where those special genes are hiding, we might have a test, but I suspect that we will not."

"Why?" Toven asked. "The entire human genome was deciphered. It shouldn't be too difficult to decipher ours."

Bridget smiled. "That's what I originally thought as well, and I even asked Kian to get us one of those machines so we could do it in-house, but then it occurred to me that the secret is in the venom. It must introduce a protein that codes for the genetic material to rearrange itself. Without the introduction of venom, the building blocks hide behind what looks like mundane human genetics, meaning that it's undetectable."

"So how would we know?" Mia asked.

"Normally, it is simple. But in your case, it might not be. What usually happens when an immortal male and a Dormant female become intimate without the use of a physical barrier type of protection, is that the transition starts anytime between two days and up to three weeks after the start of the sexual relationship. But if the Dormant is not well, the transition might not start at all."

Mia frowned. "I assume that males are induced differently?"

"You are correct. Male Dormants need to wrestle with their inducer or cause him to become aggressive by some other means. Since the venom produced in response to aggression is much more potent than the venom produced in response to arousal, that's enough to induce them. They usually start transitioning much faster than females. Roni had pneumonia just prior to his induction, and even after he recovered, his body was too weak to enter transition. It took several attempts by several immortals to induce him. He finally transitioned after Kian bit him."

Mia cast a sidelong glance at Toven. "We were under the impression that we would know in a day or two. We have been intimate without protection for nearly two weeks, and Kian scared us into coming here, saying that I might start transitioning at any moment. I told my grandparents that I'll be gone for a couple of days. I can't stay here indefinitely."

"That's still true," Bridget said. "If you don't start transitioning within a day or two, and you start using protection from now on, you will not enter transition. You can take your time deciding when you want to try again and plan accordingly."

Mia let out a breath. "That's a relief. So if I don't start transitioning, it might be because of my heart or because I don't have the right genes."

"Correct," Bridget said. "I wish I could give you a better answer, but that's how it works."

"What about Mia's legs?" Toven asks. "Can she regrow them after transitioning?"

"Again, I wish I had a definitive answer, but all I can say is maybe. How long ago was the amputation?"

"Four years."

"That's a long time. The only cases I'm aware of regrowing limbs happened to immortals that transitioned as teens, and the regrowth started immediately after the loss."

Mia's heart sank. She'd known that getting her legs back was a long shot even if she could turn immortal, and she'd thought she was okay with that, but hearing the doctor say that it might not happen at all was nevertheless disappointing.

"Then again," Bridget continued. "A transitioning body goes through such massive and rapid change that it might be just what's needed to jumpstart the regrowth."

Mia's heart soared with hope. "I'm crossing my fingers." She lifted both hands.

Bridget didn't smile. "I have to warn you, though. Regrowing limbs takes a very long time, and the transition itself takes up to six months to complete. It might take you up to a year to regrow your legs, and in the meantime, you won't be able to wear your prostheses. It will also be very painful, but I can prescribe you powerful painkillers to help with that."

Mia swallowed. "I'll be stuck in the wheelchair for up to a year?"

Bridget nodded. "You can't put any pressure on the regrowing limbs."

"Oh, boy." Mia slumped against the couch cushions. "It's going to be tough."

"The village has two virtual machines," Bridget said. "I can make it so you and Toven get priority using them. That should ease things up a little."

"It would." Mia let out a breath. "Can I stay hooked up for the entire year?"

Bridget laughed. "I don't think the rest of the village residents would be fine with that. Those machines are very popular."

"Why do you have only two?" Toven asked. "Syssi is a majority stockholder. She can get more."

"That's a question you need to address to her," the doctor said. "Is there anything else you need answers for?"

"I can't think of anything at the moment." Mia looked at Toven. "How about you?"

"Nothing comes to mind, but can we have your phone number in case we come up with more questions?"

"Of course." Bridget pulled out her phone. "Your phones are no good in the village, but you can write my number down in the notes application."

Mia's eyes widened in alarm. "There is no reception here?"

"You need a special clan-issue phone."

"I need one ASAP. I promised to call my grandparents when I got here, and I forgot. They are probably frantic with worry."

Toven

"You can use my phone to call your grandparents." Bridget handed Mia the device.

"Thank you so much." Mia dialed the number.

"Who is that?" Curtis answered.

"It's Mia, Grandpa. I'm so sorry I didn't call earlier. My phone doesn't work up here, and neither does Tom's. I borrowed someone's phone to call you. We are fine, and we are having a great time."

"Thank God." Curtis let out a breath. "Can you call us again tomorrow? Grandma was so worried about you. She drove me nuts with the worst-case scenarios she imagined."

"I will. There are plenty of people with satellite phones up here."

"And where is that?"

"Somewhere in the mountains. I wasn't paying attention during the drive."

"Well, enjoy your vacation, you two. Grandma sends kisses."

"Kisses back. I love you."

"Love you too, sweetheart."

After Curtis ended the call, Mia returned the phone to Bridget. "Is there any way Toven and I can get a phone that works up here?"

"You need to ask Kian." The doctor pushed to her feet. "Do you need a few moments alone?"

Toven nodded. "Frankly, I'm terrified of Mia entering transition."

Annani's admission that she'd helped Dormants along with her blood should have boosted his confidence in Mia's successful transition, but it also highlighted how dangerous the transition could be for an adult Dormant. Some of them had experienced difficulties severe enough to require Annani's intervention, and none of them had a congenital heart condition.

"That's understandable, but on a positive note, we haven't lost a Dormant yet, so there is no reason to panic. If Mia's body can't handle the transition, it just won't start." Bridget hesitated for a moment. "Annani gives her blessing to those who need a little help. I don't know what she does during those sessions because she insists on complete privacy, but since you're a god, you might be able to do whatever she does, and if not, you can ask her to give Mia her blessings."

He nodded. "I will ask Annani what's involved." He looked at Mia. "Blessings from two gods should be better than one, right?"

"I'll take whatever help I can get."

"That's the spirit." The doctor patted Mia's shoulder and tucked the file under her arm. "I will read as much of this file as I can today, and if I think that there is anything missing and I need to run some more tests on you, I'll let you know. I have all the necessary equipment in my clinic, so we can run them tomorrow or the day after."

"Sounds good." Mia looked at Toven. "Do you know where we will be staying?"

"Not yet." He turned to Bridget. "Is there a hotel in the village?"

"No, but there are plenty of vacant houses, which are fully furnished. I'm sure Ingrid can hook you up with one." Bridget opened the door. "I'll leave you two to talk."

When the door closed behind the doctor, Mia let out a breath. "That was intense. I don't know whether I should be hopeful or fearful. If I don't transition in a day or two, I'm not even sure that I should attempt it. Immortality with you is beyond tempting, but what if I don't make it? I'd rather have a couple of good decades with you than trade them for a dream."

Wrapping his arm around her middle, he lifted her into his lap. "The thought of losing you terrifies me. Before we met Kian and Syssi, I had reconciled myself to enjoying you for the duration of your mortal life. So if that's what you choose to do, I will be happy with that. But the truth is that I don't think I will survive it in either case. When you are gone, I will find a way to end my life."

Mia

"Don't talk like that." Mia cupped Toven's cheek. "You're scaring me even more than I already am. I can handle my life being on the line, but I can't handle risking yours as well. I'm just not going to do it."

His expression turned tortured. "That's the last thing I wanted to do."

"So promise me that no matter what happens to me, you will go on." She held on to his face, not letting him look away from her. "Promise, or I'm not going to let you induce me. I mean it."

"I will try."

"Not good enough. We are not leaving here until you promise that you will go on living, and that you will not close your heart to love. There might be other Dormants out there, and maybe I'm not the one who was meant for you."

"That's nonsense. You are my truelove mate, and since the Fates chose you for me, you have to transition successfully."

"Then it should be no problem for you to vow that you will go on."

"Fine. In the extremely unlikely event that you don't make it, I promise not to end my life, but I can't promise that I will love again."

"I can live with that." Pulling his head toward her, she kissed his lips. "Now we can go back and join the others. I want to know where we are sleeping tonight and whether they have a wheelchair-accessible bathroom."

When they returned to the living room, Bridget was gone, but everyone else was still there.

"Everything okay?" Annani asked

"Yes, thank you." Mia sat down next to the goddess. "The doctor said that I might regrow my legs, but it will take up to a year."

Across the table, Onegus winced. "It's going to be hell. Just be thankful that we have painkillers now. In my day, all we had was whiskey."

"Ouch." Mia echoed his wince.

"I have a favor to ask," Toven said to Kian. "We just found out that our phones don't work in the village. Is there a way we can get a clan phone? Mia promised her grandparents to call them daily."

"No problem." Kian pulled out his phone and started typing up a text. "I'll have our tech guy deliver two clan phones to you."

"By the way," Mia turned to Syssi. "Any idea where we are going to stay?"

Syssi's eyes widened. "I totally forgot to tell you. We had a house prepared for you right next to Orion and Alena. Geraldine and Shai are two houses away in one direction, and Cassandra and Onegus in the other. You'll be surrounded by family."

"That sounds amazing, thank you." Mia hated to sound ungrateful, but she had to ask. "Is there a wheelchair-accessible bathroom in the house?"

She'd brought her waterproof prostheses just in case there wasn't, but it was a hassle to use them.

"It's not specifically designed for that," Syssi said. "But the primary bathroom is large enough, and the shower has a no-barrier entry and is very spacious. The only problem might be the vanity which is not specifically built to accommodate a wheelchair. The commode will need grab bars, though. I can ask one of the Guardians to get them and install them before nightfall." She smiled apologetically. "It should have occurred to me to do so before your arrival."

"There was no time to prepare." Mia felt bad for making Syssi uncomfortable. "Toven only called Kian last night to tell him that we would be coming today."

"William will be here shortly with two new clan devices for you." Kian put his phone down. "After he gets here, we will show you to your new home."

"Our temporary home," Toven said. "We are not going to stay long."

"Unless Mia enters transition." Kian leveled his gaze at him. "Is there anything you need to attend to back in the human world?"

"Not really. I can write my novels anywhere. All that's pending in the human world are the negotiations for Perfect Match and taking care of Mia's family and friends."

If Mia's love for Toven was all-encompassing before he'd said that, it now expanded to a glowing halo all around her.

Kian

Kian's emotional intelligence might be borderline dysfunctional, but even he knew that statement must have delighted Mia and upset Orion.

Someone needed to have a talk with Toven and give him pointers about being a father, but it wouldn't be him. Syssi could do that much better, but she wouldn't be comfortable giving Toven advice. The only one who could and would was his mother.

Annani regarded Toven with a raised brow, but she didn't comment on his declaration. Knowing his mother, though, she was already planning on having another private talk with the guy.

Kian was still wondering what their first talk was about.

"I'm curious," Kalugal said. "How did you make all that money? I'm sure that it didn't come from your stories."

He chuckled. "If it did, I'm dropping everything I'm doing and becoming an author."

Toven regarded him with a small, condescending smile. "Everything we create and profit from starts as a story in our minds. It can be a narrative for a fictional story that delights readers just for fun, or a fictional narrative that can be sold as motivation, a religion, or politics. Or it can be an idea for an invention that would change the world. So in a way, all successful people are imaginative story-tellers."

Talk about an evasive answer. Perhaps Kian should take notes.

Kalugal wasn't about to give up that easily, though. "True, but if I sat in my office and imagined all day without taking action, I wouldn't have made a penny." He cast Toven a challenging smirk. "Which kind of narrative did you sell so successfully?"

"The one I was most familiar with. After all, I was a god, and my people strived to bring humanity out of savagery and into civility."

"Smart. You sold religion."

Toven nodded. "The irony was that I believed in what I was selling, and I hoped to succeed." He grimaced. "All I got for my efforts were rivers of blood and mountains of gold in tribute. I didn't mind the gold, but my mission was to stop the savagery, not have it escalate. It was a total failure, and after repeated attempts with different peoples, I gave up on grandiose world-changing plans."

Kalugal nodded. "My father is a ruthless dictator, but he's right about one thing. Most humans have a herd mentality, and they are not only easily manipulated and controlled, but they crave it. They don't want to think for themselves, they want to be told what to think by those they believe are their superiors."

Evidently, Kalugal's philosophy was not all that different from Navuh's. He was just more elegant about implementing it.

"That's a terrible thing to say." Cassandra glared at him. "Where did that come from?"

Kalugal shrugged. "Just look around you without rose-tinted glasses. Less than five percent of the human population is capable of independent thinking. The rest are sheep. If you want, I can direct you to studies that were done on the subject."

"By whom? You?" Cassandra crossed her arms over her chest.

Kian had a feeling that at any moment something was going to explode. Probably something in Kalugal's vicinity, and that wasn't good because sitting next to him was his pregnant wife.

Maybe it was time to intervene and defuse the tension?

Kalugal lifted his hands in the air. "The studies weren't done by me, they were done by human scientists, repeated by several different academic institutions, and used large scale sample populations. The fact that something is unpleasant to acknowledge does not mean that it is untrue."

"Send me the links," Cassandra commanded. "Your take-home value from what you've read might be skewed."

"Bravo." Kalugal started clapping. "The decision to investigate the issue and reach your own conclusions indicates that you belong to the exclusive five-percent club. Most humans would either reject my claim because they either didn't like it or it didn't agree with their worldview, or they would have accepted it without checking a single fact because it agreed with their way of thinking or they thought of me as a respectable authority figure."

Throughout the exchange, Kian had kept an eye on Toven to gauge his reaction. The god seemed impressed with his great-nephew, which had most likely been the impetus behind Kalugal's provocative statement.

What was the guy's agenda?

Perhaps that was his way of getting Toven's attention?

What did Kalugal hope to gain from Toven?

Maybe he was just trying to feel the god out?

Toven could be a powerful ally, and Kalugal must want him in his corner just as much as Kian did. By presenting himself as someone who was knowledgeable, unafraid of being controversial, and capable of providing a stimulating intellectual discussion, Kalugal sparked Toven's interest and opened the door to having a relationship with the god that was about pursuing similar goals and went beyond familial ties.

Toven probably couldn't wait to have more conversations with his *brilliant* grand-nephew.

Toven

Kalugal was a fascinating fellow who seemed to thrive on controversy. Toven was looking forward to having more talks with him. But that would have to wait for after Mia's successful transition when Toven was actually capable of having a rational discussion for more than a few minutes without his mind making rapid sprints in other directions.

Should he induce Mia, or shouldn't he? Was it fair to her to put her in the position where she had to decide whether to strive for immortality or cherish the time she had as a human?

What if her clock was ticking faster than they suspected because of her heart condition?

Cherengazi hadn't been willing to estimate Mia's longevity prospects, but Toven had read between the lines that her life expectancy wasn't great.

"Hello, everyone." A tall, slightly chubby guy rushed into Kian's dining room as if his tail was on fire. "I've got the phones for Toven and Mia."

"Thank you." Kian rose to his feet and led the guy to them. "This is William, our tech guy, and he rushed over here himself because he was curious to see you."

"Guilty." William offered Mia his hand. "Welcome to the village." He shook it briefly, and then turned to Toven. "You are a tough guy to find. We've been combing the internet searching for you."

"You were? Why?"

"After we found Orion and he told us that you were still around, we had to find you," Annani said. "I was so excited. William tried to find your books by using a software that identifies style, but you must have varied it significantly."

Toven smiled. "I doubt any of my works are published as electronic books. Most of them are not even in English."

"That would explain it." William handed him and Mia each a phone. "They are already programmed with the numbers of everyone in your family. If you have questions about using it, Roni can help you." He pushed his glasses up his nose. "I need to run back to the lab. It was nice meeting you both."

The guy was like a whirlwind, talking at a machine-gun speed and moving faster than a large man like him should be able to.

"Can I see your phone for a moment?" Annani asked.

Toven handed it to her without even turning it on.

"I will give you my direct number." She handled the device with the surety of a teenager who was born with a smartphone attached to her hand. "If you need me for any reason, call me." A moment later, her own phone rang somewhere between the folds of her gown. "And now I have your number as well." She returned his phone to him.

"I need to get back to the office," Kian said. "And the rest of your lovely family has work to do as well. Let's get you to your new temporary residence."

"Thank you for lunch and everything else," Mia said. "I'm overwhelmed by the warm welcome you and your family have shown us."

"It's my pleasure." Kian's eyes softened as he looked at her. "Enjoy your stay." He turned to Geraldine's mate. "Are you coming, or do you want to escort Toven and Mia to their house?"

Shai cast a quick glance at Geraldine, who smiled and signaled with her hand that he could go.

"I'm coming."

After more it-was-nice-to-meet-yous and goodbyes were exchanged, only Geraldine, Alena, and Orion joined Toven and Mia in the golf cart, with Okidu behind the wheel.

"No one locks their doors in here," Geraldine said. "I made a few dishes for you and put them in your refrigerator in case you get hungry between meals, but dinner is at seven tonight at my place." She grinned. "I'm only a few paces away from your house. Isn't that great?"

"It's wonderful," Toven said and meant it.

It was better than any virtual fantasy he could've designed. He had a family, they were all in one place, and except for Orion, who was still reserved, his daughter and granddaughters seemed to be fond of him. The only thing he would have changed if this was a fantasy would be Mia's transition. She would already be immortal and have her legs fully regenerated.

But this was reality, and reality was never perfect.

Mia

After Toven's relatives finally left, Mia relaxed on the couch and took her new cellphone out of her purse. Toven went for another tour of the house, this time alone, looking for God-knew what. Was he checking it for cleanliness?

It looked spotless, and it smelled fresh. Okidu had told them that he'd laundered all the bedding and towels in preparation for their arrival even though everything had been clean.

The guy, or rather cyborg, was a priceless treasure, and Mia wished she could have one. Life could be so much easier if she had a cyborg assisting her with all the things she was embarrassed to ask Toven for help with.

But since no wonderful cyborgs were available for hire, she just needed to get over her inhibitions.

When Toven crouched in front of the fireplace, the view of his muscular backside was absolutely delicious and too good not to capture. Lifting her new phone, Mia snapped a picture of the beautifully decorated room and the gorgeous man who was its centerpiece.

Well, not a man, a god, or her alien prince, or her gift from the Fates. She could go on.

When he turned toward her and arched a brow, she asked, "Can I send this picture to Margo and Frankie? The decorator has done a beautiful job with this place."

"Let me see." He walked over to the couch and sat next to her. "My face is not showing, and the interior of this house looks generic enough."

She sent the picture along with an explanation about the new phone number. "What were you looking for in the fireplace?"

"Bugs."

Mia made a face. "Are there bugs in this house? If there are, we are going home. Transition or not, I'm not staying in a bug-infested place."

She was only half-teasing.

Toven laughed. "Not those kinds of bugs. I meant listening devices. I always scope a new place for hidden cameras and microphones, but they've gotten so miniaturized in recent years that they are nearly impossible to spot."

"If there are any, I know who put them here, and it wasn't Kian. Your nephew Kalugal is shady."

He wrapped his arm around her back and hoisted her into his lap. "I don't trust either of them. In fact, I don't trust anyone."

She lifted her head and looked at him. "What about me?"

"I trust you." Something clouded his eyes. "And only you."

"I trust you too." She put her head on his chest. "I'm exhausted."

Toven's muscles tensing, he put a hand on her forehead. "You don't have a fever."

"I know. I'm not transitioning. I'm just tired. If not for the medication and your venom, my heart might not have taken all the excitement of today. I met a goddess, your children, your granddaughters, your great-grand-son, your grandnephew, and a bunch of other people. That was enough to sap my energy, add to that the talk we had with Bridget, and it would have toppled a perfectly healthy person."

"It's not just the medication or my venom," he whispered as he caressed her back. "There is one more secret I was keeping from you, and I can't keep it any longer, even though Annani made me promise not to tell you." He kept running slow circles on her back.

Mia chuckled. "I don't think any secret could be more shocking than discovering that the man I love is a god, or that he has children he didn't tell me about."

"In that respect, this secret will not be as monumental for you, but it is for me. I'm risking not only my life by revealing it, but also Annani's."

"Just tell me whether it's good or bad."

"I think it's good. Let's get the compulsion part out of the way first, okay?"

"I'm ready. Do it."

"You will not mention what I'm about to tell you to anyone other than me."

Mia felt his command settling over her, but since she agreed, it wasn't that bad. In fact, she was glad of it. If Toven and Annani's safety depended on it, she didn't want to be responsible for keeping it.

"So, what's the big secret?"

He took a long breath. "The real reason you improved so drastically is that I was giving you tiny infusions of my blood. A god's or goddess's blood can bring about miraculous healing to a human, but I discovered that its benefits were exaggerated. I shouldn't have been surprised, though. The gods always liked to aggrandize themselves."

After hearing the words blood and infusions, Mia barely paid attention to what Toven was saying.

"When did you do that? Did you compel me to forget?"

He shook his head. "Do you remember how you couldn't keep your eyes open in Switzerland? Each night, I gave you a little push to sink into a deep and restful sleep so I could give you the transfusion. I'm sorry for keeping it from you, but I couldn't tell you about the blood without telling you about what was in it. I meant to tell you the truth about myself so many times, but I kept coming up with excuses to postpone it. Part of it was fear for your heart, and part of it was fear of being loved for the wrong reasons. I wanted you to love me as you would a nothing-special human male."

Mia snorted. "Yeah, right. A nothing-special human. Good one, Toven. A movie-star-perfect man with billions in a Swiss depository who is willing to spend a big chunk of it to buy a company just so we can enjoy more virtual adventures together. Half the time I think that I'm still inside the virtual world because this can't be real."

He kissed the top of her head. "So, am I forgiven?"

She looked into his eyes. "Are there any more things that you are keeping from me?"

"I was married," he blurted. "We didn't have children, and my wife died along with the other gods."

"Was she your truelove mate?"

He shook his head. "It was what you would call a marriage of convenience, and in time, we grew to love each other, but we both knew that we weren't each other's truelove mates. I never felt for her what I feel for you, like I can't take my next breath without you by my side."

His marriage had tragically ended five thousand years ago when he became a widower. It had no bearing on their

351

relationship, but she was glad he'd told her. The guy hadn't talked with anyone about the terrible loss and had carried the pain alone for far too long.

"What else?"

"My half-brother was the so-called terrorist who murdered all the other gods and died along with them."

Oh, wow. That was much worse. Not only did Toven carry with him the pain of losing everyone he loved, but also the guilt by association.

"That's terrible." She lifted her hand to cup his cheek. "Do Kian and the others know?"

He nodded. "There was only one god capable of committing such an atrocious crime against gods, immortals, and humans. Tens, if not hundreds of thousands perished."

"Why did he do that?"

"He was insane, but don't worry. He inherited his insanity from his mother. My mother was a perfectly sane, if cold and overly formal goddess."

Toven

"You look refreshed." Geraldine hugged Mia. "Did you have a nice nap?"

"The best." Mia smiled apologetically at Toven. "I was so tired that I fell asleep in the middle of Toven telling me about the old days."

He'd given her an infusion, this time with her fully aware of it, and after that they'd lain in bed and he told her things he had never talked about with anyone. About his father and his mother and their strange relationship, about Ekin's brilliance and inventions along with his womanizing, about his mother's formal household and his father's chaotic one; he'd talked for hours, and when Mia drifted off to sleep, he kissed her lips and lay beside her, feeling lighter than he ever had.

"That's not surprising." Cassandra walked in, patted Mia on the shoulder, and kissed Toven on the cheek. "He's so old that he can probably keep talking for months about the old days."

"A walking history book," Roni said. "I would like to hear some of those tales."

"Let's sit down for dinner." Geraldine herded them toward the table. "We can hear some of those stories while we eat."

"Look at this," Mia whispered. "You are surrounded by family. But you know who's missing?"

He pulled a chair out for her. "Your grandparents, Margo and Frankie."

"You guessed it." She sat down. "Any idea how we are going to solve that problem?"

"One thing at a time." Toven sat down beside her. "First, we need to worry about your transition."

"Right." She unfurled a napkin and draped it over her knees.

Today was the first time she'd let him see her without the prostheses, and even let him carry her to bed. He didn't know whether it was because he'd laid his soul bare for her, or because she was too tired to bother with the wheelchair, but he was glad that they were finally over that hurdle.

If she transitioned successfully, or rather when she transitioned, she would need to rely on his help, and playing shy with her mate was not an option.

After the hefty dose he'd given her, her color was better, less pale than usual, and he might give her another small dose tonight before they went to sleep.

After Shai poured wine for everyone, Geraldine lifted her glass. "It fills my heart with joy to have our family gathered around the table. May there be many more such happy gatherings."

"I'll drink to that," Onegus said.

Orion murmured in agreement, Alena beamed with happiness, and Darlene looked distracted.

As Geraldine looked at him expectantly, Toven raised his glass. "I've never expected to be blessed with two children, two grandchildren, a great-grandson, and one more grandchild on the way." He turned to Mia. "I also never expected to be blessed with a truelove mate. But here I am, and my heart is overflowing with love and gratitude, but also trepidation. Let us drink to Mia's successful transition."

"To Mia," Geraldine echoed, and the others followed.

Cassandra put her glass down and looked at Mia. "I hate to be the one to point it out, but you might not be a Dormant, or you might be unable to transition. I'm just putting it out there because everyone just assumes that it's a done deal, and I really hope that it is, but it's always good to be prepared for the less desirable outcome."

"You are right," Mia said. "What happens if I'm just a regular human? Do I go back to living in the human world?"

Toven nodded. "We can go back to our house, and come visit the family whenever we want."

"Normally Kian would have objected to Mia retaining her memories of us," Onegus said. "But since you are a compeller, you can ensure she never tells anyone."

"Precisely." Toven put his hand on Mia's thigh. "Besides, it's not like Kian can command me to do anything I do not wish to do. I'm not his subject. That being said, I have no intentions of stepping on his toes."

Mia

"Thank you for a delicious dinner." Mia patted her overstuffed belly. "I need to start watching it, or I'll get fat, and in my case, it's not about vanity."

More weight would put more strain on her heart and make mobility even more difficult. The slimmer she was, the better.

"So, no pie?" Cassandra put a slice on her plate.

The delicious smell of pecans was too much of a temptation. "I love pecan pie." Mia lifted her fork. "I'll start watching it tomorrow."

It was just as good as it smelled, but a few forkfuls later, she felt nauseous and put the fork down. "You can finish it." She pushed her plate to Toven.

"Don't mind if I do." He transferred the wedge onto his plate.

"Here." Geraldine refilled Mia's teacup. "This will help you wash the pie down."

"Thank you." Mia sipped on it slowly.

Orion and Toven were still awkward with one another, and Geraldine was doing her best to engage them both in conversation so they would start talking to each other and not through her.

"Did Orion tell you that he deals in antiques?" Alena joined Geraldine's efforts. "He travels around the world to collect them. He even got a few finds on our trip to China. Have you ever visited there? It was an eye-opener for me."

"In what way?" Toven asked.

"We visited a place called Lugu Lake, and it was so stunningly beautiful. A real gem in the middle of nowhere. Have you ever been there?"

Toven shook his head. "I'm not much of a nature seeker. I'm more interested in major metropolitan areas. I've been to Beijing, Shanghai, Tianjin, Chongqing, and a few of the smaller ones. Were you in Lugu Lake on vacation?"

"We were looking for clues about the Kra-ell." Orion leveled his gaze at his father. "Have you heard of them?"

For some reason, everyone around the table fell quiet as if the answer to that was crucially important.

"I've heard of the Krall. That's one of the environments in Perfect Match. Are they real?"

"A version of them is," Onegus said. "Syssi created that environment for Perfect Match, and apparently, her imagination tapped into her foresight for ideas because we later discovered the real Kra-ell."

As Onegus went into storytelling mode, explaining about the strange Kra-ell who were a different kind of immortals, Mia closed her eyes.

She was getting sleepy again, which was probably the pie's fault. It was a sugar bomb, and she shouldn't have eaten even the little bit that she had. Except for Darlene, who was still human, the others could eat whatever they wanted.

Perhaps she could befriend the woman. She looked lonely, and she didn't talk much. To compensate, her mother talked up a storm.

It was difficult to think of Geraldine as Darlene's mother. She looked at least a decade younger than her daughter. Would Darlene look younger once she transitioned?

The lucky woman had only good stuff to look forward to, but first she needed to find an immortal dude to induce her. It shouldn't be too difficult. She was pretty enough. She just needed to smile more.

With Mia's thoughts floating around in different directions like they usually did in the moments before she fell asleep at night, the sounds of conversation became muted, and as her head became too heavy to hold up, she leaned it on Toven's arm.

"Mia?" Toven sounded concerned. "Are you falling asleep again?"

She sighed. "It was an eventful day, and the pie knocked me out."

"Do you want to go home?"

"It's okay. Keep talking. I enjoy listening to you all."

Toven

Toven put a hand on Mia's forehead even though he hadn't felt her temperature change. She felt a little clammy, but she had no fever, and her heart was beating a beautiful, steady beat.

Perhaps she was just tired.

Who could blame her?

Given what she'd learned since last night, she was doing amazingly well. His little sprite was a fierce fighter, and he couldn't be more proud of her.

"We have three Kra-ell living in the village," Onegus said. "One is currently on a mission in West Virginia, and that's another fascinating story."

Running his hand up and down Mia's arm, Toven listened to Onegus and Shai take turns telling him about the cult leader who had turned out to be a hybrid Kra-ell male, and who had escaped his mistress and, inadvertently, a subsequent massacre.

He shook his head. "It's never boring for you here in the village. It seems like there is always something extraordinary happening."

Onegus chuckled. "We haven't even told you the half of it yet."

"I'm surprised that you are telling me all of this on my first day here. But since you are the chief of security, you must not consider me a risk."

"I don't." Onegus glanced at the sleeping Mia. "You need us more than we need you. Besides, your family is here, and even though you were a cold bastard in the past, it seems like Mia has changed you on a cellular level. You are not going to betray your loved ones."

"I would never have betrayed them even before Mia restarted my heart. I might have been mostly dead on the inside, but I never would have done anything to purposely harm anyone, and especially my family. I'm nothing like my brother."

Onegus nodded. "We are well aware of that. Annani thinks highly of you, and she's never wrong."

Toven arched a brow. "Never?"

"Never," Onegus repeated. "She must have a direct link to the Fates."

"I can't argue with that." Toven smiled. "Even as a seven-teen-year-old girl, she knew that marrying Mortdh would be the end of her. Her father was blinded by his own arrogance, thinking that he could manipulate Mortdh into keeping the peace by promising him Annani. She knew better."

As Toven felt Mia's head slide down his arm, he tightened his hold on her and hoisted her up. "I think I should take Mia home."

"I'm fine," she murmured.

"You fell asleep."

He waited for her to argue, but she didn't respond, and a moment later, she started sliding down the chair.

He pulled her up. "Mia, sweetheart, wake up."

When she didn't respond, he tapped her cheek. "Mia?"

Cassandra pushed to her feet, rushed over, and lifted one of Mia's eyelids. "She's out. It's started."

Panic seizing his entire body, Toven remained frozen in place, and with his blood roaring in his ears, he couldn't hear Mia's heart.

"Onegus," Cassandra said. "Get a golf cart. Shai, call Bridget. We need to take Mia to the clinic."

"Is she breathing?" Alena rushed over.

"She is." Cassandra crouched next to Mia. "Her heart sounds nice and steady to me, but I'm not a doctor."

"She doesn't have a fever," Toven whispered. "The first sign of transition should be a fever."

Cassandra looked up at him. "Bridget says that every Dormant is different, and no two transitions are alike. Mia might be transitioning without running a fever."

Mia

Azul regarded her pregnant belly in the mirror and grimaced. "I look like a whale."

"You are more beautiful than ever to me." Tobias walked up to her and stood behind her. Circling his arms under her belly and hoisting it up, he dipped his head, rested his chin on her shoulder, and nuzzled her cheek. "Did you decide what you want to call our baby? We can't keep calling her the little one."

She smiled at him. "First of all, we don't know if it's a girl or a boy, and secondly, we have one more month to come up with a name."

"We need to make a list of potential names. I vote for Elisabeth. It's a good traditional name, and it's fit for a queen."

Azul winced. "That's boring. How about something original, like Annani?"

Tobias's smile melted away. "Where did you hear that one?"

"Nowhere. It just popped into my head, and I liked the sound of it. Why? Does it ring a bell?"

"I love you so much." Suddenly, his voice sounded like it was coming through a tunnel. "Don't leave me."

"Leave you? Why would I leave you?"

Looking at his sad face in the mirror, she saw the reflected image starting to waver as if the mirror was fogging up or her eyes were filling with tears.

Azul shut them down to clear the mist, and when she tried to open them again, she could barely lift her eyelids, and her throat felt dry.

"What's happening?" she murmured.

"Mia?" His voice sounded as if he was speaking right into her ear.

As she forced her eyes open, at first everything was blurry, but as her vision cleared, she recognized her surroundings right away. She was in a hospital room, lying on her side with Toven spooning her and his arms wrapped around her slim waist.

She wasn't pregnant, and her name wasn't Azul.

"Toven?"

"I'm here, love." He gently turned her to her back, looked down at her, and cracked a smile. "Every time you open your eyes, joy returns to my life." He kissed her parched lips, her eyelids, her cheeks. "I thank the merciful Fates and every other mystical power in the universe, who I've been praying to for the forty hours and twenty-one minutes since you started transitioning."

"I'm transitioning?"

As he nodded, the door opened, and Bridget walked in.

"Hello, Mia. I'm thrilled to see you awake for more than a few seconds." She walked over to the bed and glared at Toven. "You shouldn't be in bed with Mia. Make yourself useful and get her a cup of water with a straw. You know where everything is."

If Mia had the energy, she would have chuckled. Even in this world, doctors behaved as if they were gods.

"Yes, doctor." Toven gently extracted his arms and slid off the bed.

"You're doing very well, Mia." Bridget lifted the bed's back as Toven got busy with the water. "Much better than I expected." She cast a sidelong glance at Toven and smirked. "I have no doubt that having two gods give you their blessings helped tremendously, especially since this one has done it on a continuous basis."

Mia's eyes darted to the IV line. Had Toven been adding his blood to the bag? He'd said that Bridget didn't know about the infusions, so maybe she was referring to something else? Like in actual prayers?

Yeah, that made more sense. If Toven had given her blood during her stay in the clinic, he'd done it discreetly without the doctor finding out.

As Toven returned with the cup, Bridget motioned for him to give the water to Mia, and as he bent the straw and put it in her mouth, Mia sucked on it eagerly.

Bridget took the cup away before Mia was done. "If you can hold down what you drank, I'll give you the rest in a few minutes."

"Is that it?" Mia asked. "Am I out of the woods?"

"You were never in the woods." Bridget pulled out a measuring tape from her coat pocket. "I told Toven that you were doing better than many of the other Dormants and that he shouldn't worry, but stressed-out mates are not the most logical people."

As Bridget measured Mia's arm and noted the results, Mia gathered her courage to ask, "Did my legs start growing?"

"Not yet." Bridget shattered her hopes. "But that doesn't mean that they will not start regenerating once your transition progresses. You still have a long way to go."

"What if Mia slips back into unconsciousness?" Toven asked. "She's woken up several times before."

"I did?" Mia didn't remember waking up.

"You did, and you might again." Bridget moved to her other side to measure her other arm. "After you were brought in, your temperature kept rising, and it remained high up until this morning when it started going down a bit. I had a feeling that you would wake up for a little longer this time, and that you'd be more coherent. You were delirious the other times, which is why you don't remember it."

As Bridget put her tape measure back in her pocket and walked over to the monitors, Mia calculated in her head how long ago she'd passed out. They had arrived at Geraldine's house at around seven, had dinner, and the conversation had continued for a while. It had probably been about nine o'clock at night on Tuesday when she'd passed out, so forty hours later meant that it was Thursday morning.

Her eyes widened in alarm. "Did you call my grandparents?"

"I texted them, pretending to be you." He rubbed the back of his neck. "Bridget assured me that you were going to be okay, and I didn't want to stress them out needlessly. I decided to wait until the initial stage of your transition was over, and you were not going to slip into unconsciousness again."

Toven

The truth was that Toven didn't want them in the way. He needed to be with Mia at all times in case she needed a boost, and with her grandparents there, he would have been forced to give them time by her side, and he didn't want to risk that.

Alena kept him supplied with syringes, Geraldine brought him meals and changes of clothes, and he used the adjacent bathroom, so he never had to leave. The longest he'd been away from Mia was the twenty or so minutes while Annani had given Mia her *blessing*.

There was no need for her blood, but Annani had insisted that she needed to keep up appearances. Everyone would expect her to help Toven's fragile mate, and then attribute her successful transition to the Clan Mother's blessings.

Naturally, she hadn't given her a transfusion. Toven had done it every few hours while lying next to Mia. He'd been quite clever about it, asking Bridget to explain what the various monitors displayed and how to read the results. From then on, all he had to do was to keep them steady.

Closing her eyes, Mia sighed. "What did you tell them in the text?"

"That the reception is really bad in the mountains, but that we are having a great time and decided to stay a few more days. Your grandmother asked if you took enough medication with you, and I assured her that you did."

"Did Frankie and Margo call?"

"I texted them preemptively with the same story. There is a bunch of texts and memes from them waiting for you to read."

He took Mia's phone off the nightstand and handed it to her.

She glanced at the screen but didn't lift her hand to take the device. "I don't have the energy. Please bring my grandparents to the village. They will never forgive me for keeping them in the dark about this even if it all ends well." The last words to leave her mouth were barely intelligible, and then she was out again.

"I hate when that happens." Toven dropped Mia's phone back on the nightstand.

Bridget clapped him on the back. "Think of it as a good thing, and it will stop upsetting you. Her body is shutting down non-essential functions to preserve energy for the change. The more she sleeps, the better."

When she left the room, Toven pulled out a chair and sat down. His new phone came with a list of contacts, not of the entire village, but of everyone in his family—Kian, Bridget, William, and several others. He found Kian's number and placed the call.

"Hello, Toven. How is Mia?"

"According to Bridget, she's doing very well, thank you for asking. She woke up for a little longer just now and asked me to bring her grandparents to be with her. We discussed it before, and you said that you wouldn't object."

"As long as you're sure that you can compel them to keep us a secret, I have no problem with that. Do you want me to send someone to pick them up?"

"I thought of asking Orion or Geraldine, but if you prefer to send Okidu, that can work too."

"I'll send Anandur. He's good with people, and he will put them at ease. After you talk with Mia's grandparents, call him and coordinate the story with him. Do you want me to prepare a house for them?"

"There is no need. They can stay with Mia and me. When she's well enough to go home, she will appreciate them being there."

"Good deal. I'll tell Anandur to await your call."

"Thank you."

After ending the call, Toven spent a few moments planning what he was going to tell Mia's grandparents. He couldn't tell them that Mia had a mild cold because that didn't justify dragging them out of their house, and he couldn't tell them about her transition over the phone. Perhaps something along the lines of a new experimental treatment? Could he phrase it in a way that wouldn't be a total fabrication?

Or maybe he would just tell them that the silent partners were inviting them to their retreat?

With a sigh, Toven decided to wing it and placed the call.

"Hello, who is this?" Curtis asked.

"It's Tom. My phone doesn't work up here, remember? I also got a new satellite phone from our hosts. How are you and Rosalyn doing?"

"It's quiet here without you two. Frankie and Margo came over yesterday and had dinner with us. They are such nice girls. Where is Mia? Why isn't she calling us?"

"That's what I'm calling about. Mia is undergoing treatment in our hosts' clinic that will improve her condition even more than the new Swiss medication, and she wants you to be here with her. I'm sending a guy to pick you up, and I'll tell you more when you get here. Pack a bag for a week and don't tell anyone where you're going. I'll let Frankie and Margo know later that you're joining Mia and me, so they won't worry."

"What's going on, Tom? Why didn't you tell us that you are trying a new treatment? Is Mia okay?"

"It wasn't planned. Mia just wanted to talk with the doctor here, but one thing led to another, and she started the treatment. I really can't say more over the phone."

"I'll tell Rosy to start packing. When is your guy going to be here?"

"He can be there in a couple of hours, but if you need more time to get ready, I can ask him to wait."

"Two hours is more than enough. I want to see Mia as soon as possible. Do you need us to bring her more things?"

Toven had no idea what Mia might need, but packing things for her would make her grandparents feel useful and less stressed.

"Perhaps a few more changes of clothes."

"I'll get Rosalyn on it. Do you need me to get you stuff from your house?"

"I'm good, thank you. I have everything I need."

Annani

"Mia is in pain," Toven said quietly as Annani entered the room. "I can see it on her face."

"That is a good sign." Annani walked over to the bed and put her hand on Mia's shoulder. "It means that her body is changing. Did Bridget give her painkillers?"

"Not yet." Toven rubbed the back of his neck. "The timing is most unfortunate. Mia's grandparents are on their way, and they will be here soon. It's going to be difficult to convince them that she's doing great when her expression is so pained."

"I can try to enter her mind while she sleeps and take her pain away." She cast Toven a smile. "It is time for me to give her another blessing." She winked.

It was important to keep up appearances, and since Annani did not need to give Mia blood, she could at least help by convincing her brain not to feel pain.

"Thank you. She needs it," Toven said for the sake of the camera that transmitted everything to Bridget's office. "I'll tell Bridget to cut the feed, and I'll wait outside for Mia's grandparents." He hesitated at the door. "If you are still here when they arrive, do we tell them who you are?"

She laughed. "I will be elusive and mysterious and leave them guessing. We do not want to shock them with too much information right away."

"Good idea."

After Toven closed the door behind him, Annani leaned over Mia and brushed her fingers over the girl's forehead. "Whose descendant are you, little one?" Annani hopped on the bed and sat down next to Mia. "You remind me of my mother. She was a tiny female like you and me, with features that were delicate and seemingly fragile, but she was a formidable lady who knew what she wanted." Annani chuckled. "She lured and snagged the most powerful of gods. But while she had planned and schemed to do so, you got yourself a god without doing anything other than being yourself."

As another crease furrowed Mia's forehead, Annani reached into her mind and infused it with calm and well-being. The creases smoothed out, Mia's expression became peaceful, and Annani continued her musings.

"My mother was an only child, but perhaps her father dallied with a human and produced another immortal daughter? Perhaps you and I are distantly related?"

When the twenty minutes Annani usually spent on her blessings were up, she bent over Mia and kissed her on her forehead. "May the Fates smile upon you. Wake up soon, and be well, dear Mia."

At the door, she remembered at the last moment to tamp down her glow before depressing the handle, and as she stepped out into the waiting room, two older humans gawked at her with twin awed expressions.

"Good afternoon." She smiled at them. "You must be Mia's grandparents. I am Annani, the Clan Mother."

The grandfather shook off his stupor first. "I'm Curtis." He offered her his hand. "And you are much too young to be called the Clan Mother. Is it a religious title?"

Annani laughed. "It is an honorific title, but it is not religious." She turned to Mia's grandmother. "Your granddaughter looks a lot like you."

The woman smiled. "I was never that pretty, but thank you. I'm Rosalyn." She shook Annani's hand. "Are you a healer? I can practically feel the healing energy thrumming through your hand."

"You must be very sensitive to notice. I am not a doctor, but I have been told that my touch has healing properties, so I use it to help as best I can." Annani motioned for Alena to join her. "I wish I could stay and chat, but Alena and I need to rush to our next appointment. Toven will explain everything." She smiled brightly. "Best of luck to Mia. I will come again tomorrow to lay my hands on her and lend her my positive healing energy."

Toven

❦

After Annani and Alena left, Curtis arched a brow. "Who's Toven?"

Damn, Toven had forgotten to warn Annani about that, but it no longer mattered. He was about to tell them the truth anyway, so he might as well tell them his real name.

"That's me. Tom Hartford is one of many names I use to keep my real identity hidden."

Curtis's expression darkened. "Who are you?"

He smiled. "I'll explain everything shortly, but first, I'm sure you want to see Mia."

"Yes, please," Rosalyn said.

Toven opened the door and led them into Mia's room.

Thankfully, Annani's thrall had smoothed out Mia's pained expression, and she looked peaceful in her slumber.

"Oh, sweetie." Rosalyn rushed to her bedside and took her hand.

"What's going on, Toven?" Curtis looked at the monitoring equipment. "What are you doing to my granddaughter?"

"Nothing bad, I can assure you."

Toven went back out to the waiting room and brought back two chairs. "Please, sit down." He closed the door behind him.

When Mia's grandparents were seated, he turned the third chair in the room to face them and sat across from them.

"What I'm about to tell you will sound too fantastic to believe, but it is all true, and you can never repeat it, mention it, write about it, or discuss it in any shape or form with anyone outside this village other than Mia and me. In fact, you will not be able to even if you tried, and I'll explain how and why in a moment."

Curtis folded his arms over his chest and narrowed his eyes at Toven. "I had a feeling that you were too good to be true, but I have a feeling that I underestimated how bad you are."

"Ouch." Toven chuckled. "The meaning of my name is 'the good one,' so I can't be that bad. I'm also known as the god of knowledge and wisdom, and I've done my best throughout the seven thousand years of my life to do good. I failed many times, but I've never purposefully done anything that can qualify as truly bad."

"You are insane," Curtis murmured.

Toven sighed. "Instead of trying to convince you, I'll show you physical proof." He took the surgical knife he'd prepared for his demonstration and handed it to Curtis. "Make a cut on my hand and see it closing before your eyes. And if you don't believe your eyes, you can wipe the blood and taste it."

"That's crazy." Curtis gave him the knife. "I'm not going to cut you, and I'm certainly not going to taste your blood. I don't want to catch whatever you have. I heard that meningitis can make people crazy."

"I can do it myself, but you'll think that I tricked you. I want you to feel it."

"I'll do it." Rosalyn took the knife from her husband.

Toven smiled. "I always knew you had spunk." He offered her his hand palm up. "Watch it closely, or you'll miss it. I heal incredibly fast."

Taking a deep breath, Rosalyn supported his hand with hers and then nicked him quickly, making a tiny cut.

As the cut healed almost instantly, she wiped the blood with her finger and brought it to her nose to smell. "It smells like blood." She stuck her finger under Curtis's nose. "Smell it."

He crinkled his nose. "Alright, I smell it. Take it away." He turned to Toven. "So what does it mean to be a god, and what does it have to do with Mia?"

"I'm flesh and blood just like you, but my body's self-healing and regenerating ability protects it from senescence, diseases, and almost all injuries. I can even regrow limbs if I happen to lose them for some reason. I can still be killed, though. My people, who you know from the different mythologies, were destroyed by one of our own. I'm one of the only three surviving gods, Annani is another, and there is one more far away from here."

"Who destroyed your people?" Curtis asked.

Toven grimaced. "My half-brother. He died along with them. I was lucky to be away when he launched the attack, and I thought that I was alone in the world. I only discovered that there were others on Monday. The other thing I discovered was that some humans carry the godly immortal gene, and those can be activated. Mia is one of those humans, and since they are passed from mother to daughter, so are you, Rosalyn. Regrettably, at your age it is probably too late to activate them."

"Was that what has been done to Mia?" Curtis asked. "Did you activate her immortal genes?"

Toven nodded. "She is in the process of transitioning into immortality, and when the process is complete, she might even regrow her legs. If she does, it might take about a year, and during that time, she won't be able to wear her prostheses, which will be difficult for her and restrict her mobility, but I will be there to help her, and so will you."

Tears were streaming down Rosalyn's cheeks, and Curtis looked befuddled.

"Are you telling us that Mia will recover completely and will become immortal?" Curtis asked.

"That's precisely what I'm telling you."

"So what was the point of taking us all to that Swiss clinic?"

Toven smiled. "As I said, I didn't know that Mia was a dormant carrier of immortal genes before this Monday. When I took her to Switzerland, I believed that she was human, and I was frantically searching for ways to improve her health and prolong her life. Fate has navigated us toward each other and guided us to Perfect Match and its mysterious silent partners, who turned out to be my relatives, who I believed were all dead."

Mia

The pain woke Mia up. Everything hurt, not terribly, but enough to make her wince. As usual, Toven was draped around her back like a blanket, his warmth keeping some of the discomfort at bay.

"It hurts," she whispered.

He was awake in an instant, hovering over her. "Where?"

"Everywhere, but especially my chest, where the implant is."

As he lifted the blanket and put his hand over the spot, his eyes widened in alarm. "I think your body is pushing it out. There is a bump there that wasn't there before." He was off the bed in a split second. "I'll get Bridget."

When he opened the door, and Mia heard her grandmother asking what was wrong, she thought she had imagined it, but a moment later, her grandparents rushed into her room.

"Mia, sweetheart." Her grandmother brushed a strand of hair off her forehead. "Toven is getting the doctor. She stepped out for a few minutes to get a bite to eat."

"When did you get here?"

"Yesterday."

As her grandmother walked over to the sink and filled a cup with water, her grandfather took her place and leaned to kiss her forehead. "How are you holding up?"

"I'm okay. Did I see you already?"

Had she woken up before and forgotten that she had seen them?

Her grandfather shook his head. "We've been waiting for you to wake up since yesterday."

"Toven said that it's okay to give you a little." Her grandmother brought the straw to her lips.

Mia drank eagerly until it was all gone. "Did you spend the entire night in the waiting room?"

"No, sweetie. Toven's son took us to the house you are staying in, and we slept in the other bedroom. Toven promised to call us as soon as you woke up, but you slept through the night, and we came back here in the morning and haven't left."

"So I guess Toven told you everything."

Her grandfather nodded. "He also gave us a demonstration to show us how fast he heals. We still have so many questions, but even Toven doesn't have all the answers. He didn't know that any of his people had survived."

Mia wondered whether he'd explained the induction process and felt her cheeks warm up. Being unconscious for that was an advantage.

The door banged open, and Bridget walked in, casting her grandparents a glare that had them scurry out of the room without her having to say a word.

When the door closed behind them, the doctor pulled down Mia's hospital gown and patted the raised area with her fingertips. "Your body is repelling the implant. We need to remove it surgically before it punches through the skin."

Mia swallowed. "Will my heart be okay without it?"

Bridget nodded. "You are doing great." She pulled out her phone. "I'm calling in my staff to prep the operating room and assist in the surgery. Do you want me to send your grandparents in until we are ready for you? You have about ten minutes."

"Yes, please."

After the doctor left the room, Toven clasped Mia's hand. "You are so brave."

Her grandparents entered and walked to the other side of the bed, nodding their agreement.

She chuckled. "I'm lying here like a sack of potatoes and doing nothing. My body is doing all the work." She looked at the IV line. "I'm a little loopy. Is Bridget pumping me full of opioids?"

Toven nodded. "I'm also thralling you not to feel the pain. If you are still feeling it despite all that, it must be really bad."

Closing her eyes, Mia let out a breath. "I'm grateful for the painkillers in whatever shape or form. I don't do well with pain. But they cause curious dreams." She opened her eyes. "I dreamt that I could hear you and Bridget talking to my grandparents, and Bridget said that my stumps lengthened by two millimeters."

"You didn't dream it," her grandmother said. "You heard it, and it's true."

"I can't believe it. My legs are regenerating," she whispered. "It's actually happening."

Toven

As Annani and Alena entered the operating room's waiting area, Curtis rose to his feet and bowed to her. "Thank you for coming to pray for our Mia, Clan Mother."

She waved a dismissive hand. "Don't bow to me, Curtis, and please, call me Annani." She walked over to Rosalyn and gave her a brief hug. "I'm here as a mother and a many times over grandmother, not on official duty."

Orion's absence was a disappointment, but Toven shouldn't have expected his support. He hadn't earned it yet.

"Same goes for me." Alena embraced him.

He patted her on the back. "Bridget says that it's a simple operation, and that Mia's heart is fine without the device." He turned to Mia's grandparents and winked. "My venom is a miracle drug."

Yesterday, Bridget had saved him from having to explain the basics of the induction process, but after leaving the doctor's office, Curtis and Rosalyn had still peppered him with questions and had wanted to see his fangs. Rosalyn made a couple of references to a vampire movie series called *Twilight* and had made him promise to watch it with them when they all went home with Mia.

Rosalyn and Curtis loved the village, but they didn't want to move in. They wanted to go home and continue as if nothing had happened. For now, he would indulge them, but perhaps in time he could convince them that the village was safer for Mia. The two virtual machines they could use while her legs regenerated were a big advantage, and that alone was worth moving there.

When they'd all sat down, and an awkward silence settled over them, Rosalyn turned to Annani. "Did Toven tell you about the virtual adventure he and Mia shared?"

"He mentioned something about it, but he did not provide details. I would love to hear about it."

Rosalyn smiled at Toven. "It would be better if you tell it. My version is secondhand."

It was a good way to fill the time, and Toven dove right into it, describing the world, the return of the gods, his choice of avatar, and how fun it was to fly. He'd censored the more spicy moments, but he'd given them enough hints to get the picture.

"I was suspicious of Azul's behavior, thinking that she was hiding a husband, so I insisted on coming in and meeting her parents. I had no idea that they were producing illegal contraceptives, and when I entered and realized what was going on, Azul got frightened, which caused Mia's heart to act up in the real world. Long story short, it was my fault that she ended up in the hospital, and that the Perfect Match people forbade her from ever participating in a virtual adventure again. But I guess that everything happened for a reason. Otherwise, Mia and I would still be enjoying ourselves in the virtual world, and I wouldn't have met her in person and discovered that she was my truelove mate."

Curtis shook his head. "I don't know if I should punch you in the face or kiss you."

"I wonder if that was the only reason for that particular scenario to play out like it did." Annani rested her hands on her knees. "Perhaps the Fates are trying to tell us something about the big picture and to not just play matchmakers." She looked at Alena. "Can you do an internet search about declining birthrates?"

"I've already done that," Toven said. "It's happening, and when I plugged in the percentage of decline over five centuries, I arrived at a world population of fifty million. But before we panic, let me remind you that things seldom move in a straight line. The trend might reverse in a decade or two from now, and in a century, there could once again be talk about overpopulation."

"That is true," Annani said. "But we should watch the trend and be mindful of it. If it does not reverse on its own, we might need to give it a nudge."

"How?" Rosalyn asked.

"The way we have always done it." Annani smiled. "The power of stories that turn into beliefs. Not too long ago, having three or more children was the way to go, and that is what was shown in movies, television series, and told in books. But now movies and stories are no longer about families but about individuals, and many choose not to have children at all."

Alena sighed. "They do not know what they are missing. Motherhood always filled me with joy. I love children." She rubbed her belly. "Ever since I found out that I'm pregnant again, I'm practically walking on a cloud."

When the door opened and Bridget walked in, all eyes turned to her.

"The surgery went well, the device is out, and Mia's heart is beating beautifully without its help. She's in recovery, but she's still sedated. One of you can come in and be with her."

"Toven should go," Rosalyn said. "We will wait here and take turns later."

Mia

The sight that greeted Mia when she opened her eyes was better than any dream. Toven's smiling face was so full of love and hope that she didn't need to ask how the surgery had gone.

"Welcome to your eternal life, my love." He leaned down and gently kissed her lips.

That hadn't been what she'd expected. "How long ago was the operation?"

"A couple of hours."

"And in those two hours, I turned immortal?"

"Not entirely," Bridget said from behind her. "But the implant is out, your heart is perfect, and the incision healed within minutes. Do you want to see?" She handed Toven a handheld mirror.

Still grinning, he pulled the sheet a little lower and angled the mirror so Mia could see where the scar from her first operation used to be and where the new one should be.

There was no trace of the original or the new, her skin looking smooth and perfect as if she never had been operated on.

She lifted her eyes to Toven. "What else has changed?"

"For now, that's it." He returned the mirror to Bridget. "But if you remember what we talked about before you were taken to surgery, your legs grew by a couple of millimeters."

The lack of pain registering, Mia got worried. As the saying went, no pain, no gain, and if she wasn't hurting, she wasn't regenerating her legs.

"How come I don't feel any pain?"

Bridget chuckled. "If you want it, I can lower the dosage of the painkillers."

"No, that's okay. I was just worried that I stopped growing."

Bridget threw her a small smile. "Let's hope that the growth continues. If it does for at least a week, we can assume that your legs are regenerating."

"I'm crossing my fingers." Mia tried to do that, but she could barely move her hands. "When am I going to feel stronger? Better yet, when can I go home?"

"You will probably feel strong enough to take a shower by the end of the day." Bridget used a remote to raise the back of Mia's bed. "And if by home you mean the one in the village, I can release you tomorrow. But if you mean your home in Arcadia, then the answer is a week from now. I want to keep an eye on you until I'm sure you no longer need me."

"We will stay a week in the village and then go home." Mia looked at Toven. "If that's okay with you. We didn't talk it through yet."

"Whatever makes you happy, my love."

"What about your happiness? You just discovered that you have a family. I'm sure you want to spend as much time with them as possible."

Bridget cleared her throat. "I'll give you a few moments alone, and then I'll send in your grandparents. They are anxious to see you."

"Thank you, doctor. For everything."

"It's my pleasure to welcome new baby immortals into our world." Bridget headed toward the door.

"Thank you," Toven said as Bridget pulled it open. "I am forever in your debt."

"You are welcome."

When the door closed behind Bridget, Mia smiled. "If we have a daughter, we can name her Bridget. I like her assertive personality."

"Yeah, me too." He sat on her bed and took her hand in his. "We have plenty of time to decide on that."

"Thanks mainly to you." Mia's eyes darted to the camera hanging near the ceiling.

Toven's blood had saved her life, she had no doubt about that. If she had been found by a regular immortal, she would have never made it through the transition. The Fates had paired her with the only immortal who could save her.

Following her eyes, Toven glanced at the camera and then back at her. "I am forever grateful to the Fates for guiding me to you and nudging me to do right by you." He leaned closer and nuzzled her cheek. "And I'm also going to do right by your family."

Her eyes widened. Did he mean that he was going to give his blood to her grandparents?

"Oh, Toven. I love you so much." She managed to lift her hand and cup his cheek. "I'm the luckiest girl on the face of this planet."

Toven

~

"We should get a motorized wheelchair," Rosalyn held the door open for Toven.

Mia looked up at her grandmother. "I'm not always going to be this feeble. Bridget said that in a few days, I should start feeling stronger than ever."

Toven pushed the wheelchair past the threshold. "A motorized wheelchair would be a great solution in the village. The paths are not smooth, and wheeling yourself manually over them will become tiring."

Mia shook her head. "We are not staying long enough to justify the expense, and at home, I don't need it. My minivan is modified to use with a wheelchair, so I can get myself places."

The decision was to go home to Arcadia and re-evaluate after a few weeks. Mia's grandparents were willing to move into the village provided that they would be free to come and go as they pleased, and Kian had approved it, but Mia needed more time to decide.

Once she became fully immortal, with all the little oddities that came with it which she would need to hide, she might be more inclined to move into the village. But Toven was not in a rush. They could visit as much or as little as they wanted, and the truth was that he preferred it that way as well.

He'd been alone for far too long to become a team player overnight. He needed a period of adjustment nearly as much as Mia did.

"How is the pain level?" he asked when he noticed her wince.

"I'm not in pain thanks to the meds Bridget gave me, but the itching is driving me nuts. I want to scratch but I can't."

"I can go back and ask Bridget for an anti-itch lotion," Rosalyn offered.

"She doesn't have it in the clinic. Gertrude went to get some from a pharmacy in town, and she'll bring it to the house later." Mia looked over her shoulder at Toven. "I'm so grateful to everyone for taking such good care of me. Your family is incredible, the close and the extended."

"I'm grateful to them as well, and to the Fates that brought us to them. I don't want to think what would have happened if you had started transitioning without me knowing what was happening."

He was so glad that the decision to induce Mia's transition had been taken out of his hands, because he wasn't sure he would have had the guts to do it once he knew the risks involved.

"It's such a beautiful day." Rosalyn waved at a trio of clan ladies passing them by. "Bridget wanted to send us home with a golf cart, but I figured that the fresh air would do you good." She leaned closer to her granddaughter. "Besides, it's a great way to meet people."

"I don't mind." Mia adjusted her skirt, so it was evenly spread over the chair. "What I mind is not having my prostheses. I should have asked Bridget if I could wear them just for the aesthetics without them pressing on my growing limbs. I feel awkward."

"Oh, sweetie." Rosalyn patted her shoulder. "You'll get used to that."

Mia shook her head. "I need to call Frankie and get her advice, but how am I going to explain why I can't wear my prostheses?"

"You can tell her that Toven, aka Tom, found you another groundbreaking, experimental secret treatment that can regrow your legs." Rosalyn waved a hand. "Something with using stem cells and grafting and whatever fancy terms you can think of."

"That's not a bad idea, Grandma. Good thinking."

"I keep telling your grandfather that all of my ideas are good. He should have realized that after being married to me for so long."

"Speaking of Grandpa." Mia looked up at Rosalyn. "Are you sure that he's okay installing grab bars in the bathroom? When was the last time he worked with power tools?"

The truth was that the grab bars had been installed days ago, and the reason Curtis wasn't with them was that he was helping Geraldine and Cassandra prepare a surprise party for Mia.

"He's fine." Rosalyn patted her shoulder. "Using a power drill is like riding a bike. Once you learn how to do it, you never forget."

Mia

When Toven opened the door and wheeled Mia in, the first thing she saw was a bunch of balloons floating around the living room. She was about to make a comment when people jumped from behind the furniture and the counter, yelling, "Surprise!"

As she laughed and clapped, it occurred to her that only a week ago, no one would have dared to give her such a fright.

"Thank you."

Next followed the hugs and kisses, and when all that was done, Toven wheeled her to the dining table.

"I only helped set it up," Cassandra said. "Geraldine, Darlene, and Ruth cooked everything."

"Hi." A small, dark-haired woman offered Mia her hand. "We haven't met yet. I'm Ruth, Sylvia's mother. Roni wanted to barbecue for lunch, but since you can't eat anything heavy yet, I told him that I'll help prepare a light lunch."

"That's very sweet of you, thank you."

"Ouveeoy!" A baby babbled from somewhere in the room. "Ouveeoy!"

As Mia turned toward the sweet sound, Syssi walked over with Allegra in her arms. "Someone is demanding to say hi." She lowered the baby so she could look at Mia.

"Hello, little lady." Mia brushed a finger over her soft cheek. "It's so nice to meet you. I would like to hold you, but I should wait a day or two until my arms feel stronger."

"Ouveeoy," Allegra answered, and the different tone she used sounded like an agreement.

"Welcome to immortality," Syssi said. "I'm so happy to see you on the other side."

"I'm glad to be here."

"Congratulations." Kian took Allegra from Syssi. "So, what have you decided? Are you moving into the village or going back to the human world?"

"I need to go back for now. I have two dear friends who have been with me through thick and thin, and I can't just abandon them."

"You won't," Syssi said. "Even if you live in the village, you can visit them anytime you want."

Mia shook her head. "It wouldn't be the same. The two of them stop by my grandparents' house nearly every evening and have dinner with us. We are practically like sisters."

"I've been thinking," Toven said. "If the theory about the special feeling of affinity between immortals and Dormants is true, then Frankie and Margo might be Dormants. I'm not the type who befriends people easily, and yet those two felt like old friends right from the start. Then again, they are Mia's best friends, and she loves them, so I'm not objective. Is there a way to test it?"

"There might be." Kian sat down with the baby in his arms. "Lisa, my brother-in-law's sister, claims to be able to identify Dormants. Once you go home, you can invite her and your friends for dinner. If she says that they are Dormants, we can take it from there and test it further."

"How?" Mia asked.

Kian smiled. "Start introducing them to clan males and hope for the best."

Mia

⁖

One week later.

"Mia!" Margo rushed through the door and ran to hug Mia as if she hadn't seen her for months. "Why are you in a wheelchair? Are you still feeling sick?" She leaned away to take a better look at Mia's face. "You don't look sick. You look like someone who just got back from a very restful vacation."

Mia hadn't told her friends anything yet. The excuse for the long absence was a cold that had kept her in bed all week long, forcing her and Toven to accept their hosts' hospitality for much longer than was originally planned. Her grandparents also had to come to help Toven take care of her.

"I have a lot to tell you, but let's wait for Frankie."

"Okay." Margo didn't look happy about it, but then she noticed the table that had been set up for eleven people. "Who else is coming?"

"Tom's family. He discovered an entire branch of his family who lives right here in Los Angeles, and he has many cousins. Two of them are coming over for dinner tonight along with their spouses and his niece."

Geraldine and Cassandra were going to pretend to be Toven's cousins, and Lisa was tasked with checking whether Margo and Frankie were Dormants.

"I thought that you didn't have any family." Margo embraced Toven. "How did you find them?"

"Turns out that one of my cousins is the mysterious silent partner."

"Wow." Margo let go of him to hug Mia's grandparents. "That's an amazing coincidence."

As a knock sounded on the door, Toven walked over to open up for Frankie.

"Oh, Mia." She trotted toward her on her high heels. "Are you still not over your cold?" She bent to hug her.

"I'm fine. The reason I'm in the wheelchair has nothing to do with me being sick. The opposite is true." She motioned for her friends to sit on the couch and wheeled the chair to face them. "I didn't have a cold. I was getting a new experimental treatment that's not approved, and therefore it's illegal."

"You can't tell anyone about it," Toven said, using his compulsion voice. "It's top secret, and Mia is breaking protocol by telling you."

Margo put two fingers over her heart. "I swear not to breathe a word of it to anyone outside this room."

"Same here," Frankie said.

Mia grinned. "My heart is fixed, and I'm growing new legs."

Frankie gaped at her. "How?"

"Stem cell, grafting, growth drugs. I don't understand half of what they told me, but the bottom line is that I can't use the prostheses because that would impede the growth. I'm stuck in the wheelchair for the next year."

"Who cares?" Margo jumped off the couch and hugged her. "It's worth it."

"I think so too." Mia looked at Toven. "I owe it all to Tom. None of this would have become available to me without him."

"What about the wedding?" Frankie asked. "You wanted to get married in six to nine months, but now you probably want to wait until your legs regenerate so you can walk down the aisle."

Toven put his hand on Mia's shoulder. "As far as I'm concerned, we can get married tomorrow, but I'll leave it up to Mia. Whatever she decides, is fine with me."

Margo gave him a dreamy smile. "Are any of your newfound cousins single? Because I want one just like you."

Toven grinned. "I have quite a few who I would love to introduce to you."

As Margo gave him the thumbs up, the doorbell rang, and as Toven turned around to open the door for his family, Mia wheeled herself to greet them with Margo and Frankie following right behind her.

"Good evening, everyone." Cassandra walked in with a big bouquet of flowers in her hand.

"Oh, my gosh," Frankie exclaimed. "You're Cassandra Beaumont from Fifty Shades of Beauty." She shifted her gaze to Onegus. "And you are Onegus McLean, the billionaire. I saw your pictures in all the gossip magazines after the charity gala. Which one of you is Tom's cousin?"

Mia had no idea that the two immortals were famous. Weren't they supposed to be secretive and hide behind pseudonyms?

"I am," Cassandra said. "And you are?"

"Frankie." She offered Cassandra her hand.

The rest of the introduction continued, with Lisa being the last one.

"Hi, I'm Lisa." The Dormant detector offered her hand to Margo. "I'm Tom's niece."

"Nice to meet you." Margo shook her hand.

"You don't look anything like Tom." Frankie shook the girl's hand as well. "You look more like Onegus's niece or Shai's."

That was true. While Toven, Geraldine, and Cassandra were all dark-haired, Lisa was so blond that her hair was almost white.

Lisa smiled. "There are so many members in our family that everyone is either a cousin or an aunt or uncle regardless of how they are really related."

"My family is the same," Frankie said. "I have about a hundred cousins, and I don't think I'm really related to half of them."

"Can we move this lovely conversation to the dining table?" Mia's grandmother shooed them away from the door.

As everyone made their way toward the dining room, Lisa leaned toward Mia and whispered in her ear, "I really like your friends. I felt the affinity as soon as I shook their hands."

Mia's heart leaped, did a double somersault, and then danced a victory dance.

How lucky could one girl get?

She was immortal, her fiancé was a god, and her best friends might be dormant carriers of the immortal genes and could join her in the new world that had opened up to her.

The best virtual fantasy could not rival her new reality.

At the table, Toven rose to his feet with a wine glass in hand. "To family by blood and family by heart, old and new, life is good when we are all together."

THE ADVENTURE CONTINUES
WILLIAM & KAIA'S STORY IS NEXT
THE CHILDREN OF THE GODS BOOK 62
DARK WHISPERS FROM THE PAST

TURN THE PAGE TO READ THE EXCERPT—>

JOIN THE VIP CLUB
To find out what's included in your free membership,
flip to the last page.

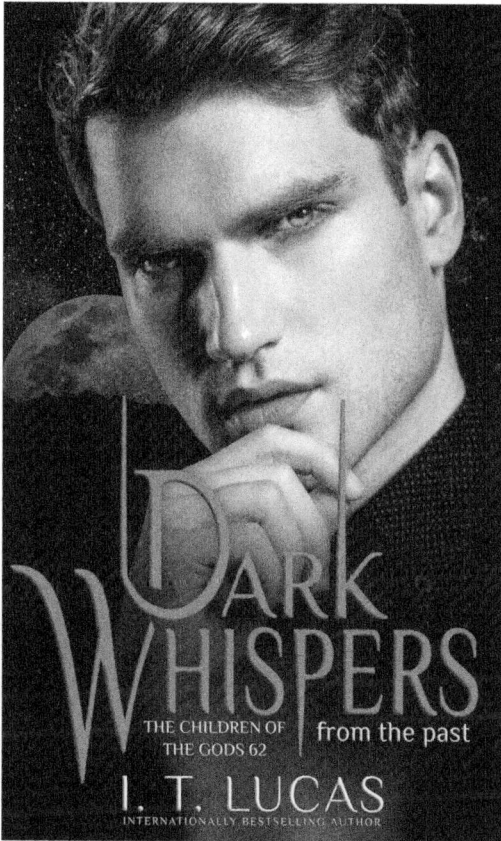

A brilliant scientist and programmer, William lives for his work, but when he recruits a young bioinformatician to help him decipher the gods' genetic blueprints, he find himself smitten with more than just her brain.

A Ph.d at nineteen, Kaia is considered a prodigy and expects a bright future in academia. But when William invites her to join his secret research team, she accepts for reasons that have nothing to do with her career objectives. Wiliam's promise to look into her best friend's disappearance is an offer she just can't refuse.

Jade

The trees were a blur as Jade's booted feet ate up the miles. Propelled by the rage simmering inside her, she ran faster, pushed harder, and let her instincts guide her through the dense forest without colliding with obstacles or stumbling over them.

Leaving her hunting party behind, Jade veered to the right, leaped over a boulder, and dodged a fallen log. Her speed and agility could only be matched by her second-in-command, who was barely keeping up, while the rest would be left to fend for themselves, including her daughter and Kagra's sons.

Their offspring might be pureblooded Kra-ell and possess the most powerful and ruthless of warrior genes, but they didn't have the furnace of rage to push them beyond their comfort zone. Besides, what Igor's offspring failed to realize was that being a powerful Kra-ell was about more than genes. It was about smarts and honing their brains along with their bodies, and it was about honor and following an ancient code of conduct given to the Kra-ell by the Mother of all Life herself.

Exertion usually took the edge off, but today it failed to burn through the rage, fueling it instead. Her lungs gobbling up the mist and her heart pumping blood into her tiring limbs, Jade added a burst of speed and pushed harder.

Not to be outdone, Kagra sped up as well. Her long lean limbs working in perfect synchronization, her dark braid flying behind her like a devil's tail, she was a sight to behold. Watching her protégé blossom into the leader she'd been born to be filled Jade's chest with pride. She wished her daughter could be more like Kagra, but Drova was her father's daughter through and through. Just like Igor, she pissed on the Mother's teaching and ignored even the most basic tenets of the Kra-ell code of honor.

Despite Drova's lowlife murderer of a sire, Jade had had high hopes for her daughter, but even with all she'd invested in teaching and training the girl, it seemed that her nurture could not outdo Igor's nature.

Thank the Mother for guiding her to choose Kagra even though her second had been a pain in the ass at times. She wasn't a *yes* female, and she challenged Jade left and right, but she was loyal and honorable, and her mind was strong enough to withstand Igor's influence and retain some of its autonomy.

Kagra had always been a strong-willed, capable female, but during their twenty-two years of captivity, she'd become a force to be reckoned with. In a decade or two, she might match or even surpass Jade's power, but it would do her no good. It would only make her even more desirable to Igor, who wanted his offspring to be born to the strongest females, leaving the other captives to serve his henchmen and produce more of them for his army, so they could raid more Kra-ell tribes, steal their females and slaughter their males.

In a way, the weaker ones had it easier, their susceptibility to Igor's compulsion allowing him to subdue their grief and rage and make them more malleable, but Jade wouldn't have traded places with them for anything, not even her freedom. As long as her anger and grief burned within her heart, she would never stop plotting her revenge.

Although she and Kagra were the two most powerful females in the compound, able to retain some of their free will and autonomous thinking, neither of them would ever be able to break Igor's hold on their minds. They would never get free, and their need for revenge would probably remain an unappeased inferno of fury burning in their guts. But as long as Jade still had breath in her lungs and a mind capable of thinking, she would never abandon hope of one day killing Igor in the most painful and horrific way.

How could the Mother have given such an evil male such an incredible gift?

How could she look upon her children and watch her once proud daughters subjugated and exploited?

Perhaps the devil that the humans believed in was real, and he'd been the one who had bestowed upon Igor the power to bend others to his will. The Mother of all Life was supposed to look after her loyal creations and bestow her gifts upon her most deserving daughters, and very rarely on her most deserving sons as well.

"Slow down," Kagra panted beside her. "You can't outrun your anger."

"I can try." Jade continued at a breakneck speed for several more miles, slowing down only when her legs threatened to give out.

Stretching, she waited for Kagra to catch up.

"You're killing me." Kagra put her hands on her hips. "I'm going to throw up."

"You should thank me for pushing you. What's the only way to get stronger?"

Kagra rolled her eyes. "Train, and train, and then train some more until you can't move, and then do the same thing the next day, over and over again."

"You're lucky that I'm too tired to punch you for that eye-roll." Jade stretched her calves and motioned for Kagra to do the same. "We need to catch a big prey to replenish our reserves. I've burned through everything I had, and I'm starving."

"Let's rest a little first," Kagra said. "I'm thirsty more than hungry." She sniffed the air. "I smell water."

As Kagra beelined for the nearest stream, Jade followed.

Karelia was a beautiful region, densely wooded and rich in water and game, but it didn't make living under Igor's thumb any more tolerable. To have her family and her freedom back, Jade would have traded Karelia for a life of near starvation on barren and desolate land.

Anything would be better than the nightmare she was living in, even death. But since Jade was still in her prime, the end of her life wasn't coming any time soon, and even if taking her own life wasn't dishonorable, the option had been taken away from her along with every other personal liberty and right.

For a Kra-ell, the only way to die honorably was either in battle or in a duel to the death, but Igor had made sure that she could do neither, and he'd also closed every other loophole that could lead to her death or that of her charges.

Sitting on the rocky riverbank, Kagra took off her boots and socks and put her feet in the water. "It's as freezing as usual, but it feels good."

"Summer is coming." Jade sat next to her and started removing her boots as well. "It's getting warmer."

Kagra moved her foot in circles, creating little spirals. "What if you push me in? I might wash up somewhere far away from here, and perhaps Igor's influence wouldn't reach that far?"

"Yeah, and you'll be saved by a frog prince who will kiss you and turn you into an ugly toad."

That got a laugh out of Kagra. "I love it when you take human fairytales and parables and turn them on their heads, but I'm serious. I can't jump into the water with the intention of running away, but if you push me, then it's an accident."

"I can't push you because that would be aiding your escape, which I'm under strong compulsion not to do. Secondly, you might freeze to death before you wash up. And thirdly, if you are not back in the compound within forty-eight hours, he will activate the damn collar." Jade pushed a finger under hers, rubbing it against the chafe marks on her neck.

Most of the time, she managed to forget about the titanium circle around her throat, the symbol that marked her as Igor's slave, but when she ran, the damn thing abraded her skin.

"The remote won't work from that far away," Kagra argued. "Besides, I don't think that there are explosives in the collars. The bands are not thick enough to contain anything. I think Igor just put them on us to torment and humiliate us."

"I'm just glad that they don't have listening devices in them. If I couldn't talk freely with you, I would explode." At first, Jade had thought that the collars contained tracking and listening devices, but after cursing Igor out on multiple occasions and not getting punished for it, she realized that no one was listening. "But I bet that he has location trackers in them in case someone manages to throw off his compulsion." Jade lifted the collar of her shirt and tucked it under the metal. "Not that I can imagine anyone strong enough to do that. If you and I can't break free of his compulsion, no one can. He might have put the trackers in just to make us feel even more helpless, and he succeeded. After twenty-two years of examining every loophole and thinking of every way I could kill him, even at the expense of my own life, I know that there is no way out. We are going to die here, and so will our children."

"Maybe they will come for us," Kagra whispered. "The queen was supposed to send more settlers."

Jade sighed. "No one is coming. And even if they did, they wouldn't know where to look for us."

William

As William took the stairs to Kian's office two at a time, he was proud of himself for being able to do so without getting winded but at the same time annoyed with himself for being predictably late. He'd planned to arrive at least half an hour early, but as usual, he'd gotten distracted, and now he had less than fifteen minutes left before the meeting to discuss with Kian all the issues that were of no interest to the other participants.

"Good morning." He rushed into the boss's office. "I know that I'm early, but I need to talk to you before the others arrive."

Kian smiled indulgently. "I assume this has to do with your recruitment efforts?"

"Yes." William pulled out a chair next to the conference table and dropped into it.

"How is that going?" Kian asked. "Are the increased incentives attracting better-qualified people?"

William chuckled. "Nearly doubling what we were offering certainly helped attract a higher caliber of candidates, but the qualifications are the lesser problem. The bigger one is finding bioinformaticians who are willing to accept work on a secret project that requires them to live in isolation for several months. They are in such high demand that they can pick and choose, and the good ones are more interested in prestige than money. A secret project they can't talk about or even mention will not help their future career prospects because they can't put it on their résumé."

Kian pursed his lips. "It's only going to last a couple of months, and it's not such a daunting prospect given that the isolated location is Safe Haven, which we've turned into a high-end resort. They can enjoy the beach and the gym, and we even hired a gourmet cook to prepare healthy meals for them."

The gourmet cook and the facilities would be shared with Eleanor's paranormals, but William saw that as an advantage rather than a disadvantage. His team would have only three to five members, and that wasn't enough to keep people from going stir crazy from isolation. And since the paranormal enclave was inside the most secure zone, it wasn't a safety issue either.

William pushed his glasses up his nose. "I hope they don't notice the security measures that can put Area 51 to shame. The so-called resort is guarded better than a top-security prison."

"They won't notice." Kian waved a dismissive hand. "We went to great lengths to keep all of it hidden, and if they see the occasional drone, they will assume it belongs to one of the lodge's guests."

"I hope so." William released a breath. "I lined up several good candidates from Stanford, most of them recent graduates, and I'm meeting with them tomorrow and Wednesday."

"Where?" Kian asked.

The boss didn't like him leaving the village without a Guardian escort, and William braced for a confrontation. None of the other council members were forced to travel with bodyguards, and he saw no reason for being singled out.

"The Bay Area, of course. I meant to tell you last week that I would be flying out tomorrow, but I forgot." He hadn't, but he hoped that it would be too late for Kian to insist on a Guardian escort.

Kian frowned. "Your time is too valuable to waste on traveling to interview prospects. You can use teleconferencing to interview them."

That was an angle William hadn't anticipated, mostly because what Kian was suggesting was absurd. He couldn't choose his team members based on a video call interview. As an immortal, he had extrasensory perception that could only be used in close physical proximity.

"My time is indeed valuable, but so is the information we are trying to decipher with the help of these recruits. I've done most of the groundwork via emails and phone calls, but you know as well as I do that there is no substitute for face-to-face meetings."

Kian lifted a brow. "Are you so desperate that you plan on thralling them into accepting the job?"

William wondered whether the boss was suggesting that he do that or warning him not to do it. Kian could go both ways.

"Thralling humans for our benefit is against clan law, and it's also immoral, but I'm ashamed to admit that the thought has crossed my mind." He sighed. "The reason I want to meet with them in person is that I need to get a sense of who they are as people. Their academic abilities are not the only deciding factor. I'll be spending a lot of time with them over several months, and it's important that I get along with them, and that they get along with each other. If I manage to have a team of three to five bioinformaticians assembled by the end of Wednesday, I'll consider it time very well spent."

Kian regarded him with a smile. "Let me guess. Your nineteen-year-old prodigy refused to come to you for an interview, and you hope to convince her to join your team in person."

That was true, but William wasn't going to apologize for wanting Doctor Kaia Locke on his team. "She's my best candidate, but I would have gone even if her parents weren't an issue."

"What's their problem?"

"They think that she's too young to leave home, which is absurd since the girl is an adult and has a PhD. I hope that after they meet me, they will agree to let her join." He waved a hand over his face. "My harmless, nice-guy appearance will finally be good for something."

Kian chuckled. "You *are* a harmless, nice guy. I hope you convince her to join. Is she pretty?"

William shrugged. "I'm not the kind of guy who allows himself to be blinded by physical beauty. Kaia's beautiful brain is of much more interest to me than her physical appearance." Especially since she was nineteen, and William had never been drawn to young women.

He preferred mature females who knew what they wanted and didn't waste time on games.

"Kaia what?" Kian flipped his laptop open.

"Doctor Kaia Locke." William shook his head. The guy was a two-thousand-year-old immortal, but he was acting like a frat boy.

Most men, including the mighty Kian, judged people, and especially females, based on their looks. William wasn't indifferent to beauty, but he deemed exceptional brains and strength of character much more important than a person's appearance.

Kian typed in the name, lifted a brow, and kept reading. "Doctor Locke has a very impressive résumé, and I suspect that under those monster frames, she's a looker."

William had seen Kaia's graduation photo, and even though her dark-framed enormous eyeglasses hid most of her face, he couldn't help but notice her lush, sexy lips, and the secretive smile that hinted at a sense of humor. But since she was only nineteen, Kaia Locke would never become anything more than a colleague.

Taking off his glasses, William rubbed the lenses with a corner of his Hawaiian shirt. "I believe that Doctor Kaia Locke is more concerned with science than she is with trivial things like fashionable frames and makeup."

Kian lifted his hands in the air. "I meant no offense. Are you taking the jet?"

"I don't need the jet to get to the Bay Area. I booked a commercial flight."

Kian shook his head. "I want you to take the jet, and I'm sending a Guardian with you."

That was what William had been afraid of. "Why?"

"Did you forget? We lost Mark in the Bay Area."

William winced as a spear of pain pierced his heart. Given their shared field of expertise, Mark and he had been close, and he still mourned his loss.

He wasn't the only one.

Mark's murder had shaken up their family. It was the reason Kian had decided to pull all of their people from the Bay Area, build a hidden village for the clan, and have everyone living where they were protected and safe.

But that had been four and a half years ago, and a lot had changed since.

"I didn't forget, and I never will, but we haven't heard from the Doomers in months. Lokan says that Navuh is busy breeding the next generation of smart warriors, and until he achieves that, he isn't going to come after us."

Kian leaned forward and pinned William with his intense eyes. "That might be true, but we know that they run drug and prostitution rings in California. You could accidentally bump into a Doomer, and you are not a warrior. Cancel the flight. You're taking the private jet and a Guardian. End of discussion."

Folding his arms over his chest, William glared at Kian. "None of the other council members have to travel with bodyguards." He sounded like a kindergartener, but he really didn't want to have a Guardian going with him on the interviews.

"What do you want me to say, that you are more valuable?" Kian leaned back in his chair, but his eyes were still holding William's captive. "I value all the council members tremendously, for their skills and as my closest friends, but if tragedy strikes, they can all be replaced. No one can take your place."

"I'm training Marcel. He's almost as good as me." That was a gross exaggeration, but Kian wouldn't know that.

"Almost doesn't cut it, and we both know that Marcel doesn't have that extra something that you have. Shai knows every aspect of the clan business as well and better than I do, but he can't take my place for the same reason. I know in my gut when to make a deal and when not to. Things are rarely clear cut, and I don't base my decisions solely on numbers and charts, just as you don't base yours on calculations alone or rely on tried and tested solutions. You think outside the box."

Regrettably, that was true, but that didn't mean that he should be kept in a cocoon. "I'm not going to show up to meetings with a bodyguard."

"The Guardian can pretend to be your chauffeur."

William snorted. "Do I look like the kind of guy who has a chauffeur?" He flapped his Hawaiian shirt, which was two sizes too big on him. He'd lost about thirty pounds since he'd started training with Ronja and Darlene, but he needed to lose at least thirty more, and it would be a waste of time and energy to shop for new clothes only to do it again in a couple of months.

Kian eyed the shirt with a frown. "Get some new clothes before you go. If you want to impress your candidates, and especially Doctor Kaia Locke and her parents, you can't show up looking like a schlump."

Kaia

"Don't cry, sweet pea." Swaying on her feet, Kaia held her baby brother to her chest and rocked him gently. "Whoever decided that babies needed to get six vaccines at twelve months old was a sadistic bastard. They should have spread them out over several months."

Her mother rocked Ryan, who was hiccuping between sniffles. "It's better to get it over with all at once."

Kaia strongly disagreed. When she had children, she wouldn't allow them to be tormented like that.

Poor boys.

Throughout the ordeal the twins had been screaming their little heads off, and when they'd gotten exhausted, they'd switched to pitiful whimpering and casting accusing looks at Kaia and their mother for allowing the nurse to give them ouchies.

"Gilbert should have been here with his sons. I don't want them to associate me with needles. I want Evan, Ryan, and Idina to always think of me as the cool, fun big sister."

Usually the nanny accompanied their mother to doctor visits with the twins, but Idina had come down with a cold and couldn't go to preschool, so the nanny had to stay home with her.

Her mother sighed. "He wanted to be here for them, but he had an important inspection at a job site that he couldn't leave to the supervisor. He had to attend it in person."

Kaia twisted her lips in a grimace. "Yeah, I bet."

It wasn't the first time Gilbert had come up with a convenient excuse to wiggle out of performing his less-than-pleasant fatherly duties, which included changing poopy diapers and wiping little noses. The guy was only forty-eight, but he acted like a throwback to the fifties.

He was a great guy, and he loved Kaia and Cheryl as if they were his own daughters, but he wasn't very helpful with the little ones, leaving all the work of raising them to their mother and the nanny.

It would have been semi-okay if their mother was a stay-at-home mom, but she wasn't. Karen Locke was a sysadmin for a large defense contractor, which was a demanding position with a salary to match. It wasn't fair for her partner to leave all the work of managing the household and taking care of his toddler daughter and twin baby sons to her, and by extension, to Kaia and Cheryl.

Well, mostly to Kaia because Cheryl was still in high school while Kaia was home, exploring her employment options.

She'd had offers from several universities and a dozen or so private research facilities, but she was probably going to accept a position at Stanford so she could keep living at home.

Her mother and Gilbert didn't want her to move out, and she didn't want to do that either. How could she possibly leave her sweet baby brothers, Idina and Cheryl? She would miss them too much.

On the other hand, starting college at fourteen and finishing her doctorate at nineteen, all while living at home, meant that Kaia had missed out on the whole college experience. It would have been nice to try something different instead of doing more of the same for the rest of her life.

She stifled a snort. If her memories of her past life as a mathematician were real and not imagined, she was doing more or less the same thing during two lifetimes, or maybe more. What if she'd been stuck in the same groove throughout her soul's existence? She might have gone through many life cycles, and in each of them, she'd been consumed by the beauty of numbers and the endless patterns they formed. All of creation was based on numbers, and it fascinated her, but there was more to life than research, and she'd learned that lesson in her past life as well as in her current one.

Her previous self had been single, childless, and lonely, while Kaia had a wonderful family and was surrounded by love. Losing her father at a young age had reinforced the lessons learned in her previous life, making her hold on to the people she loved because she could never know how long she would have with them.

Maybe that was why Kaia appreciated her chaotic home life and was in no hurry to leave.

"Come on." Her mother slung the strap of her enormous baby bag over her shoulder. "Let's take the boys home."

By the time they got to the car Evan had fallen asleep, exhausted from all the crying, and Ryan had quieted down but was still sniffling pitifully.

After strapping the twins into their car seats, Kaia got behind the wheel. "I guess we are not stopping by the supermarket on our way home."

Her mother turned to look at the babies in the backseat. "Not with the twins. We can order what we need online and have it delivered."

Kaia grimaced. "They always mess things up, and they drive me nuts with all the messages about approving substitutions. I prefer to drop you off and go by myself. The guy from the secret research project is coming tomorrow, and all we have to serve are Skittles and gummy bears."

"I don't know why you agreed to see him." Her mother folded her arms over her chest. "We've talked about it, and we agreed that you are not going to accept his offer no matter how good it is. You are just wasting his time and ours."

"I'm curious to hear more about the project. What if it's about something so crucial and necessary that I would later beat myself up for not being part of it? Besides, the guy sounds so desperate for me to join that he might present me with an offer that I can't refuse."

That was all true, but there was a third reason for her wanting to meet William, and it had to do with Tony's disappearance. Her mother and Gilbert would freak out if they knew that she was getting involved in that, and her mother wouldn't allow the recruiter anywhere near the house if she suspected that he had anything to do with Tony's fate.

Kaia didn't know whether William had been involved in Tony's case or not, but she was desperate for any clues that could help her find out what happened to her friend.

The thing was that William's offer was very similar to the one Anthony had received a little over a year ago. The highly classified research project had been supposed to take four months, and yet no one had heard from Anthony in over a year. It was a long shot to think that William had been Tony's recruiter as well, but bioinformatics wasn't a huge field, and there weren't that many players outside of academia and major research institutions. William could have heard something, or he might know the people who had hired Anthony.

Order Dark Whispers From The Past today!

Join the VIP Club

To find out what's included in your free membership, flip to the last page.

The Children of the Gods Series

Reading Order

THE CHILDREN OF THE GODS ORIGINS

1: GODDESS'S CHOICE

When gods and immortals still ruled the ancient world, one young goddess risked everything for love.

2: GODDESS'S HOPE

Hungry for power and infatuated with the beautiful Areana, Navuh plots his father's demise. After all, by getting rid of the insane god he would be doing the world a favor. Except, when gods and immortals conspire against each other, humanity pays the price.

But things are not what they seem, and prophecies should not to be trusted...

THE CHILDREN OF THE GODS

DARK STRANGER

1: DARK STRANGER THE DREAM

2: DARK STRANGER REVEALED

3: DARK STRANGER IMMORTAL

DARK ENEMY

4: DARK ENEMY TAKEN

5: DARK ENEMY CAPTIVE

6: DARK ENEMY REDEEMED

Dark God

Dark Whispers

A brilliant scientist and programmer, William lives for his work, but when he recruits a young bioinformatician to help him decipher the gods' genetic blueprints, he find himself smitten with more than just her brain.

A Ph.d at nineteen, Kaia is considered a prodigy and expects a bright future in academia. But when William invites her to join his secret research team, she accepts for reasons that have nothing to do with her career objectives. Wiliam's promise to look into her best friend's disappearance is an offer she just can't refuse.

William knows that his budding relationship with the nineteen-year-old Kaia will be frowned upon, but he's unprepared for her family's vehement opposition.

Family means everything to Kaia, so when she finds herself in the impossible position of having to choose between them and William, she resorts to unconventional means to resolve the conflict.

64: Dark Whispers From Beyond

The sacrifices Kaia and her family have to make for a chance of gaining immortality might tear them apart, and success is not guaranteed.

Is the dubious promise of eternal life worth the risk of losing everything?

Dark Gambit

65: Dark Gambit The Pawn

Temporarily assigned to supervise a team of bioinformaticians, Marcel expects to spend a couple of weeks in the peaceful retreat of Safe Haven, enjoying Oregon Coast's cool weather and rugged beauty.

Things quickly turn chaotic when the retreat's director receives an email with an encoded message about a potential new threat to the clan.

While those in charge of security debate what to do next, Safe Haven's first ever paranormal retreat is about to begin, and one of the attendees is a mysterious woman who makes Marcel's heart beat faster whenever she's near.

Is the beautiful mortal his one truelove?

Or is she the harbinger of more bad news?

66: Dark Gambit The Play

To get to Safe Haven's inner circle, the Kra-ell leader sacrifices a pawn. He does not expect her to reach the final rank and promote to a queen.

67: Dark Gambit Reliance

Marcel takes a big risk by telling Sofia his greatest sin. Can he trust her to keep it a secret? Or maybe it's time to confess his

crime and submit to whatever punishment Edna deems
appropriate?

Three miserable centuries of living with guilt and remorse are
long enough.

Once the dust settles on the Kra-ell crisis, he will gather the
courage to put himself at the court's mercy.

DARK ALLIANCE

68: DARK ALLIANCE KINDRED SOULS

A daring operation half a world away devolves into a full-scale
crisis that escalates rapidly, requiring the clan's full might and
technological wizardry to manage and survive.

Hardened by duty and tragedy, Jade is driven by a burning
desire for revenge. When Phinas saves her second-in-command,
Jade's gratitude quickly becomes something more.

69: DARK ALLIANCE TURBULENT WATERS

When a dangerous foe turns the tables on the clan,
complicating the Kra-ell rescue operation in unforeseeable
ways, Kian and his crew bet all on a brilliant misdirection.

On board the Aurora, Phinas and Jade brace for battle while
enjoying a few stolen moments of passion.

Drawn to the woman he sees behind the aloof leader, Phinas
realizes that what has started as a calculated political move has
evolved into a deepening sense of companionship.

Jade finds reprieve in Phinas's arms, but duty and tradition
make it difficult for her to accept that what she feels for him is
more than just gratitude and desire.

After all, the Kra-ell don't believe in love.

70: DARK ALLIANCE PERFECT STORM

After two decades in captivity, Jade is finally free, her quest for revenge within grasp, but danger still looms large. A storm is brewing on the horizon, gathering momentum and threatening to obliterate Jade's tenuous hold on hope for a better future.

Dark Healing

71: Dark Healing Blind Justice

The sanctuary is Vanessa's life project. The monumental task of rehabilitating the traumatized victims of trafficking doesn't leave much time for personal life, let alone dating or finding her one and only.

When Kian asks her to help the Kra-ell, she's torn between her duty to the sanctuary and a group of emotionally wounded aliens who no other psychologist can treat.

She's the only immortal with the necessary training to get it done.

The Kra-ell culture and the purebloods' nearly androgynous alien looks shouldn't appeal to her, and yet, she finds one of them disturbingly attractive.

Is it the dangerous vibe he emits?

Does it speak to her on a subconscious level?

Or is it her need to put the broken pieces of him back together?

And why is he interested in her?

She cannot offer him a fight for dominance like a Kra-ell female would, but some strange and unfamiliar part of her wishes she could.

72: Dark Healing Blind Trust

Riddled with guilt over the crimes he was forced to commit, Mo-red is ready to stand trial and accept the death sentence he believes he deserves, but when the clan's alluring psychologist offers a new perspective on his past and hope for a better future, he resolves to fight for his life.

73: DARK HEALING BLIND CURVE

Kian is still reeling from the shocking revelations about the twins when a new threat manifests, eclipsing everything he's had to deal with up until now. In light of the new developments, Igor, the other Kra-ell prisoners, and the pending trial are no longer at the forefront of his mind, but the opposite is true for Vanessa. As her relationship with Mo-red solidifies, she is determined to save the male she loves, even if it means breaking him free and living on the run.

DARK ENCOUNTERS

74: DARK ENCOUNTERS OF THE CLOSE KIND

Convinced that her family is hiding a terrible secret from her, Gabi decides to pay them a surprise visit.

Something is very fishy about the stories her brothers have been telling her lately. Her niece, a nineteen-year-old prodigy with a Ph.D. in bioinformatics, has gotten engaged to a much older guy she met while working on some top-secret project, and if Gabi's older, overprotective brother's approval of the engagement wasn't suspicious enough, he also uprooted his family and moved to be closer to the couple.

What Gabi discovers when she gets to L.A. is wilder than anything she could have imagined. Her entire family possesses godly genes, her brothers and her niece have already turned immortal, and she could transition as soon as she finds an immortal male to induce her. Finding a suitable candidate in a village full of handsome immortals shouldn't be a problem, but Gabi's thoughts keep wandering to the gorgeous guy she met on her flight over.

Could Uriel be a lost descendant of the gods?

He certainly looks like them, but that doesn't mean that he's a good guy or that he's even immortal. He could be a descendant of a different god—a member of an enemy faction of immortals who seek to eradicate her family's adoptive clan, or what is more likely, he's just an extraordinarily good-looking human.

75: DARK ENCOUNTERS OF THE UNEXPECTED KIND

Who is Uriel?

Is he a lost descendant of the gods or just a gorgeous and charming human who has rocked Gabi's world?

76: DARK ENCOUNTERS OF THE FATED KIND

As Aru and his team embark on a perilous mission, their past and present converge in a meeting that holds the key to their fate.

DARK VOYAGE

77: DARK VOYAGE MATTERS OF THE HEART

As Annani and Syssi set out to unravel the mysteries of Syssi's visions about the gods' home world, the long-awaited wedding cruise sets sail with Aru, Gabi, and Aru's teammates on board.

While the gods find themselves surrounded by immortal clan ladies eager for their affections, they soon discover that destiny has a different plan for them.

THE CHILDREN OF THE GODS SERIES SETS

BOOKS 1-3: DARK STRANGER TRILOGY—INCLUDES A BONUS SHORT STORY: THE FATES TAKE A VACATION

BOOKS 4-6: DARK ENEMY TRILOGY —INCLUDES A BONUS SHORT STORY—**THE FATES' POST-WEDDING CELEBRATION**

BOOKS 7-10: DARK WARRIOR TETRALOGY

BOOKS 11-13: DARK GUARDIAN TRILOGY

BOOKS 14-16: DARK ANGEL TRILOGY

BOOKS 17-19: DARK OPERATIVE TRILOGY

BOOKS 20-22: DARK SURVIVOR TRILOGY

BOOKS 23-25: DARK WIDOW TRILOGY

BOOKS 26-28: DARK DREAM TRILOGY

BOOKS 29-31: DARK PRINCE TRILOGY

BOOKS 32-34: DARK QUEEN TRILOGY

BOOKS 35-37: DARK SPY TRILOGY

BOOKS 38-40: DARK OVERLORD TRILOGY

BOOKS 41-43: DARK CHOICES TRILOGY

BOOKS 44-46: DARK SECRETS TRILOGY

BOOKS 47-49: DARK HAVEN TRILOGY

BOOKS 50-52: DARK POWER TRILOGY

BOOKS 53-55: DARK MEMORIES TRILOGY

BOOKS 56-58: DARK HUNTER TRILOGY

BOOKS 59-61: DARK GOD TRILOGY

BOOKS 62-64: DARK WHISPERS TRILOGY

BOOKS 65-67: DARK GAMBIT TRILOGY

BOOKS 68-70: DARK ALLIANCE TRILOGY

BOOKS 71-73: DARK HEALING TRILOGY

MEGA SETS

INCLUDE CHARACTER LISTS

The Children of the Gods: Books 1-6

The Children of the Gods: Books 6.5-10

TRY THE SERIES ON

AUDIBLE

2 FREE audiobooks with your new Audible subscription!

PERFECT MATCH SERIES

Vampire's Consort

When Gabriel's company is ready to start beta testing, he invites his old crush to inspect its medical safety protocol.

Curious about the revolutionary technology of the *Perfect Match Virtual Fantasy-Fulfillment studios*, Brenna agrees.

Neither expects to end up partnering for its first fully immersive test run.

King's Chosen

When Lisa's nutty friends get her a gift certificate to *Perfect Match Virtual Fantasy Studios*, she has no intentions of using it. But since the only way to get a refund is if no partner can be found for her, she makes sure to request a fantasy so girly and over the top that no sane guy will pick it up.

Except, someone does.

> **Warning:** This fantasy contains a hot, domineering crown prince, sweet insta-love, steamy love scenes painted with light shades of gray, a wedding, and a HEA in both the virtual and real worlds.

> Intended for mature audience.

Captain's Conquest

Working as a Starbucks barista, Alicia fends off flirting all day long, but none of the guys are as charming and sexy as Gregg. His frequent visits are the highlight of her day, but since he's never asked her out, she assumes he's taken. Besides, between a day job and a budding music career, she has no time to start a new relationship.

That is until Gregg makes her an offer she can't refuse—a gift certificate to the virtual fantasy fulfillment service everyone is talking about. As a huge Star Trek fan, Alicia has a perfect match in mind—the captain of the Starship Enterprise.

The Thief Who Loved Me

When Marian splurges on a Perfect Match Virtual adventure as a world infamous jewel thief, she expects high-wire fun with a hot partner who she will never have to see again in real life.

A virtual encounter seems like the perfect answer to Marcus's string of dating disasters. No strings attached, no drama, and definitely no love. As a die-hard James Bond fan, he chooses as his avatar a dashing MI6 operative, and to complement his adventure, a dangerously seductive partner.

Neither expects to find their forever Perfect Match.

My Merman Prince

The beautiful architect working late on the twelfth floor of my building thinks that I'm just the maintenance guy. She's also under the impression that I'm not interested.

Nothing could be further from the truth.

I want her like I've never wanted a woman before, but I don't play where I work.

I don't need the complications.

When she tells me about living out her mermaid fantasy with a stranger in a Perfect Match virtual adventure, I decide to do everything possible to ensure that the stranger is me.

The Dragon King

To save his beloved kingdom from a devastating war, the Crown Prince of Trieste makes a deal with a witch that costs him half of his humanity and dooms him to an eternity of loneliness.

Now king, he's a fearsome cobalt-winged dragon by day and a short-tempered monarch by night. Not many are brave enough to serve in the palace of the brooding and volatile ruler, but Charlotte ignores the rumors and accepts a scribe position in court.

As the young scribe reawakens Bruce's frozen heart, all that stands in the way of their happiness is the witch's bargain. Outsmarting the evil hag will take cunning and courage, and Charlotte is just the right woman for the job.

My Werewolf Romeo

The father of my star student is a big-shot screenwriter and the patron of the drama department who thinks he can dictate what production I should put on. The principal makes it very clear that I need to cooperate with the opinionated asshat or walk away from my dream job at the exclusive private high school.

It doesn't help matters that the guy is single, hot, charming, creative, and seems to like me despite my thinly-veiled hostility.

When he invites me to a custom-tailored Perfect Match virtual adventure to prove that his screenplay is perfect for my production, I accept, intending to have fun while proving that messing with the classics is a foolish idea.

I don't expect to be wowed by his werewolf adaptation of Red Riding Hood mesh-up with Romeo and Juliet, and I certainly don't expect to fall in love with the virtual fantasy's leading man.

The Channeler's Companion

A treat for fans of *The Wheel of Time.*

When Erika hires Rand to assist in her pediatric clinic, she does so despite his good looks and irresistible charm, not because of them.

He's empathic, adores children, and has the patience of a saint.

He's also all she can think about, but he's off limits.

What's a doctor to do to scratch that irresistible itch without risking workplace complications?

A shared adventure in the Perfect Match Virtual Studios seems like the solution, but instead of letting the algorithm choose a partner for her, Erika can try to influence it to select the one she wants. Awarding Rand a gift certificate to the service will get him into their database, but unless Erika can tip the odds in her favor, getting paired with him is a long shot.

Hopefully, a virtual adventure based on her and Rand's favorite series will do the trick.

Note

Dear reader,

I hope my stories have added a little joy to your day. If you have a moment to add some to mine, you can help spread the word about the Children Of The Gods series by telling your friends and penning a review. Your recommendations are the most powerful way to inspire new readers to explore the series.

Thank you,

Isabell

FOR EXCLUSIVE PEEKS AT UPCOMING RELEASES & A FREE COMPANION BOOK

JOIN MY *VIP CLUB* AND GAIN ACCESS TO THE VIP PORTAL AT ITLUCAS.COM
TO JOIN, GO TO:
http://eepurl.com/blMTpD

INCLUDED IN YOUR FREE MEMBERSHIP:

YOUR VIP PORTAL

- READ PREVIEW CHAPTERS OF UPCOMING RELEASES.
- LISTEN TO GODDESS'S CHOICE NARRATION BY CHARLES LAWRENCE
- EXCLUSIVE CONTENT OFFERED ONLY TO MY VIPs.

FREE I.T. LUCAS COMPANION INCLUDES:

- GODDESS'S CHOICE PART I
- PERFECT MATCH: VAMPIRE'S CONSORT (A STANDALONE NOVELLA)
- INTERVIEW Q & A
- CHARACTER CHARTS

IF YOU'RE ALREADY A SUBSCRIBER, AND YOU ARE NOT GETTING MY EMAILS, YOUR PROVIDER IS

SENDING THEM TO YOUR JUNK FOLDER, AND YOU ARE MISSING OUT ON **IMPORTANT UPDATES, SIDE CHARACTERS' PORTRAITS, ADDITIONAL CONTENT, AND OTHER GOODIES.** TO FIX THAT, ADD isabell@itlucas.com TO YOUR EMAIL CONTACTS OR YOUR EMAIL VIP LIST.

Check out the specials at
https://www.itlucas.com/specials

Printed in Great Britain
by Amazon